The JADE BOY

Cate Cain

templar

First published in the UK in 2013 by Templar Publishing,

an imprint of The Templar Company Limited,

Deepdene Lodge, Deepdene Avenue,

Dorking, Surrey, RH5 4AT, UK

www.templarco.co.uk

ISBN 978-1-84877-229-8

Printed and bound by CPI Group (UK) Ltd, Croydon, CR0 4YY

For my husband, Stephen, and my dad, John

Prophecy

The single candle beside the curtained bed flickered and a tall shadow moved on the panelled wall beyond. Just for a moment the shadow appeared to be that of a horned creature. The little flame danced madly then it sputtered and died, leaving the room in complete darkness.

"Now, tell me, what do I need?" The man's voice was soft, sibilant and oddly cracked.

Silence.

The man spoke again, his voice laced with something that sounded like amusement. "Tell me, Lady Elizabeth. I command you. I don't need to tell you, of all people, how I found you, do I? Or what I might do next?" The last words were spoken slowly and very deliberately. After a moment a young girl answered, but as she spoke, her light voice deepened and seemed to echo in the blackness. Gradually the girl's voice became that of a grown woman – a woman chanting from somewhere far away.

*"Oak grove burns and old stones sing
Old stones sing for green blood
Green blood flows in old veins
Old veins fill with new life
New life born as oak grove burns."*

When the chanting stopped there was a rustling noise and an odd halting, thumping sound as if something lame moved across the creaking boards.

"Thank you, my lady. That was most illuminating."

A jangling sound. A key fitted to a lock.

Just before the door opened, the woman's voice came again, this time so distant and faint that it was impossible to catch every single word, although the last sentence seemed to hang and sing in the air like the ghost of a peal of bells.

"You must seek the boy of Jade..."

CHAPTER ONE

London, February 1666

"Oi! Yer spindle-shanked, thieving gypsy! If I find one more of them pies missing, I'll skin yer alive and turn yer miserable carcass on a spit over the fire until yer eyeballs pop!"

Jem ducked as a heavy ladle clanked down the long wooden table towards him, narrowly avoiding a direct hit.

Pig Face was having one of his bad days.

Muffled sniggers from a couple of smut-faced scullion boys over by the hearth accompanied the fat cook's display of temper. When Pig Face turned his attention back to the huge side of beef turning on the spit, they screwed up their pinched little faces and waggled their tongues at Jem.

Pig Face lifted another ladle from a pot bubbling away beneath the meat and poured dollops of golden fat over the fragrant roast.

Jem was momentarily fascinated by the map-like pattern of sweat and grease covering the grey cloth stretched across the man's ox-broad shoulders.

As if he could sense Jem's stare, the cook spoke again, his voice surprisingly thin considering the mountain of flesh from where it came.

"An' don't think I ain't counted them syllabubs in the cold store, yer pimple-cheeked beggar. If just one of 'em goes missing I'll hack yer fingers off with a meat cleaver!"

The scullions sniggered again and one of them flicked an old chicken bone at Jem's head.

Jem bit down on his anger, squared his shoulders and rubbed furiously at the huge silver object standing on the stone floor in front of him. He knew better than to protest his innocence. After all, no one would believe him. He was an outsider among the servants in Ludlow House and was never allowed to forget it.

As the boy worked away at the blackened silver with a rag, a reflection began to appear in the bulbous stem of the candelabrum. First a pair of dark eyes that burned like embers stared angrily back at him, then a long, straight nose above a wide mouth set into a grim line appeared. Finally, a handsome face topped by a mop of thick black curls was revealed. Whatever Pig Face might say, Jem wasn't pimply at all, but his olive skin – golden now, even in the depths of winter – was enough to mark him out as an oddity among the whey-faced servants.

'Gypsy' was the least offensive of their insults.

Jem pushed the hair back from his forehead and shifted uncomfortably on the stool. Despite the roasting, it was gloomy and freezing at this end of the kitchen and his hand was cramped from all the polishing. He'd already worked on eight of the metal monsters – there were still four more to go.

George, the Seventh Duke of Bellingdon and Jem's employer, was determined that tonight Ludlow House, his ancient London home, should outshine the court at Whitehall: King Charles himself was visiting.

Everyone was preparing for the great feast and nowhere was busier than the kitchens. Pig Face was bad tempered on the sunniest of days, but this last week his mood had been blacker than the stinking water in the midden pits at the back of the yard where the servants emptied the household chamber pots.

Above stairs, the housemaids and the footmen had been scrubbing for days. Each morning brought new deliveries of splendid carpets and magnificent hangings intended to disguise the old walls and patched floorboards.

The duke was out to impress his royal guest and no expense was to be spared. Even the hallway was to be lit by twelve magnificent candelabra, each bearing a score of costly bees wax candles. Ludlow House was to be made fit for a king, but before he arrived Jem had a lot more polishing to do.

The boy stretched his fingers and blew on his hands. He reached up to the narrow band of cloth tied around his neck and scratched at the skin beneath. The livid red birthmark he took such pains to conceal always itched when he was angry.

"Scratchin' at the Devil's stamp, are ye?"

Old Susan, the laundry woman, was watching him from her grubby, rag-piled corner. Her tiny eyes twinkled with malice as she raised her hand and brought her thumb and index finger together to make the sign of the evil eye.

She blew sharply at Jem through the gap and hissed, "May God's holy wind carry ye far from this place. T'ain't right that one pricked as Satan's own should live among decent Christian folk."

Jem was aware of more muffled laughter from the scullions and a bloody chicken foot flew through the air, landing at his feet. He kicked at the gristly object and it skittered across the flagstones, rattling under the table to the feet of Simeon, the youngest and smallest of the house servants.

The thin-faced boy gave a yelp of surprise and took a step back, tripping over the ladle Pig Face had hurled at Jem. As Simeon fought to stay upright, a towering decorated cake – a work of confectionery art on which the moody cook had lavished many curses and painstaking hours – wobbled dangerously on the platter he was about to carry up to the banqueting chamber.

Simeon's eyes grew round with horror as he zig zagged backwards, fighting to stay on his feet and keep the cake on the platter in his hands. The kitchen was suddenly silent as everyone watched the inevitable calamity unfurling. Only a matter of seconds passed, but to Jem it felt as if the seconds had slowed to hours.

Jem sprang to his feet, knocking over the great candelabrum, where it bounced off the stones and clanged like a tolling bell. He vaulted over the table and deftly grabbed the platter from Simeon's hands, just as the boy finally lost his balance and toppled to the floor.

With the cake safe on its silver platter, Jem looked down at Simeon and winked. The terrified boy scrambled to his feet – and everyone let out a great breath of relief that quickly turned to mocking laughter.

As Jem placed the platter back on the table, Simeon tugged his sleeve and whispered, "Thank you."

Jem, who was no stranger to punishments in Ludlow House, didn't like to think about what the consequences might have been if Pig Face's masterpiece had been destroyed. He knew better than most what would happen to the small serving boy.

"No harm done, Sim. Look, there's not a sugar flower or a marchpane figure out of place," he said loudly.

"I'll be the judge of that." Pig Face lumbered over and squinted at the cake. Little drops of sweat plopped from his brow to the table as he scrutinised every inch and every curl of sugared icing. After a moment he made a harrumphing noise that almost sounded like disappointment.

Spinning around remarkably swiftly considering his bulk, the fat cook clipped Simeon sharply round the ear before turning on Jem.

"There's no time for chatter in my kitchen, brat. And I'll warrant that silver is dented after the way yer flung it to the stones. There'll be a fine for that.

Well, what are yer standing there gawpin' fer? On with it!"

Jem gritted his teeth and returned to his stool. Lifting the heavy candlabrum upright, he concentrated on the tarnished silver, rubbing with such a burst of fury that he caught his knuckles on the metal ridges and they began to bleed.

If Sarah, his mother, were here, Pig Face wouldn't dare to talk to him like that, Jem fumed inwardly.

Unfortunately, Sarah rarely ventured down to the kitchens at Ludlow House. As wardrobe mistress to the duke's wife, Mary, her place was above stairs and many of the kitchen servants viewed her and, consequently, her son, with jealous suspicion.

Even worse, when Jem tried to talk to Sarah about his treatment, she always seemed anxious and eager to get away from him. Just last week, when Old Susan had passed on yet another malicious lie about his conduct, Sarah had lectured him.

"I don't want to hear stories about you from the under-servants. Do you understand me, Jem? You undermine my position in this household – and your own."

Jem had watched his mother swish angrily away down the panelled corridor. And not for the first time, he had found himself wondering just what his position in the household actually was.

Jem stopped polishing for a moment, winced and clenched his fist. He wiped specks of blood from his ragged knuckles on his coarse breeches. That made them hurt even more.

Thwack!

Jem yelped with pain and clamped his hand to his left ear. Another sharp blow rapped across his stinging knuckles.

"So, Jeremy Green is a lazy sluggard as well as a pie thief, I see."

The words were sharp and clear. Everyone stopped working for a moment and stared.

Wormald, the duke's steward, was standing just behind Jem's stool. As usual, he'd appeared from nowhere. He always wore felted slippers to muffle the sound of his tread, which made him a silent but deadly menace.

Curtains of lank grey hair hung from the centre of Wormald's head, brushing the stiff white collar he wore over his dusty black doublet. With his prominent, beaklike nose and sharp grey eyes, the duke's steward resembled a bird. Certainly, he was vicious as a hawk.

The man appeared to be quivering with righteous anger, but Jem also sensed pleasure. There was nothing Wormald enjoyed more than punishing Jem – mainly because he regarded Sarah as his arch enemy. While the duchess relied on Jem's mother, the duke relied on his steward and as the duke and the duchess had not been on good terms for many years now, the two servants were themselves bitter rivals. Unable to hurt Sarah, Wormald contented himself by torturing the next best thing – her son.

Wormald swept the kitchen with a steely gaze, making sure that everyone was watching, before continuing, "We will discuss a suitable punishment for your idleness later, boy."

Then the steward bent lower to ensure that his next words were for Jem alone, "You can leave off that. The duke is calling for you. Now."

Jem was confused. Surely there must be some mistake. Why would the duke call for him?

The steward's eyes narrowed as they took in Jem's bloodied knuckles and grimy jacket.

"You're wanted in the great salon, boy, so you'd better smarten yourself up. And you can take this to the duke while you're about it."

Wormald handed Jem a pewter jug filled with

aromatic wine. Jem noticed that the man looked furious – his thin lips were pursed into a tight line of cold disapproval.

Aware that twenty pairs of eyes were locked upon him, Jem rose uncertainly. He wiped his fingers and pushed his untidy hair back, before dusting down the dark green velvet jerkin made for him by his mother. It had been her gift at his last birthday and he was painfully conscious that already the sleeves were too short. At twelve years old, Jem was a head taller than most of the other kitchen lads.

"Look sharp now. His Grace isn't one to be kept waiting."

Wormald jabbed Jem in the back with a bony finger. Jem was too used to Wormald's cruelty to give the man the satisfaction of another yelp. But as he crossed the flagstones of the kitchen and carried the wine carefully up the winding stairs leading up to the upper part of the house, Jem was a little afraid.

The duke had only ever called for him once before, two years ago. He had been made to remove his shirt and stand, shivering, in the centre of the great salon while the duke had examined him with detached interest. He had felt like a curiosity, like some new object the duke had bought to impress his friends.

Most particularly he had examined Jem's birthmark, which itched and glowed under the scrutiny. And all the while Sarah had stood to one side, wringing her hands.

At the time, Jem thought that she looked as if she'd been crying too. It had been a horrible, humiliating experience. What if it was about to happen again?

He stumbled on the stairs and spilled some wine. He tried to scuff out the stain with his foot, terrified that Wormald would see it.

Wormald!

Jem's stomach gave a little flip, Wormald would be furious that he was being singled out for special attention by the duke.

"I'll pay for that later, too," the boy thought gloomily as he entered the great hall.

CHAPTER TWO

The hall was a blur of activity as an army of maids prepared for the evening ahead. The great oak staircase was already glowing like a freshly hatched conker and new Turkish carpets overlapped on the black and white marble floor. Bowls of lavender and spices filled the air with the scent of prosperity.

Avoiding the clucking maids, Jem made his way up the broad stairs and turned left at the first landing where a magnificent portrait of the duke dominated the hall below.

It was an open secret within Ludlow House that the Duke of Bellingdon was not satisfied with his home. It was old, dark, not of the finest style and not in the most fashionable part of London. To compensate for its shortcomings, the duke filled his home with magnificent things – the most magnificent thing of all, of course, being himself.

Jem placed the wine jug on the floor outside the door to the duke's chamber and knocked.

"Enter."

The boy swallowed, straightened his jacket again

and, bending to retrieve the jug, opened the door. He stepped into the room and bowed his head. After the chill of the kitchens, it was good to feel warm. A huge fire crackled in the hearth, throwing off heat and flickers of gold.

The duke's great salon was shadowy in the weak February light and the flames danced off the opulent furniture, making the room seem to shiver and move. Heavy brocade curtains hung at the windows, portraits lined the walls and comfortable chairs with gilt arms sat before the fire.

The duke was standing with his back to Jem on the far side of the hearth. Today he was wearing a lavishly embroidered frock coat and the curls of his magnificent golden periwig hung to halfway down his back. The man was burnished with wealth. Jem looked down at his own ill-fitting jerkin, ashamed.

"Leave it there, boy."

The duke waved a lazy arm in Jem's general direction and a waterfall of lace rustled over his hand. The words were clearly addressed to Jem, but the duke didn't turn to look at him. Instead, he was examining a vast painting propped against the wall. The painting showed a beautiful woman in a stormy landscape. She appeared to be riding a stag.

Jem wanted to take a step closer for a better look.

"So this is the boy then, George? How very interesting for you."

Jem spun round, surprised that the duke was not alone.

The air at the far end of the salon seemed to shudder for a moment and then an impossibly tall figure stepped out of the shadows and into the circle of firelight.

Jem felt his whole body tense as the duke's towering visitor took another halting step towards him. The man was richly dressed in pale grey silk with a dark cloak falling from one shoulder. The hem of the cloak rustled as it dragged along the floor.

Jem now saw that although the man was unusually tall, his great height was emphasised by an inky black wig that rose to two peaks on the top of his head and tumbled in oily curls to below his shoulders.

Leaning heavily on a long staff that seemed to be formed from knobbled blackened wood, the man limped one step closer. His wide mouth curved into a smile and Jem saw that the man's lips were painted the same brilliant red as the flash of lining from the cloak over his shoulder. At the top of the visitor's staff was a gleaming bird head carved from crystal.

The bird's eyes sparked in the firelight and when Jem looked up, the man's eyes glinted in the same way.

Jem tried to look away, but couldn't. The visitor's eyes were locked on to his and something in the man's expression reminded the boy unnervingly of Caesar, the duke's ferocious mastiff dog, when Pig Face dangled a juicy bone in front of his kennel.

"And you say that the king will like this, Cazalon?" The duke clasped his hands behind his back, rocked on his exquisite heels and continued to examine the painting. "Can't say I like it myself." The duke leaned closer to inspect the brushwork. "But, then again, my dear Count, you always seem to find the very thing."

The duke took a step back to admire the woman on the stag from a distance. "She's certainly a pretty piece. His last work, d'ya say?"

Count Cazalon's eyes narrowed as he turned away from Jem to look at the duke. The count smiled again, and his thin red lips spread across his face like a gash.

"I assure you it is quite unique, George. There will never be another like it. The artist died of the plague mere hours after putting the last stroke to the canvas. The lady, I believe, vanished without trace soon after."

Jem noticed that Cazalon's voice had an odd sing-song note to it that sometimes slid into a long, fat hiss.

"Well, well. How diverting. You have a remarkable knack for bringing me the most rare items, Cazalon."

The duke took out pair of golden pince-nez and scrutinised the painting again. He nodded to himself.

Cazalon was now staring intently at Jem once more. He limped forward, supporting himself on the peculiar twisted staff and caught Jem's chin in his hand, tipping the boy's head back to catch the firelight.

"Your name?"

"J– J– Jem, sir."

"And what else?" Cazalon asked lazily. He turned to the duke. "What family name was the boy given, George?"

As if noticing Jem properly for the first time, the duke looked over and laughed. "His mother calls herself Mrs Green. He's known here as Jeremy Green. We call him Jem."

Jem felt uncomfortable. Under the cloth, his birthmark began to itch.

"Jem *Green*, you say?" The count was suddenly interested – his grip tightened on Jem's chin.

Despite the heat in the room, the boy shivered. Count Cazalon's red-gloved hand smelled strongly of roses, but beneath that there was another sour, putrid scent. It clawed at the back of Jem's throat and gave him a sharp reminder of the time he'd been ordered to clear a spotted, maggot-riddled cheese from the cellar store.

Jem caught his breath. Close to, he now saw that the count's face was painted deathly white, like one of the actresses at Drury Lane. The thick lead make-up was cracked, like a spider web of wrinkles. The man's obsidian eyes were long, slanted and outlined in black. In their glimmering mirror Jem could see two tiny doll-like versions of himself.

Cazalon smiled again and looked Jem up and down. The boy rubbed nervously at his throbbing knuckles, and as the count caught sight of the bloody rawness there, just for a second, his eyes seemed to widen and blacken completely, like ink seeping through water.

Cazalon drew a sharp rasping breath and took a step back.

"And how old is the boy, George?"

The duke commanded Jem to answer for himself.

"I– I am twelve, my lord."

Cazalon nodded and pursed his painted lips. "And when is your birthday, child?"

"In September, sir."

Jem was amazed, no one ever took any notice of him, let alone of his birthday.

The count continued, "Do you know the exact date?"

"I was born on the fourth day of September in the year sixteen hundred and fifty-three, sir."

At this Cazalon smiled so broadly that his long angular face seemed to split in two. He brought his crimson-gloved hands together as if he was praying and Jem thought he heard the man murmur softly, "Perfect…"

In the hearth a log flared into a shower of brilliant red sparks and popped loudly.

A sudden scuffling noise came from the far end of the room, where one of the tapestries lining the wall now appeared to be twitching.

Jem watched as a tiny black and white shape emerged from behind the fabric and clambered onto the golden bar from which the tapestry hung – a monkey.

Count Cazalon followed Jem's astonished gaze.

"Ptolemy, bring Cleopatra down," he ordered in a slow, bored voice.

Another figure emerged from the gloom at the far end of the salon. All this time Jem hadn't realised there was a fourth person in the room, but now an elaborately dressed, turbaned pageboy with the darkest skin Jem had ever seen stepped into the firelight.

The page simply stared at the monkey for a few seconds before the little creature swung down, almost toppling a Chinese vase as she leapt to settle on his shoulder.

Eyeing the rocking vase, the duke cleared his throat. "Er, you've seen the boy now, Cazalon. Perhaps it would be better if your servant and the animal leave us while we conclude our business? I wish to speak to you in private."

Cazalon laughed. It was a cold metallic sound like the cry of a fox. He gestured at his black-skinned servant and the monkey.

"My servant moor is mute, George. In all the days I have had him he has never spoken a word. He is little more than an animal. But if you are worried about the monkey making a mess in your *exquisite* home, then can I suggest that your boy here, Master Green, should take them both to the kitchens and find them a morsel of food."

The duke nodded and glanced at Jem. "Take them to the kitchens."

He turned back to the painting. "She really has the most unusual eyes, Cazalon. I think tonight, the king will appreciate my generosity."

But Cazalon wasn't listening to the duke. Instead, he bent his head low so that his masklike face was level with Jem's, before whispering in his oddly distorted voice, "I do *so* look forward to our next meeting, Master Green."

When Cazalon spoke Jem thought, just for a moment, that he caught sight of the man's tongue flickering between his painted lips. It was, he could swear, black and pointed.

As the great salon doors closed behind him, Jem felt a rush of relief to be away from the stifling room and the stifling attentions of the duke's peculiar and unsettling visitor.

He took a gulp of fresh cold air and stared frankly and curiously across the hallway at the count's servant. He tried to remember the boy's odd name. What had Cazalon had called him – Tollymee?

Jem had never seen anyone like him before. The boy was tall like Jem, with long, lean limbs. He was dressed in fine material like his master, the shades of red and grey echoing Cazalon's clothing. But it was the boy's face that fascinated Jem most. His skin was as dark and luminous as the river at night and his huge eyes seemed to bore into Jem's soul.

The monkey on his shoulder began to chatter excitedly. She leaned across the gap between the two of them and playfully grabbed a handful of Jem's thick hair. The black boy grinned broadly, and Jem decided that he liked the look of him.

"Cleo likes you."

Jem nearly jumped out of his skin. The words had sounded clearly and distinctly in his head like notes of music, but there was no one else in sight. The other boy hadn't said a thing or even moved his lips – and, anyway, Cazalon said his servant couldn't speak.

Jem looked up and down the corridor and then stared suspiciously at the boy and the monkey. The dark boy's smile stretched even wider as he turned on his red-heeled shoes and set off up the corridor. At first the monkey batted her little paws at the red feather that sprouted from the top of the boy's turban. Then she twisted herself round on her master's shoulder and stared back at Jem.

"Come on then. Show me the way," came the mysterious disembodied voice again. *"I'm very hungry."*

CHAPTER THREE

"Will you look at that?" called out one of the servants as the boys and the monkey made their way down the staircase. "Our gypsy lad has found himself a friend."

For a moment all the scrubbing, polishing and bustling stopped as twenty pairs of eyes locked onto the trio. Jem kept his head down and led the way across the hall to a small door concealed by a tapestry.

"Lord preserve us. The moor's got a rat on 'is back," hissed one of the maids.

"That ain't no rat, 'tis a badger," said a footman as the strange little party disappeared into the passage behind the door.

"Your friends are clearly very stupid."

Once again, Jem heard the words clearly in his head. He spun round and looked at the dark boy – who grinned and arched an eyebrow.

"They are not my friends," Jem blurted out, horribly aware that it looked like he was talking to himself.

The voice came again.

"Any fool can see that Cleo is a monkey. Would you like to carry her?"

The dark boy reached out his arm so that it rested on Jem's shoulder. The little monkey chattered before scampering across the bridge between them, settling herself by Jem's ear.

"See, as I told you – she likes you. Now, what about that food?"

Jem was astonished. "I– I…" he began, before words rang out in his mind again.

"You don't have to talk out loud. Just think and I'll hear you."

Jem thought about the door at the end of the passage leading down to the kitchens and then he thought about the pile of forbidden venison pies in the pantry.

"Perfect! We shall dine like princes," came the reply. *"Lead the way, my friend."*

Luckily, apart from a sleepy spit boy, the kitchen was now deserted. Everyone was upstairs preparing the banquet chamber. A new batch of pies, fresh from the oven, gleamed in golden rows on the table. Jem took one for himself and handed another to the visitor. The spit boy rustled to life in his sooty corner.

"You ain't to touch them pies. Pig Face'll kill me if he knows I let yer take 'em, an' then he'll beat seven bells outta the both of us."

The boy shuffled closer then stopped, mesmerised, as Cleo leaned down from Jem's shoulder and grabbed a nugget of steaming pastry crust in her little hand.

"'Ere, what yer got there? That's an evil spirit, that is."

The dark boy made a slight movement with his hand. Instantly, Cleo hunched herself up and leaned forward, baring her sharp white teeth. She looked like one of the gargoyles around the roof of St Paul's Cathedral.

Gobbets of pastry spattered from the monkey's mouth over Jem's coat. She reached out and yanked a greasy lock of the spit boy's hair so hard that it came away in her paw. The boy squealed in pain before turning on his heels and racing to the safety of the yard beyond the kitchens.

As the door slammed behind him, Cleo settled back again and started to stroke Jem's ear.

I think you are not well treated here, my friend?

Jem heard the words clearly in his mind. He nodded glumly. He looked at the other boy, who was hungrily assessing the rows of pies on the table. He had twice called him 'friend' – no one had ever called him that before.

"Well, just time for one more pie, I think,"

said the visitor, reaching out to help himself.

Jem was amazed.

"You *can* talk!" he exclaimed. For, indeed, the boy had actually spoken the words aloud.

"Of course I can, but only when I choose and only to those I choose to hear me."

Cleo jumped to the table from Jem's shoulder and began to tug at her master's silk sleeve.

The dark boy put down the pie and nodded. Then he reached up to the folds of his turban and removed a shining brooch that was pinning the feather in place. It was shaped like a glittering scarab beetle. He placed it carefully in the centre of the table.

He took a step back and put his hand on Jem's arm to pull him away too. All the while he kept his eyes locked on the elegant jewel. Not for the first time that day, Jem felt completely baffled. What on earth was the strange boy doing now?

The air around the beetle seemed to shimmer and fizz. Gradually, Jem became aware of a low humming noise and as the sound strengthened, the jewel began to pulse with light and colour.

Suddenly its wing case parted with a crack and a plume of purple smoke began to waver from the split along the beetle's back and into the air above the table. The plume whirled faster and faster and as it did so it seemed to wind itself into a vapoury form with a head and limbs.

The smoky figure began to glow with an eerie green light.

"Shield your eyes, Jem. *Now!*"

The dark boy shouted the instruction just as the shining figure billowed and grew so tall that it appeared to reach the stone arches of the ceiling. There was a blinding flash, a plaintive musical sound and the scent of violets.

"At last! I thought you were never going to set me down, Tolly!"

The voice belonged to girl. A small, but very cross girl.

She was standing on the table – in exactly the spot where the beetle had been.

Jem's first instinct was to run. This was witchcraft – and he wanted no part of it. He pulled his arm roughly from the dark boy's grip, but the boy caught hold of his wrist and held tight. Jem was wiry, but the other boy was surprisingly strong.

"Jem, wait. We mean you no harm," he said aloud.

Jem stared up at the girl in disbelief.

She looked down at him, frowned and darted an

anxious look at the dark boy. He nodded and Cleo chirruped. Then the girl smiled. Jem noticed that she had a little gap between her front teeth. She was wearing a ragged green dress that would once have been fine and expensive but was now shabby. It was obviously too small for her. Her eyes were a brilliant shade of emerald green and shone with a peculiar intensity that made Jem want to look away, and then look back again immediately.

But the most unusual and unsettling thing about the girl on the table, quite apart from the fact that she had appeared from nowhere, was that her thick waist-length hair was pure white and gleamed like moonlight. Jem had never seen anyone like her before.

"You were so interested in those pies, Tolly, I thought you'd forgotten me. Well, aren't you going to help me down?"

Tolly released his grip on Jem's wrist, then took the girl's hand and helped her jump from the table. She still sounded cross, but Jem noticed that Tolly was grinning at her.

The girl straightened her skirts and turned to look closely at Jem.

"So this is the one?"

Tolly nodded. "I am certain he is the boy the master has been seeking. He is called Jem *Green*."

The girl's eyes widened and she took a step towards Jem.

"So the boy of jade is a kitchen lad?" she murmured, scanning his face and frowning. Then she reached for a pie.

This was too much.

"Look," Jem blurted out. "I don't know who you are or what's going on here, but at any moment now Pig Face is going to come back downstairs and then we'll all be in big trouble. I– I…" he faltered as Cleo jumped to his shoulder and started to stroke his ear.

The girl took a crumbly bite from the pie and then held out a flake of golden pastry to the monkey. Cleo gripped it in her tiny paw and started to nibble.

"It's all right, Jem. Ann is my friend," Tolly said. "She has taken a great risk coming here to Ludlow House today to find you."

Ann shot Tolly an odd look.

"You're speaking aloud to him. Is it safe?"

Tolly nodded. "I… that is to say, *we* know he can be trusted. Cleo's never wrong, is she?"

Ann stared intently at the dark boy then she

offered Jem her hand and dipped her head. "Then that is good enough for me. I am Lady Ann Metcalf, ward to Count Cazalon."

The girl stared at him expectantly. After a moment he took her hand and, feeling slightly self-conscious, he gave a shallow formal bow.

When he looked up again her eyes were closed. She gripped his hand more firmly and then began to speak in a rush.

"This house is not your home, Master Green. You are loved, but not protected. You have a place here, but you do not fit it. You live in shadow. Your mother is a good woman, but she is ashamed of her sin... she is ashamed of *you*. Your father—"

"Enough!" Jem bellowed the word and wrenched his hand from Ann's grasp.

All the blood drained from his face as he stood rigidly in front of the girl, clenching his fists so tightly that the nails dug into his palms.

No one, not even Wormald or Pig Face had made him feel like this before. He glared at the girl, but she didn't open her eyes. Tolly took a soft step back and Cleo jumped from Jem's shoulder to the table where she cowered behind Ann, covering her eyes with a paw.

After a few seconds Jem spoke quietly, his voice low and dangerous.

"Who are you to speak of my mother? As for my father, he is… dead." The word tasted bitter in Jem's mouth. "How dare you come here and…'

"And what Jem?" Ann's odd green eyes snapped open and she stared up at him. "I've spoken the truth, haven't I? This place is not your home. And your mother, she loves you, but there is a shadow between you, isn't there?"

Jem was silent for a moment as a whirl of confusing feelings and memories tumbled through his mind. Why wouldn't Sarah ever speak about his father? Why wouldn't she ever take his side against Wormald and Pig Face? Why did she try to avoid him?

And how did this girl know all this?

He stared sullenly at the floor.

Ann took his hand again and squeezed it tightly. "Isn't there Jem?" she asked softly, tipping his head up with her other hand so that he looked her full in the face. Jem didn't answer. His anger was fading but it was being replaced by confusion and something like fear.

Cleo gave a little chirrup, jumped to Ann's shoulder

and nuzzled into the girl's thick white hair, chattering into her ear.

Ann smiled. "I know Cleo. I have been rude and abrupt. But we have such little time. Please forgive me, Master Green. I only wanted to make you trust me, but I fear I offended you in the process…"

Jem swallowed and looked uncertainly between the girl and the dark boy. What kind of trick was this? How had this girl known so much about him? Things that even *he* didn't like to put into words.

Tolly laughed and reached over to tweak a tendril of Ann's white hair. "She's always the same – so eager to show off her skills. But you must listen to us. We've been searching for you."

Ann broke in. "And you don't have to call me Lady Ann, Jem. Can I call you Jem? I can't bear formality among friends. Can we begin again? Please?"

She took his hand once more and squeezed it.

Jem felt an unexpected jolt of warmth. He smiled warily at the girl and then at Tolly.

"I don't wish to be rude," he began, "but could one of you tell me what's going on?"

For a fleeting moment he wondered if this was a dream – or perhaps a fever? Maybe he was actually in his truckle bed sweating out the nightmares brought on by the ague?

"You are perfectly well," said Tolly, reading his thoughts. "But you must listen to Ann. She has reason to believe that your life is in danger. Tell him."

Ann sat on the edge of the table and Cleo jumped from her shoulder to curl up in her lap. The girl stroked the monkey's head as she spoke softly.

"I know this must seem very odd, Jem, but you must believe that we mean you no harm. In fact, we need your help."

She paused and looked up at him. "What do you think of Cazalon?"

He noticed that she clenched her left fist as she forced herself to say the name.

Jem remembered his encounter in the duke's study and shuddered. He thought about giving a brave answer, but looking at the expression on Ann's face he decided to be honest.

"I thought he was… sinister and peculiar."

Tolly laughed, but it wasn't a happy sound.

Ann continued. "My guardian is a collector. He is fascinated by all things unusual, powerful, strange, ancient and wondrous. His house is full of the most hideous and unnatural things. Things that even I, with all my... skills, cannot understand.

"Recently, he has become obsessed with a new find – a new object to add to his collection. Please don't ask me how I know this, I just..."

Ann came to a halt and Tolly reached out to take her hand. Cleo looked up, her button-bright eyes anxiously scanning one face then the other.

Ann shook her head as if trying to clear cobwebs from her thoughts. She continued, "For months now, he has been seeking *the boy of jade*. At first we thought it was an object made from the precious green stone, but our investigations led nowhere, and now we think it is a person. We think it is you, Jem *Green*."

Ann emphasised Jem's name when she spoke and looked at him intently. She smiled tightly at Jem's baffled expression before continuing, "Oh, I know he seems so controlled and powerful, but behind that arrogant painted exterior he has been utterly desperate. Jem, I must know, if you are the boy of jade, what is it about you that has driven Cazalon into a frenzy of desire?"

Ann stared at him expectantly.

Jem looked blank. He was a just lowly servant. Apart from his mother, and when he was much younger, the duchess, no one had ever showed the slightest interest in him – except to humiliate and punish him. He wracked his brains, but couldn't think of a single thing that might make him interesting to the count.

"I have no idea what you are talking about. There's nothing special about me. I'm just a *gypsy brat*." He answered sourly, mimicking Pig Face's reedy voice.

The room was quiet for a moment.

Ann reached across the table and took another pie. She began to eat it in a dainty way, but after the first couple of neat bites she started to cram the pastry and spiced meat into her mouth.

"These are very good," she said through a mouthful of crumbs. "Tolly, have another one, quickly."

The dark boy didn't hesitate. Jem realised that the two children and the monkey were ravenous. He looked at the table and felt a pang of fear when he saw how many pies were now missing. There was no doubt who Pig Face and Wormald would blame... They would take it in turns to beat him later.

Suddenly Cleo leapt from Ann's lap and scampered to the end of the table. Her small body went rigid as she stared at the door, then she raced back to Tolly's feet and started to chatter furiously. He scooped her from the floor.

"Ann, someone is coming, we must be ready," he said anxiously.

The girl wiped crumbs from her skirts and stood up. She turned to Jem and took his hand again.

She held her head to one side, frowned and then smiled broadly. "You don't like the steward here, W– Wormy? Is that his name?"

Jem nodded. "Er yes, sort of, but how…?"

Ann grinned mischievously. "Never mind how for the moment, let's just say that Mr Wormy is about to develop a rather embarrassing condition. I'm so glad we've found you, Jem. And I'm sorry too – there's much more to say, but we have no time left. We need your help – and I think you're going to need ours."

Ann took a step back, raised her arms and began to spin slowly on the spot.

"Wait!" called Jem, but it was already too late.

Little flickers of blue light began to spark from the tips of her fingers and the air around her started to shimmer. Jem heard her voice as if from somewhere far away.

"You are right to fear Cazalon. He is a monster…"

The girl's last words were little more than a whisper as she spun faster and faster. There was a blinding flash and she disappeared.

Tolly bent down to retrieve a small glittering beetle from the flagstones. Carefully he lifted it up to his turban and Jem watched, fascinated, as he nestled it into the folds of material. It was now a jewelled clasp again.

The door to the kitchen swung open and Wormald appeared. He paused and sniffed the air suspiciously before stalking over to the boys. When he saw Cleo, his nose wrinkled in distaste.

"You, monkey boy. Your master is calling for you and that noxious, repulsive beast. Out. Now!"

Tolly straightened his coat, drew himself up to his full height, lifted Cleo to his shoulder and began to saunter confidently across the kitchen.

"A moment!" Wormald's voice crackled with spite. "Do I see crumbs on the floor? How many pies have you stolen, boy – you and that ungodly creature on your back?"

Tolly stopped and looked questioningly at Jem.

Wormald's bony hand slipped under his black frock coat to his belt, where he kept a small thin whip clipped next to an ornate silver ring that contained keys to every room in the house.

The ring of keys jangled as the steward slowly produced the whip and walked towards the table.

The man was fizzing with dangerous excitement. Jem's stomach knotted. How many pies had Ann, Tolly and Cleo eaten? Six, maybe seven?

He shifted position in front of the table so that he masked the gaps in the gleaming rows and began to speak.

"Er... Mr Wormald, sir, the duke ordered me to feed the count's servant. He specifically said that I was to—"

Wormald's eyes narrowed. "And fed your own greedy guts in the process I'll be bound. If I don't see sixty pies on that table you'll go without food for a fortnight... after I've beaten you *and* these repellent creatures. Stand aside!"

Little flecks of spittle spattered into the air as the steward screeched his order.

Jem took a sidestep and turned to look at the table, dreading the worst.

Rows and rows of golden venison pies glowed with warmth on the long wooden trestle top. Not a single gap could be seen, not a single pie was missing. Wormald made a hasty count.

"Sixty!" he almost spat the word. "It seems I caught you in good time."

At that moment, Cleo made a noise that sounded

very much like a chuckle. She rocked on Tolly's shoulder and snickered loudly. Tolly tried to muffle her, but she leapt down to the table where she bared first her teeth at the steward and then her bottom.

Jem gulped. From long experience he knew this wouldn't turn out well.

Wormald's jagged face set into a mask of controlled fury. He brandished the whip like a kitchen knife as he advanced slowly and softly along the table towards the chattering creature. Tolly stepped forward to gather her into his arms, but the monkey scampered to the far end of the table where she kept up her mocking, chirruping sounds, all the while keeping her bright black eyes locked on the approaching steward.

Tolly darted a stricken look at Jem.

"The little beast won't think it so funny when I beat its brains out," Wormald said in the soft, wheedling voice he usually reserved for his dealings with the duchess.

"Here, monkey," he crooned as he got nearer and nearer. "Come here, you repulsive, misshapen abomination."

When he was just a couple of feet away he jerked the whip into the air ready to lash out.

Jem couldn't bear it.

"No!"

He sprang forward and knocked the whip from Wormald's hand. It flipped up into the air and fell at Tolly's feet. The dark boy kicked it away in disgust.

The steward spun round and glared – his grey hair crackled with static making it rise around his head like a grimy halo. From the deep pocket of his frock coat he now produced a short serrated cane that Jem recognised with a shudder.

Wormald took a step towards them and his eyes sparked with malice.

"Oh, you've done it now, my lad. I *was* going to be merciful and just use my whip. But now—"

His words were cut short by the most enormous farting noise that ripped through the kitchen with such force and energy that it actually produced a ringing echo from the copper pans ranged along the shelves.

The steward's face turned sickly green and he bent double to clutch his stomach. Then, as yet another colossal fart exploded from his breeches he started to scuttle urgently and inelegantly towards the kitchen door, all the while bending and pulling his frock coat around him as if to muffle the thunderous sounds.

As Wormald disappeared into the darkening afternoon, presumably making for the servants' middens at the far end of kitchen yard, they heard his choked voice fading across the cobbles.

"Don't think that I'll forget this! That smug grin will be wiped off your face, kitchen brat, when I've finished with you. When the king arrives tonight you shall not be permitted to watch from the gallery with the rest of the servants. And... and that's just the beginning."

Stunned for a moment, the boys stared at the swinging yard door, then they began to laugh so hard that they couldn't speak. Cleo chattered and jumped onto Tolly's rocking shoulder, where she batted at the red feather of his turban with an air of nonchalant victory. Jem sank to his knees and slapped the stone floor.

Finally Tolly wiped a tear from his cheek and spoke aloud.

"So that's what she meant by embarrassing condition. Brilliant, wasn't it?"

Jem grinned and nodded. "I'll pay later, but it will be worth it. Did Ann really give Wormald the gripes?"

Tolly nodded and laughed again. "She did it for you."

The sound of clattering hooves leaving the stable yard warned the boys that Cazalon's carriage was being brought round.

"We have to go now," said Tolly, offering Jem his hand.

It was as if something in the dark boy's broad handsome face suddenly closed as he added, "Your steward is not the only cruel master."

With that he adjusted Cleo's position on his shoulder and strode towards the door.

Just as Tolly and Cleo disappeared into the winding staircase leading up to the house, Jem caught the faintest whiff of violets and a girl's voice whispered in his ear.

"Your father is alive, Jem."

CHAPTER FOUR

Jem was surrounded by a ring of ice-blue flames that burned his skin like the east wind in January. Tongues of frosty fire licked hungrily at his boots as the dancing circle grew smaller and smaller. Somewhere far away, a woman called his name. His feet felt like blocks of ice as a deadly numbness began to creep up his legs.

"Jem! Wake up!"

His eyes snapped open. Sarah stood at the end of the bed. She had tugged the thin blanket off his body and now his exposed feet were frozen. A single candle in her hand threw flickering shadows into the corners and crevices of the beamed attic.

"Pull on your coat, too, Jem," she said, bending to retrieve a woollen sock from the floor.

He was supposed to be sorting rags for use in the privies – a punishment set by Wormald. There was a great pile of them on the floor and on the bed, but the task was so dull Jem had become drowsy. He had kicked off his boots, crawled under the patched sheets and fallen asleep.

Now he was aware of a distant humming, as if the house, usually so silent in the hours of darkness, had somehow come alive.

"Be quick about it," his mother whispered, "we don't want to miss him."

"Miss who?" asked Jem sleepily.

"The king, of course. He is expected at any moment. I know that Wormald has forbidden you to watch with the rest of the servants, but I…"

Sarah stopped and busied herself with the heaps of privy rags.

Jem grinned. Despite her coolness towards him when they were in the company of others, he knew she loved him. There were still times, like now, when she made sure that Wormald didn't get his own way.

Jem struggled into his tight jerkin and Sarah drew a sharp breath, "You're growing so fast. You'll soon be as tall as your—"

She paused and started to straighten the bed, tutting when she found a book smuggled from the duke's library buried in the knot of sheets. When Jem was small, Sarah had spent many hours teaching him to read. Now he escaped from the drudgery of the kitchen whenever he could by losing himself in books Sarah borrowed for him from the duke's magnificent library. Tales of ancient heroes, travellers and far-off lands were his favourites.

"You've had this for at least a month now, Jem. I'll have to take it back."

She tucked the book under her arm and continued to straighten the bedding. As she bobbed and bustled, little wisps of pale gold hair escaped in spring-like tendrils from under her lace cap.

Jem frowned. He felt sure she had been about to mention his father, but had stopped herself – as usual.

"Your father is alive."

Those four whispered words had echoed in his mind for hours until he almost felt he was going mad. Had he imagined it? Was it true… was it even possible?

The most he knew was his father's surname – Green – and the fact that he had been a soldier. Sarah had said he had died before Jem was born. Anything else on the subject was firmly locked away in his mother's heart – and Jem knew better than to ask.

He thought back on the events of the afternoon – had that really happened or had it been part of a dream too?

"Come on dormouse. It's almost time." Sarah

thrust a pair of woollen socks into his hand. "You'll need these, it's a cold night."

Jem pulled a face, but then he smiled. Sarah hadn't called him dormouse for years. Not since the days when he had shared her room and huddled in her bed. That was a long time ago now.

He shivered and pulled on the socks as Sarah opened the door cautiously and checked the corridor. No other servants were about – they were all in position, awaiting the arrival of the king. Mother and son hurried down the narrow stairs from the attic rooms and made their way through a series of dark passages before entering a long gallery that hung like a balcony four floors above the great hall. The distant humming suddenly became a cacophony of voices and laughter. Somewhere, musical instruments were being played.

Two levels below, Jem could see the rest of the under-servants crowded together on a lower gallery, all craning for a better view. Little Simeon looked up for a second, and, catching sight of Jem, waved. Jem shook his head and put his finger to his lips, motioning to Pig Face and Old Susan, who were standing just a few paces away from the boy. Everyone knew he had been banned from watching the spectacle.

Jem held tight to the rail and looked down. He didn't much like heights. Even though he knew he was perfectly safe up on the balcony, he still gripped hard and concentrated on the solid boards beneath his feet.

The hall below was glittering with light and colour. He had never seen so many finely dressed people. Even from this distance, he could smell the burning beeswax candles mingling with the scents of the expensive perfumes and oils worn by the nobility. He could smell sweat, too, as the overdressed and overheated bodies below pushed and jostled for position.

"Look, there's the duchess," said his mother, pointing.

The delicate duchess was wearing sapphire blue silk with a coil of heavy pearls at her neck.

"The dress looks well on her," Sarah added, proud of her needlework.

Jem nodded uncertainly. He knew his mother and the duchess were unusually close. When he was small, the childless duchess had almost been like a second mother to him, but recently something in her had changed. Sometimes it was as if she could hardly bear to look at him. He wondered if he was a painful reminder of the children she had never had.

Her moods had become unpredictable and often she was sharp and irritated. As Jem looked down he realised that the woman he had once thought so beautiful now looked disappointed and bitter. She also looked angry – and Jem could see why.

In the centre of the room, the duke was holding the hand of a pretty woman. He was evidently being very amusing because every now and then she laughed, throwing back her head so that her glossy black ringlets bounced and caught the candlelight.

Suddenly a call went up.

"The king!"

Three loud raps sounded and the huge doors to Ludlow House were swung back.

Jem's grip tightened as he leaned further over the balcony. Everyone in the room was suddenly silent as the royal party entered. Like a flock of tropical birds the court women came first, with their jewel-coloured silks and fluttering fans. They were followed by a swagger of capes and ruffles as the king's male friends and companions made their entry.

Finally the king himself arrived. Charles II was taller than anyone else in the room. He was a handsome man with bright, merry eyes and a rather prominent nose.

Charles strode across the hall and slapped the duke on the back.

"So this fine lady will be my dancing partner tonight? What a generous gesture, George!"

The king beamed at the preening beauty standing at Bellingdon's side. His voice was deep and low, but every word carried to the upper balcony.

Jem glanced over at his mother. She too was straining to get a better view and he noticed with surprise that she was clinging to the rail so tightly that her knuckles showed white through the skin. For a fleeting moment he wondered if she was uncomfortable with heights too, but his thoughts were interrupted by an elaborate trumpet fanfare.

He looked down again and watched as the king, Bellingdon and a small party of favoured courtiers moved off into the banquet chamber. The crowd of guests below immediately ebbed and swayed to follow them like the frothy wake of a boat.

The duchess remained in the hall but Jem could see she was not alone. As a man in a dark cloak shot with iridescence like the wing case of an insect leaned in to whisper in her ear, she bowed her head and laughed coquettishly behind her fan. The man was wearing such an extravagant wig that it was impossible to see his face.

The duchess nodded and the man raised his head slowly and began to scan the upper balconies. He was obviously searching for someone.

Eventually he looked up to the level where Jem and Sarah stood.

The duchess's companion was Count Cazalon.

The count's black eyes locked on Jem's and the man performed an elaborate bow, twirling his gloved hand in a theatrical display of politeness. Jem had the disturbing feeling that all along Cazalon had known he was there, watching.

Cazalon said something else to the duchess and she looked up too. Catching sight of Jem and Sarah, she nodded again enthusiastically, patting Cazalon's arm with her fan before pointing it in Jem's direction.

The man bowed deeply to her and then turned his attention back to Jem, staring intently at the boy, but looking amused.

Suddenly Jem felt dizzy. He lost his grip on the rail and slumped forward. He wanted to be sick and felt the cold prickle of sweat beading his forehead. The world began to spin and whirl around him and a series of peculiar images rushed through his mind – the sun raced across a blood-red sky, stars wheeled around the heavens, the moon crashed into the sea, a great pointed building rose from nothing on a desert plain and a huge stone woman with the body of a lion turned slowly and terribly to stare at him with eyes that burned like coals.

Jem was distantly aware of a roaring sound in his head and the tiled floor below seemed to roll like waves on the ocean before it rose up to meet him.

As he fainted, he heard Ann's words ringing in his mind.

"You are right to fear Cazalon. He is a monster."

CHAPTER FIVE

The duke's great banquet was the talk of London. Everyone who mattered agreed that it had been the most magnificent event the city had seen since the coronation itself. Meanwhile, the duke's servants, who did not matter, privately agreed that the feast had caused an enormous amount of extra work. They grumbled for days as everything was cleared away and order regained.

Sarah had clucked and fussed about winter fever as she guided Jem back to his bed after he fainted on the balcony, but by mid-morning next day he had recovered enough to feel hungry.

She tried to smuggle some cheese and meat up to the attic, but when Wormald caught her in the corridor carrying the small covered tray, he demanded that the boy be set back to work immediately. Sarah was furious, but had no choice other than to allow it.

Within an hour Jem was hard at work on a series of never-ending chores. In fact, he had so much to do there was little time to think about what he'd seen.

The arrival of the king had been exciting, but any pleasant memories of his birds'-eye view of the proceedings were eclipsed by the moment he had found himself scrutinised, once again, by Count Cazalon. *Monster* – that was what Ann had called her guardian. It was a thought that unsettled him so much that he tried to put it from his mind.

The morning of the third day following the banquet found Jem still hard at work in the kitchen. His task was to polish the silver salvers and tureens so that they could be safely locked away again in the vaults. It was bitterly cold and the thin February light struggled to reach the gloomy corners of the echoing, stony room. Jem blew on his chilblained fingers, tightened the scrap of bandage that covered his still-bloody knuckles and rubbed even harder at the platter on his knees.

He felt a tap on his shoulder and was surprised to see his mother standing there. Sarah rarely came down to the kitchens.

"You are to leave this now, and go to the duchess," she said. "Be quick about it, Jem. She is waiting in her parlour."

The duchess sat at a desk in front of the tall window overlooking the gardens. Today, the formal walkways and flower beds were invisible beneath a layer of snow.

"Ah Jem, good," she said as he entered the room. He noticed that her pale cheeks were flecked with bright spots of colour.

"I need you to deliver this note to… a friend."

She handed him a sealed square of paper and looked him directly in the eye before continuing, "This is a very private business matter, you understand, Jem? No one, not even your mother, is to know where you are going or what you are doing for me."

Her voice seemed tight and a little strained.

Jem took the note and bowed. He had a twisting feeling in the pit of his stomach and was horribly aware that somehow, he knew exactly where this errand would take him.

The duchess continued, "I want you to deliver this to the house of Count Cazalon in Southwark. I realise that you don't know the way, so we…" she paused, "that is to say *I*, have arranged for Cazalon's pet moor to meet you at the steps to London Bridge at noon. He will guide you to the house and then the count will want you to carry a most important package back to me."

"But, ma'am, I… my duties—" Jem began, trying

desperately to think of a way to avoid this errand.

"Are cancelled for today," said the duchess firmly, adding, "I have already sent word to Wormald that I need you."

Jem groaned inwardly. What would the steward make of that? Whatever the duchess had told Wormald, it would certainly merit another beating. He bowed and backed towards the door.

"Wait. Come here, Jem," the duchess called out. "Here is your toll for the bridge."

She took a small leather pouch from the folds of her dress and counted three coins into the palm of his hand.

"The rest of the money in here is to be given to the count himself and no one else." She gave him the heavy pouch.

"Look sharp now. Off you go… And remember, Jem. No one is to know about this."

❃ ⚊ ❃

Muffled against the bitter cold in a thick woollen scarf and two layers of mittens, Jem left Ludlow House through the yard gate behind the kitchens. He took the passage normally used by the delivery men so that no one would notice him go.

He was confused and angry. And there was something else that troubled him too – the duchess had seemed oddly furtive. What could she possibly be up to that she couldn't even tell his mother about it? Jem didn't like to admit it but he was also scared. He would choose a joint beating from Wormald and Pig Face over a visit to Count Cazalon.

The city was crusted with soot-blackened snow and ice. Even in the darkest narrow streets, where the upper storeys of timbered houses jutted out so far over the road that they almost touched, grimy flakes had still managed find a way through chinks of sky to settle on the ground.

Jem thrust his hands into his pockets and walked quickly, his head buried deep in the folds of his scarf. Despite the chill, the city streets were filled with noise and bustle. Carts and carriages rocked past on the frozen ruts, ragged street vendors called out their wares and knots of red-faced merchants warmed their hands at braziers set up on every corner.

Jem thought about buying himself a ha'penny bag of roast chestnuts just so that he could hold something hot. In fact, he was just about to pay a smut-faced boy tending a street griddle when he realised that he didn't know the toll.

Even if he could get across London Bridge, the thought of not having enough money to get back again – and safely away from Cazalon – chilled his blood more than the biting February wind.

At the bottom of Foster Lane he turned left into Cheapside, the vast black bulk of St Paul's now looming at his back. Slipping and sliding at every step, he pushed his way through the crowds. As he passed a group of rowdy soldiers outside a tavern he remembered Ann's words again. If what she had said was true, his father could be right here in the city and he'd never know it.

He stopped for a moment and stared. Sensing the boy's interest one of the men turned and grinned.

"Fancy yerself a soldier, do yer, longshanks?" The man took a step back and made a play of assessing him. "Well, you've got the height and build for it, lad – and that looks like a good sword arm there."

The soldier winked and turned back to his comrades. Jem felt his frozen cheeks flush with unaccustomed pleasure. No one had said anything like that before. If his father really was alive perhaps he'd be proud of him? Perhaps he'd teach him how to ride, how to handle a sword – all the things Jem secretly longed to do.

As he crunched on his way, Jem was so lost in thought that he was suddenly surprised to find himself on the banks of the Thames. He'd passed through the maze of stinking alleyways that led down to the river without even noticing where he was.

Jem pushed through the crowds towards the entrance to London Bridge, where a mass of laden carts and people jostled to cross over to the south side of the river. The air here was thick with smoke from all the fires in the crooked houses and shops that straddled the bridge.

It was already past noon. The city bells had rung out the hour not long ago.

"I'm down here."

A familiar voice sounded in Jem's head. He turned to scan the surging crowd around him.

"Not there – I'm down here. *Look to your left. I'm on the river."*

Jem jostled his way over to the edge of the Thames and saw Tolly standing on the ice just below.

The dark-skinned boy grinned and waved. Today he was wearing a thick chequered cloak and he was alone. Cleo was nowhere to be seen. Jem felt a pang of disappointment.

"Monkeys don't like snow!" Tolly's voice rang

out in Jem's head. It sounded slightly scornful. *"Don't waste your pennies when you can walk on water. It's perfectly safe. The Thames has been frozen for weeks now. Look..."*

Tolly stamped hard on the ice then gestured behind him. Hundreds of people were actually standing on the now-solid river. More than that, the ice was covered with stalls, tents, huts and even small fires.

Jem scrambled across a low stone parapet and down the slippery slope to join his friend.

"How much have you got there?" asked Tolly.

Jem was about to answer out loud but decided to follow Tolly's lead and be silent. He grinned and simply opened the palm of his gloved hand to reveal the coins given to him by the duchess.

"Excellent," came the reply. *"There's something over here I want to see. Come on."*

Tolly led the way as they skittered across the ice to a ring of people gathered midway across the river. The crowd were standing behind a rope barrier and staring into the depths.

A giant of a man wearing a long fur coat was calling out to passers-by. His single golden earring, a hoop the size of a sovereign, jiggled against the folds of his fat neck as he boomed out, "She is the very miracle of our age! See the mermaid of the Thames, trapped beneath the waters with no hope of release! Not even her scaly sisters can reach her now."

Fascinated, the boys moved closer.

"If you two ain't got a penny to see my mermaid, you can clear off now," said the man, blocking their view.

Tolly gave Jem a nudge and, reluctantly, Jem offered the man a shiny coin.

The man grabbed it eagerly, gave a toothless smile and crunched aside on the ice, allowing them to join the crowd.

The river ice at the centre of the ring had been polished and cleared of snow. It was so smooth and round that it looked like a vast mirror. About twenty people were kneeling or standing around the edge and peering intently into the water.

"I can see 'er tail," said one woman, while another crossed herself and said loudly that such a sight wasn't 'fit for God-fearin' folk' before bending down for a better look.

At first Jem couldn't make anything out in the still greyness. Then, as his eyes adjusted to the murky view, he saw her.

About three feet below the surface a young woman appeared to be suspended in the water. Her arms were outstretched above the billowing brown folds of her skirts and apron. Jem realised that what he originally took to be strands of weed was hair streaming out from her head.

A basket was attached to her shoulder and around it Jem now saw a variety of floating objects, including a mirror, ivory hair combs and skeins of unravelling ribbon. Everything was motionless, trapped in the ice.

The woman's face was turned upwards and her blank eyes were open. Her mouth appeared to be caught in a black 'o' of perpetual surprise.

Jem shuddered. This was no mermaid, it was a frozen pedlar woman fallen through the ice.

At his side, Tolly was absolutely still. He appeared to be spellbound. His eyes were locked on the dead woman's face.

Suddenly, Tolly sprang up and bolted from the horrible scene. He slipped and slid as he did so, pushing into the other people around the ice window. Two of them fell over.

The crowd shouted angrily after him and one of the women rounded on Jem. "You should keep your savage on a lead," she spat. "Animals like that should be locked in a cage."

Jem backed away from the furious crowd and then he too broke into a run. Ahead of him he caught glimpses of the red and black squares on Tolly's cloak as the boy fled to the furthest bank of the river.

When he finally caught up, Jem was breathless. Tolly was leaning against the base of one of the arches of the bridge, his breathing fast and shallow. Jem saw that he was trembling. He tapped the dark boy's shoulder and was shocked to see tears streaking down his face.

"I heard her," Tolly choked the words out loud. "She spoke to me."

Furiously smudging away the tears with the backs of his hands, Tolly straightened up and inhaled deeply.

"She didn't know," he continued as if to himself. "Why didn't she know?"

Jem felt embarrassed. He shuffled his feet and patted his friend's shoulder again. "What that woman said about putting you on a lead was rude and ignorant. But you shouldn't pay attention to people like that, Tolly – London is full of them.

People call me gypsy boy – and worse – all the time."

Tolly looked at Jem oddly. "No, you don't understand, not—" But then he stopped himself, shook his head and pointed at the sickly yellow sun.

"I have been foolish," he said. "And now we are late and my master will be angry. Come."

CHAPTER SIX

Jem had never been south of the Thames before. As the boys trudged along he felt a hundred pairs of eyes boring into him from behind rag-covered windows. Tolly's voice told him to look down at the road, walk quickly and ignore everything.

"*Where exactly are we going, Tolly?*" thought Jem.

The silent reply came immediately. "*To Malfurneaux Place, Count Cazalon's London residence.*"

After a few seconds the voice came again. "*Be on your guard, Jem. I cannot read my master, but I know he means you no good.*"

Tolly led the way down a dark, shabby street and stopped at a wide-arched gate set into a crumbling wall. He pushed at a hinged board in the wooden doors of the gateway and stepped through. Jem followed.

He found himself in a long snow-covered courtyard. Unlike the gardens at Ludlow House, no trees or flowers grew here. Instead, he saw rows of mournful hooded statues interspersed with huge snow-crusted blocks of marble that reminded him of the old tombs that lined the nave of St Paul's. Just occasionally the stone ranks were punctuated by the shattered remains of a broken pillar that pushed up through the snow like a petrified tree.

Tolly's voice sounded in his head.

"*This used to be an old abbey, Jem. The master chooses to live where the past and the present exist as one. Come.*"

He led the way up a central path. As they crunched past one of the statues the shroud of snow covering the figure's cloaked head and shoulders fell away to reveal a grinning skull set deep in stony folds.

Jem shuddered and forced himself to look away.

He realised that the courtyard was completely silent. Apart from the crump of their footsteps, not a sound came from beyond the walls and despite the open sky no birds sang here.

At the far end of the courtyard, the boys passed through a jagged ruined archway and into a smaller yard. Tolly turned to the right, but Jem's feet were rooted to the spot.

The vast blackened bulk of Malfurneaux Place reared up at the far side of the yard.

Ancient, dark and twisted, the tottering levels of the house seemed to reach out over the courtyard blocking any possibility of light from the bleak sky above.

Jem forced his feet to move again, and as he approached the house, he saw that the great black skeleton of timbers binding it together was heavily carved. Women with slanting eyes and wings rode serpents that had grotesque heads emerging from their mouths. A hunting scene streamed across a huge beam, showing a horned man leading the chase, surrounded by slavering wolves and astride a horse with an impossible number of legs. And, Jem realized, peering closer, there were hundreds of carved human figures huddled in the knots and crevices of the wood, as if they were trying to escape from the horrible creatures around them.

As the boy stared at Malfurneaux Place it seemed to shift and move. When he blinked, it was as if the building had subtly rearranged itself, so that what he thought was there was gone – or had changed.

"Don't look at it. Keep your eyes on the ground and follow me. The house is playing with you."

Tolly's voice sounded sharp and nervous.

Jem took a step forward, uncomfortably aware that dozens of arched blank windows ahead of him seemed to be watching his progress.

Tolly's voice came again, "*Whatever happens, remember that we are here too, Jem. You are not alone.*"

A man's voice rang out through the stone courtyard.

"You are late, Ptolemy."

Jem looked up to see a small hump-backed figure standing at the top of a flight of steps leading to a wide, open doorway. The man scuttled down the steps towards them. He was dressed in a tattered black frock coat that made him look like a crow, his skin was wax-yellow and his blind eyes were white as milk. He was bent and bony and his head jutted forward and skewed to the right so that he appeared to squint permanently sideways from beneath a pair of alarmingly springy eyebrows. He was wearing a matted grey wig that kept slipping to the right, causing him to repeatedly jerk his head like a bird to flick it back into place.

The little man sniffed deeply and spoke again. "You've got the lad, then."

It was not a question. He clutched a spindly stick, which he scraped back and forth in the gravel.

"Inside."

He turned and led the way up the steps into the shadowy hallway and the boys followed.

The doors clanged shut behind them and the room was instantly plunged into total darkness.

"I suppose you'll be wanting a candle?" came the man's voice. "Don't need one myself. Old Tapwick knows all the ways here."

A candle flame flared and Jem jumped back in alarm as a skull seemed to float in the air just beneath his chin.

But no, it was Tapwick, and he appeared to be staring up at him. He was so close that Jem could see the hairs sprouting out of his nose. The nostrils flared and the man inhaled deeply.

"Ah, I've got you now," he said, adding, after a few seconds, "I never forget a smell."

The man's breath stank of sour milk. Revolted, Jem took another step back.

Tapwick gave a wheezy laugh and pushed the boy towards a staircase that reared up into blackness from the centre of the hall.

"Master's been waiting for you this last hour. And he's not one to be kept waiting."

The man turned to Tolly. "And you, you black devil, you are to wait here until I say so. Come."

Jem followed as the old man moved easily towards the staircase, taking the thin light from the single candle stub with him. Although Tapwick used his stick as a guide, he hardly needed it – he moved like one who could see.

Just before Tolly was swallowed by the blackness, he smiled encouragingly at Jem, but the expression didn't reach his eyes.

Jem gulped and felt horribly alone. Nervously he started to turn the loose coins over and over in his pocket.

"Stop that clinking. Can't hear myself see," said Tapwick irritably.

At the second landing they came to, Tapwick turned left into a passageway lined with what seemed to be colossal statues. Jem looked at the first of these as they passed, but was so frightened by the dimly lit form captured in stone that he decided to concentrate on the little light moving just ahead of him. He was almost sure that the statue had opened its eyes and stared at him.

They came to a door midway down the passage and Tapwick stopped.

"You are so late that you will have to wait in here while I check that the master is still ready to receive," he said, handing the candle stub to the boy. "Don't touch anything," he warned as he pushed

Jem into the room and shut the door.

Jem listened as Tapwick's footsteps and the scraping of his stick faded down the corridor. He stood at the threshold to the gloomy room, his heart pounding away so heavily under his ribs that he imagined he could almost hear it. The air was foul – it smelled as if something old and sick was rotting here. Jem took a deep breath and raised the candle.

He was in a long, narrow gallery, much like the room at Ludlow House where the duke displayed his latest treasures – only, this room had no windows. The weak light from the little flame picked out several large, oddly shaped objects standing in the corners. They were all smothered under grey dusty cloths.

Feeling uncomfortably aware that he was being watched from above, he jangled the coins in his pocket and raised the candle higher.

Jem gasped and shrank back against the door.

A gigantic, snarling black cat loomed over him. The animal's huge eyes glowed with blank ferocity and its unsheathed claws seemed unnaturally long and sharp. The creature seemed to be about to spring, but Jem realised with a surge of relief that it was long dead and was actually suspended from wires on the ceiling. A skilful hand had frozen the animal's body in an eternal, deadly pounce.

He breathed deeply and stumbled to the side to get away from the horrible thing above him. As he did so his boot caught in a heap of fabric spooling on the floor from the largest of the odd covered objects standing about the room. The object began to rock and the cloth covering slumped heavily to the floor.

Jem coughed as a rancid smell suddenly hit his nostrils, then blinked as he tried to make sense of the sight before him. It was another animal, and at first, it appeared to Jem to be a crouching lion. But, instead of snarling jaws, the creature had the open beak of an enormous bird, like an eagle. A pair of vast golden wings sprouted from the lion's back and Jem shuddered as he saw the cruel jagged stitches punched into the animal's skin, where the wings were attached with splints of wood and thick black thread. This work was done by a far less skilful hand, and the creature smelled as if it were rotting from the inside out.

It's a gryphon, he thought, remembering a picture he'd seen in one of the duke's books.

In the far corner, beyond the gryphon, Jem's

candle revealed another draped form. He hesitated for just a moment, then stepped forward. He had to know... He raised the candle and tugged at the musty cloth covering. As it fell, he found himself standing beneath the hooves of a rearing horse. Jem gagged. The terrible smell was even worse now.

This animal had once been a noble stallion, but now it was dirty and grey.

As he looked at the horse, Jem felt tears prickle in his eyes and bile rise in his throat.

But worst of all was the twisted, bony horn that grew from the centre of the stallion's head, just above the sightless eyes. Jem could see immediately this wasn't a real unicorn – the ivory horn was clamped into place by four metal bolts hammered into the animal's skull. He felt blind fury that someone could do such a thing to a beautiful animal.

This sad, dead creature in its forgotten corner was slowly rotting away, just like all of the other monstrosities that were no doubt hiding beneath the other cloth shrouds in the room.

Jem shuddered and hastily backed away. This was horrible, the work of a madman. He felt disgust, and pity for the unnatural creatures around him.

Ann's words suddenly came to him. *"My guardian*

is a collector. His house is full of the most hideous and unnatural things."

He wondered how his friends could survive here surrounded by such… evil. Yes! That's what he felt. This place was truly evil.

"Enjoying the master's toys, are we?"

Tapwick's question sounded more like a sneer. The bent little man was standing at the entrance to the room staring sightlessly at Jem.

"Master's ready for you now."

Jem's breathing became fast and shallow, he could feel the muscles in his legs twitching and little spurts of white-hot energy cramped his stomach.

If Cazalon could do all this to these poor animals, what might he want to do to *him*?

Every fibre of his being told Jem to run, but something else told him that escape would be impossible.

"He is waiting. Come!"

Jem followed Tapwick deeper into Malfurneaux Place through a maze of passages and stairs. He wondered if he would ever be able to find his way out.

"Nearly there."

Tapwick held back a thick velvet curtain and ushered Jem into an arched corridor.

After the brooding silence of the rest of the house, Jem suddenly found himself deafened by the ticking sounds of hundreds of clocks and ancient timepieces. How had he not heard them on his approach? Jem shook his head in amazement.

Some were beautiful golden treasures, others were dark metallic contraptions with their open workings twitching and moving. They seemed oddly alive.

"Master calls this *the passage of time*." Tapwick sniggered as he brushed past Jem. "Keep up."

At the far end of the corridor, where it turned off to the left, Jem made out a greyish column propped against the wall. As he got closer, the weak light from his little candle showed that the object was in fact a grotesquely delicate clock constructed entirely from bones.

Small bones, large bones, grey bones, yellow bones – they were stacked together to create a hideous filigree box topped by a smooth ivory dial.

Fascinated and repelled in equal measure, Jem saw that the broad dial was covered in writing and strange symbols. Instead of showing the time, the single hand – formed from what looked like a small human arm, hand and fingers – seemed to point at dates and years.

He heard a scuffling noise near his feet and looked down. At the base of the clock, nestled among the bones, Jem saw a bird. The little creature blinked its black eyes and cheeped. Despite himself, Jem smiled and bent closer.

The bird ruffled its feathers... and scuttled off into the darkness on what looked like the four, pink hairless feet of a rat.

Jem brought his hand to his mouth to muffle a yelp of horror.

Tapwick laughed and started to scratch his stick backwards and forwards on the floorboards.

As the scraping sound echoed around the corridor, the ticking of the clocks grew louder and louder. Jem brought his hands to his ears to block the painful noise.

Then all the sounds stopped at once, as a door at the far end of the lefthand passage clicked ajar. A dull pulse of red-gold light spilled out through the crack in the door and across the bare boards.

"I'm to leave you here," said Tapwick, snatching the candle stub.

He shoved the boy towards the door and then turned back into the clock-lined passage, disappearing into the blackness.

Jem stood alone. The tips of his boots glowed dully in the faint light from the door. He looked closer. Next to his foot there was a pile of white crystals. In fact, now that he was becoming accustomed to the gloom, he could see that instead of a pile of crystals, it was actually part of a semi-circle of small white granules running across the floorboards, arcing from one side of the door to the other.

Jem bent down to touch it. Salt. *Pig Face would never allow such extravagance,* he thought. Salt was expensive and hard to come by. He took a pinch between his thumb and forefinger and as he did so, the door opened wider and a wave of tremendous heat rolled into the passage.

For a moment Jem found it difficult to breathe – but it wasn't just the heat that caught at his throat. The air was filled with the tang of something sweaty, old, musty, decayed and horribly sweet.

"Master Green, you are sinfully late."

Cazalon's weirdly accented, sing-song voice sounded from the depths of the room. "But as we are destined to become so very close, I will forgive you. Come here, boy, where I can look at you."

Jem swallowed hard, stood up and stepped over the semi-circle of salt and into the room.

CHAPTER SEVEN

Jem found himself in a long, wide chamber with a vast painted ceiling. The only source of light came from a fire crackling in the hearth of a magnificent carved chimney breast halfway down the room. In the gloom he couldn't quite make out what the painting high overhead represented, but he was aware of hundreds of glittering eyes staring down at him.

"Come, warm yourself, Master Green. You must be chilled to the marrow."

The lazy hissing voice was unmistakably Cazalon's, but he was nowhere to be seen.

Jem began to walk nervously towards the hearth. Even though the fire was at least thirty paces from the door he could feel intense heat from the dancing flames on his face. With every step, his eyes grew more accustomed to the dimness.

Like the room where Tapwick had left him earlier, Cazalon's chamber had no windows. On the left, the wall was hung from floor to ceiling with a series of tapestries. Jem recognised the dark woven forms of centaurs and goat-legged satyrs from the duke's books of Greek myths.

On the right, the room was lined with a row of squat black chests. Standing on the top of the first chest was a large plaster model that appeared to show a ring of tumbled stones set in a field. On the next, Jem saw something that looked like a Roman temple, with rows of horizontal steps and vertical columns.

Finally, he recognised the building displayed on the last chest – it was a model of St Paul's Cathedral.

"I see you are admiring my playthings, Master Green."

As Jem turned towards the voice, every fibre of his being was strung tight as a viol.

Cazalon was seated in a tall-backed chair beside the fire. The chair's back was to the door, which was why Jem hadn't noticed him.

A gloved hand pointed to a spot in front of the fire.

"Stand there. I want to look at you."

Jem noticed that Cazalon's hand trembled. As he turned to face the count, Jem saw that he was wearing a long red gown that spooled out across the floor. A black curly wig hung from one of the carved points at the top of the chair and his head was close-shaven, apart from a single plait that snaked from the top of his crown and was draped over his right shoulder. In the firelight the plait appeared to be blue.

Cazalon didn't move. He was slumped oddly in the chair and his painted face looked gaunt and tired. But his slanted, mirror-like eyes glinted with dangerous energy as they flickered over the boy's face. At last, the count spoke.

"So very like your father."

Jem was startled. Despite his fear, he couldn't stop himself from blurting out eagerly, "You knew my father, sir?"

Cazalon smiled slowly. "Well, you are nothing like your small, fine-boned, golden-haired mother – Sarah isn't it? Companion to the duchess?

"You, on the other hand, are olive-skinned, black-haired and tall for your twelve years. So I conclude, Master Green, that you must look like your father. It is a simple deduction."

Suddenly Jem was angry. Everyone seemed to have something to say about his father – except him. Forgetting his fear he took a step forward.

"My father died before I was born. I don't know what he looked like… sir."

He scowled and fell silent. How dare this strange man speak of his mother, let alone his father. He had no right.

Cazalon leaned forward to poke at the fire with his knobbled staff and the flames danced and crackled.

"I seem to have upset you, Master Green, and I am sorry. Perhaps we can begin again?"

Jem shifted uncomfortably. All he wanted to do was hand over the duchess's note, collect her package and get away from Malfurneaux Place as quickly as possible.

Cazalon stared at him. After a moment the man tapped the tip of his staff lightly on the floor and the crystal bird's head sparked with firelight.

"I enjoy games, Master Green, they help to pass the time. I hope you enjoy games too. Can you guess from what this staff is made?"

He twirled it slowly on the spot so that the odd twisted knobbles seemed to move up and down its length like snakes around a branch. Jem found himself mesmerised, unable to look away.

"It is the petrified backbone of a shark. Do you know what a shark is?"

Jem shook his head.

"Then I shall tell you. A shark is a fish – a most

dangerous specimen, the sharp-toothed wolf of the sea. I trust you will remember that useful fact. Do you like quizzes, boy?"

Jem looked at his feet. He didn't want to talk to this man. He just wanted to leave.

"Sometimes, sir. It depends on the subject."

Cazalon leaned forward in the chair and smiled.

"Good, then let us start with observation. What have you noticed about my house?"

Jem was silent. He had noticed so many revolting, unsettling and frankly terrifying things about Malfurneaux Place. What answer did Cazalon expect?

"Well… Jeremy? I think I shall call you that."

Jem replied warily, "It's… it's very dark, sir."

"And what else? What about the people here?"

Jem considered the only people he had encountered inside Malfurneaux Place, before replying uncertainly. "Er… your page cannot speak and your steward cannot see?"

"Good, Jeremy. Good. We spoke earlier about deduction. What do you deduce from your last statement?"

Jem was lost. He looked around the room trying to find inspiration in the models and tapestries.

At the far end of the room there was a huge black shape in the shadows. Jem realised it was a vast canopied bed topped with a crest of dark feathers and gilded with figures. The thick velvet curtains were pulled shut around it.

Cazalon coughed.

"I would appreciate it if you would concentrate on my question, Jeremy. Think."

Jem thought very hard, before stammering, "It tells me that you are a good master to employ those who are so afflicted."

Cazalon coughed again and then began to laugh. This wasn't the thin metallic laugh Jem had heard before. This was a laugh that grew to a deep, wild howl that seemed to wrack Cazalon's body so violently that the man had to cling to one of the chair arms to steady himself.

Cazalon slapped the arm.

"Osiris, did you hear that?" he wheezed, still rocking with mirth.

Behind him, Jem suddenly heard a rushing sound like wind moving through tree tops. The hot air from the fireplace seemed to shift over his head as a huge white bird swooped close to his ear and came to settle on Cazalon's chair.

The bird turned its milky pink eyes on Jem and opened its ugly beak to reveal a yellow tongue that wriggled like a fat worm. Osiris leaned forward, raised its tail and deposited a steaming squirt of foul-smelling liquid on the floor.

"Such a messy pet," said Cazalon affectionately, adding, "but what can one do? An albino raven like my beauty here could not live in the wild. His kind would tear him apart."

Cazalon looked directly at Jem.

"So, in some ways, young man, your answer to my question was quite correct. Despite their afflictions, Tapwick and Ptolemy are both singular people and I value their particular... qualities."

He leaned forward and Osiris began to sway excitedly on the chair behind him.

"But what I value most, Jeremy Green, is that one of them cannot see what happens within these walls and one cannot tell of it. And that is the lesson I want you to learn today."

Grasping his bird-headed cane, Cazalon raised himself to his full height. The movement seemed to cause him pain.

"I understand that you have seen some of my toys today, Jeremy?"

Jem nodded, thinking that 'toy' was strange choice of word to describe the wretched deformities he'd seen earlier.

As if reading his thoughts, Cazalon smiled slowly and spoke again. "When I was… younger… I travelled the world to find the creatures of ancient myth and make them my pets. I am sure that an inquisitive boy like you would be as disappointed as I was to find that gryphons, unicorns, manticores and merfolk did not exist. They were merely stories – the work of imagination.

"Ah, but then, Jeremy, I thought to myself, if such creatures could be created in the mind, why should I not create them in the flesh?"

Cazalon paused for a moment and his eyes bored into Jem's.

"It was such a pity," the count concluded, dropping his words slowly and deliberately into the air like stones into a deep well, "that none of them survived beyond a month."

An image of the white horse with the horn bolted cruelly to its forehead flashed into Jem's mind. The animal had been alive when Cazalon experimented upon its body. He wanted to be sick.

Cazalon watched him carefully. "And so I believe

we understand each other, Jeremy. If you and I are to become…" Cazalon paused and appeared to test a phrase in his mouth before uttering it, "… *bonded in friendship* before you leave today, I must extract a promise of discretion from you."

Jem nodded dully. His mouth had gone very dry. Somewhere a small, hopeful voice told him that Cazalon had talked about him leaving.

Leaning heavily on the staff, Cazalon took a step closer to Jem and caught the boy's chin between his fingers. Again Jem smelt the odd perfume of sweetness masking putrefaction. He stared up. Cazalon's eyes were closed and his dark-painted lips were moving.

Suddenly Jem began to choke. His throat felt blocked and dry. Pulling himself free from Cazalon's grip, he bent double as his stomach heaved. He began to retch – and sand poured from his mouth. He spluttered and coughed, fighting for breath, but to his horror, the sand kept falling and falling.

Then suddenly, it stopped.

Jem gasped and swallowed a lungful of air. It felt as if his chest was bound with iron bars. He braced his hands on his knees and tried to control his ragged breathing, then he wiped at his mouth and straightened up.

Cazalon was smiling.

For a second any fear was driven from Jem's mind as he burned with hatred. He thought about lunging at the count – perhaps he could grip the plait and pull the man to his knees?

But Cazalon thumped his staff heavily on the floor and the fire in the hearth began to flare and pulse.

Jem felt his eyes begin to scald, his very eyeballs seeming to boil in their sockets. He could see and feel nothing but searing flames, as a pair of hot coals burned in his head.

Then, as quickly as it had begun, the pain stopped. Jem stood shuddering before the hearth. Around him, the room was swimming and everything appeared to be red. He blinked hard and winced at the sudden shot of pain that speared his temples. His head throbbed and tears were now streaming from his eyes. He wiped them away and then pulled to loosen the linen band covering the birthmark at his aching throat.

Cazalon barked a short, hoarse laugh.

"Just a taste of what I can do to those who displease me, Jeremy. I trust that you are now aware of what might happen if you were ever to reveal the secrets of my extraordinary…"

The count broke off as he noticed Jem's bandaged hand. Most particularly it seemed that Cazalon noticed the fresh blood that had seeped through the scrap of cotton over Jem's raw, scraped knuckles.

His eyes widened and he grasped the staff more tightly.

After a moment he spoke in an eager cajoling voice. "But where are my manners? You are injured and as I am, among many other things, something of a physician there is nothing I should like more than to help you. Show me your hand."

Jem didn't move. He stared sullenly at the floor.

"Your hand, boy. I haven't got all day."

Cazalon's voice was light, but there was an oddly strained quality to the words that made Jem look up. The man was staring intently at him, his pupils were dilated with concentration – for a second it almost seemed that his eyes were completely black. Jem felt compelled to raise his bandaged hand and hold it out to the count.

Cazalon leaned forward and tutted as he unwrapped the bloody scrap and examined Jem's scabbed knuckles. The tip of his thin black tongue appeared as he moistened his cracked lips.

"You should keep the wound clean to guard

against infection. And you should allow it to breathe." Cazalon scrunched up the blood-speckled bandage and quickly stuffed it into the folds of his gown. "You will not be needing this again, Jeremy."

Jem noticed that the man smiled broadly as he patted the place where he had secreted the bandage and smoothed the material.

Then Cazalon stared intently at him and he had the strangest sensation that he could feel the count inside his mind. Not in the way that Tolly spoke to him, but rather as if something was sneaking around in his deepest thoughts and trying not to be noticed. It was like the faint itchy feeling when a tiny insect lands on your skin.

Osiris bobbed excitedly on the pole. The bird opened its pale yellow beak, dribbled and let out a single 'kraak' of approval.

Cazalon nodded and looked over at his vile pet. He murmured something that sounded to Jem like, "Soon, my dear heart, my own soul."

The count clapped his gloved hands.

"And now to business, my young friend. I suppose the great duchess will be expecting her cure?"

Jem felt in his jacket pocket for the duchess's note. He handed it over.

Cazalon took it between the thumb and forefinger of his right hand and held it away from him as if it were something unpleasant. Then, without warning, he quickly crumpled it into a ball and tossed it into the flames without even reading it.

"And the money?"

Jem dug into his pocket and produced the coin pouch. He was about to hand it to the man, but Osiris swooped swiftly and silently, and snatched up the little bag in his bent grey claws.

The count gave a satisfied smile and limped over to the fire. He reached up into the carvings of the chimney breast and retrieved a small polished black jar with a lid shaped like the head of a hawk.

He turned.

"Do you know what this is, Jeremy?"

Jem shook his head.

"It is a canoptic jar from taken from the tomb of a long-dead king of Egypt. A pharaoh, in fact. This little jar once held the mummified remains of the king's heart, so that when he made the great journey to the afterlife he might..."

Cazalon stopped. He whispered, "Afterlife," once more, then laughed. It was a bitter, angry sound.

The count removed the cap and poured a handful

of black dust from the jar into a small pouch. He continued, "This substance is mummia, boy. It is made from the powdered skin, bones and corpse wrappings of the pharaohs. It is the most ancient and valuable medicine – a physick that can prolong youth and life.

"Your mistress is to add one spoonful of mummia every day to a single glass of wine and drink it immediately."

Cazalon's eyes narrowed as he handed the pouch to Jem.

"One spoonful only, mind. That is most important. You must make that very clear to her, Jeremy. If the duchess uses more than the amount I have prescribed…"

Cazalon paused and drew his hand across his forehead. He stumbled back and sank into the chair beside the fire, staring silently into the flames. He clapped his hands again.

Moments later, Tapwick entered the room.

"Take him," muttered Cazalon without looking round. "Ptolemy will show him the way back."

The count's eyes closed and at that very moment Osiris took flight upwards to the painted ceiling of the room, letting out another piercing 'kraak'.

CHAPTER EIGHT

The door to Cazalon's chamber closed silently behind them.

Tapwick sniffed, jerked his wig back into place and scuttled off up the corridor. Jem found that he almost had to run to keep up with the little man, who carried the only source of light. They went back through the passage of clocks and then down several flights of stairs.

The boy and the steward were racing along a particularly long dark passageway when something very odd occurred. Tapwick, who was four paces ahead of Jem, stopped dead. He was frozen in the middle of a step with his left foot hovering inches above the floorboards. It happened so instantly that Jem nearly knocked into him from behind.

The boy cleared his throat, "Er... Mr Tapwick, are you all right?"

There was no reply. Confused, Jem walked round to stand in front of the old man.

Tapwick's milky eyes were open and unblinking. From the scruffy wig on his head to the springy hairs in his nostrils and the unravelling threads dangling from his ragged cuffs, nothing about him moved. Even more oddly, the tiny flame of the candle he carried was utterly motionless, too. Like an old clock, Tapwick had simply stopped.

Jem wasn't sure what to do. He tried to prise the candle from Tapwick's hand but it wouldn't budge. He stared into the blackness ahead but couldn't make out a thing.

"Tolly!" he whispered, as loudly as he dared.

There was no reply.

He tried with his mind instead. "*Tolly… are you there?*"

Nothing.

He had to get away.

Jem took a deep breath and stepped away from the frozen man and into the gloom. Within just ten paces he was engulfed in the hungry blackness of Malfurneaux Place. He swallowed hard, held his hands out in front of him and cautiously continued forward.

"Take five more paces and then turn right."

A light musical voice sounded in the dark. Ann!

"Don't be frightened, Tolly's here, too."

In confirmation, Jem suddenly felt a small tug

on his coat and a familiar chirrup as Cleo jumped lightly to his shoulder and began to stroke his ear.

He edged carefully forward and turned right, after the fifth step. The dark was somehow thinner here. Jem could now see another long corridor ahead of him. At the far end, Ann stood at the open door of a lighted room. She motioned for him to join her. Cleo leapt from his shoulder and raced to her. Gratefully, Jem followed. When he reached the door, Ann quickly ushered him inside.

Jem found himself in a tiny, cramped bedchamber. Rags hung at a tiny barred window set high in the wall and the room was almost empty apart from a narrow bed and several piles of books. Patches of brown mould spotted the walls, making the chamber smell musty and damp. The only sources of light seemed to be a single candle set in a sconce on the wall by the bed and a little fire crackling in the grate.

Ann smiled brightly, but she looked even smaller and thinner than he remembered. Her wide green eyes shone with a sort of feverish intensity and her white hair seemed to glow like a halo.

"Welcome to my room, Jem. As you can see, as befits the ward of such a great man, I live in the lap of luxury."

She smoothed down the skirts of her tattered green dress. Jem saw it was the same one she had been wearing the last time they had met.

Ann smiled bleakly, before continuing. "I am sorry I cannot offer you a delicious pie, or even a glass of water. But you can, at least, warm yourself. Here Tolly, use this one to feed the fire. I've read it now. I'll remember it."

She tossed a book to the other side of the room. Jem now saw that Tolly was crouched in front of the tiny hearth. Tolly tore at several pages, scrunched them into balls and pushed them into the grate. Then he grinned at Jem and spoke out loud.

"You survived, then?"

The words were light but Jem noticed the quick anxious look that passed between the dark boy and the girl.

"Tolly, we don't have much time," said Ann quickly, "You know I can't hold Tapwick for long. Ask Cleo to keep watch."

Tolly called the monkey over and bent to stroke her ears. Cleo chirped softly and scampered over to the door. Ann let her out and wedged the door ajar with a book, then she turned to Jem and demanded abruptly, "Do you know anything about the rites of binding?"

Jem shook his head, he had no idea. He felt confused and frightened. Even though he was relieved to see the others again, instinct told him to run as fast and as far as possible from Malfurneaux Place.

"I don't know what you mean," he said. "Please, I just want to get out of here. This place is… is… *evil*."

He almost whispered the last word. He had a strange feeling that the house might be listening. Then another thought blazed in his mind.

"What did you mean about my father, Ann? You know – when you came to the duke's house… That was you, wasn't it? I wasn't imagining it? You said he was alive."

Ann ran a hand through her luminous white hair, pushing it back from her pointed face. "I am sorry, Jem, but we don't have time for explanations. You must tell us everything about your meeting with my– my g– guardian."

She faltered over the last words and Tolly rose to join her by the door. He took her hand and squeezed it. Jem felt oddly excluded.

"You two seem to know so much already. I think it's me who deserves some answers."

Ann sighed and shook her head.

"Now is not the time Jem, but I promise to

explain everything to you later. As much as we know, that is. But for now, you must listen to us. I've sealed Tapwick into a moment of time, but I can't hold him long – I've not practised enough. I *need* to know what happened in that room. What did my guardian say to you? Everything is a clue."

Jem looked from Ann's troubled green eyes to Tolly's serious brown ones and knew that he could trust them. But all the same, he felt they were both keeping something from him.

"Please, Jem." Tolly poked another crumpled page into the grate. "I understand why you are reluctant to help us, when we won't answer your questions, but now is not the time for explanations."

Ann took a step forward. "Jem, start from the beginning. Try to remember everything you saw and heard after you left Tolly in the hall – and do it quickly, before Tapwick comes looking for you."

Jem began to speak. Once he started, the words tumbled from his lips as he described the horrors of the house, the mutilated animals, the passage of clocks and the rat-footed bird.

When he got to the interview with Cazalon, he lowered his voice to a whisper, as if repeating the man's words could conjure him up. When Jem finished, Ann's eyes were round as saucers.

"I haven't seen those rooms," she said. "Officially I'm a prisoner in here, but even when I've managed to get out and explore – I usually only make it as far as the library…" she pointed at the piles of books, "I've never seen the chambers or the poor creatures you describe. What about you, Tolly?"

The dark boy looked troubled.

"I've seen my share of strangeness here – the library itself is strange enough," he looked knowingly at Ann and she nodded, "But I've never seen those animals, Jem. I think the house shows people what it wants them to see. Only Tapwick and Cazalon can truly navigate its maze."

Jem shuddered. "Malfurneaux Place and its master should be burned to the ground. I can't understand why you two stay here."

Ann laughed bitterly. "Where would we go, Jem? Look at us. A penniless girl and a moor. Where would we find a place to hide? Who would help us? We would be starving on the streets, and worse. This house is our only home. When my mother and grandmother were taken, I had no choice. I…" a huge sob stopped her words and Ann hid her face in her hands.

Tolly put a protective arm about her shoulders and glared at Jem.

"It is not so easy to be free," he said angrily.

Jem bit his lip. His words had been thoughtless.

"You're right. I'm sorry, I didn't mean…"

Ann fished a grimy rag from the folds of her skirt, blew her nose and smiled weakly.

"Don't worry," she said, sniffing. "Besides, Tolly and I *have* to be here, Jem. We think my guardian is about to do something terrible, but we don't know what it is or why he wants to do it. The only clue we have is that he needs the boy of jade to make it happen. We're certain that's you."

She stopped for a moment and frowned. "Jem, think. When he spoke to you did he take anything of yours?"

He shook his head. "No, nothing… unless you count the bandage."

The air in the room seemed to freeze.

"What do you mean?" Ann's voice was tight.

Jem described the moment when Cazalon examined his knuckles and stuffed the blood-stained bandage into the folds of his gown. Ann turned paler than ever. The bones of her tiny face seemed to be straining against the skin that covered them, her tapering fingers picked at the fabric of her dress.

"Jem – remember how I asked you about the rites of binding?"she said.

"Yes." He had a bad feeling that he had already failed an important test.

"The rites of binding are used in the old magic to tie a person to your will and your desires. Once you have tricked a person into fulfilling the five rites you have complete power over them. You will be able to make them do what exactly what you want. They will become your creature.

"Giving someone something from your body – like hair, spittle, blood – that's one of the rites. Because Cazalon has your blood, Jem, it means that he will now be able to enter your thoughts. He will read your mind."

Jem shivered as he remembered the peculiar, irritating feeling inside his head that started just at the moment when Cazalon took the bandage.

"Is there a way to stop him?"

"You must be wary at all times when you are near him," said Ann. "If you feel him in your mind, concentrate hard on one single, secret thing – a happy or perhaps a sad thought, a wish or a desire. It should block him for now, until I can find a way to protect you."

"Is that what you two do?"

Ann and Tolly exchanged a swift glance, making Jem feel excluded again.

"What about the other rites, Ann? What must Jem be on the look out for?" Tolly ignored Jem's question, but still smiled encouragingly.

"Of course. How stupid of me."

Ann took hold of both of Jem's hands. She began to speak slowly, all the while staring into his eyes as if willing him to remember her words.

"You must not accept food from him. You must not kneel to him and you must not give him an article of your clothing."

Jem nodded, repeating the instructions in his head.

"And the fifth rite?" he asked.

"You must not cross a barrier of salt at his invitation."

Jem dropped her hands.

"But I– I… have already done that. I crossed a half circle of salt at the entrance to his chamber when he called me in."

The little room was silent for a moment.

"I've already completed two of the rites, haven't I?"

"Jem, you weren't to know. It's not your fault." Tolly's voice was warm and calm. "Now you'll be on your guard. It will be fine – you are ready for him."

Ann nodded. She smiled, but Jem saw fear in her eyes.

"We need you to keep *all* your wits about you at all times," she said, "because although my guardian is fascinated by you – his *jade boy* – he is also plotting with your master, the duke. That's right, isn't it Tolly?"

Tolly nodded. "Usually the duke makes Cleo and me leave the room when Cazalon visits Ludlow House – he's terrified she'll break something. But I've heard enough to know that they're up to something. And from what I've been able to read in the duke's mind, I know he's excited – and nervous too. They are planning something together, but the duke's head is muddled. I'm not quite a mind-reader Jem – I mostly sense people's feelings."

"So you see, Jem," said Ann, "we must find out what they're up to. There's a puzzle here, but we can't solve it without your help."

Jem stared at the other two children.

"How do you know?" he began. "I mean, how did you find out about this jade boy stuff and what makes you think…" but before he was able to finish the sentence Cleo came bounding through the partially open door. She chattered furiously and leapt onto Tolly's shoulder.

"Quickly, Tapwick will wake at any moment," whispered Ann. "Take this candle and find your way back to the exact place where you stood when I stopped him. Tolly – you too. You must be in position down in the lower hall where Tapwick first left you."

She grabbed the single candle from the sconce on the wall and pressed it into Jem's hand.

"Run!" she ordered, and the boys and the monkey barrelled from the room leaving Ann lit eerily by the thin light of the tiny fire.

They raced down the corridor and turned to the left – then skidded to an abrupt halt in horror. Cleo shrieked and covered her eyes.

Tapwick was still motionless, frozen in mid-step, but they could not reach him.

The floor ahead was completely covered by a writhing carpet of huge black-backed insects. Millipedes, earwigs, beetles, worms – a moist shining nest of them wriggling and rippling across the floorboards, up the walls and over Tapwick's feet.

As the boys stared in horror, the little candle in the man's hand began to flicker.

CHAPTER NINE

Cleo clambered up on to Tolly's shoulder.

The seething insect carpet seemed to be flowing up the passageway towards them and all the while, the glow from Tapwick's candle pulsed stronger and brighter.

Jem heard a gasp.

Ann was now standing two steps behind them, her eyes locked on the wriggling blackness. She stepped between them and reached out for their hands.

"The house is playing tricks on us," she whispered. "If we truly believe they are not there, they won't be."

"But they *are* there. Look at them!" hissed Tolly. "There must be millions of the horrible things!"

"Don't believe your eyes. Believe your heart. Walk with me." Ann took a firm step towards the insect mass.

"I can't," Tolly replied, pulling her back.

Ann looked at Jem.

"What about you?"

Jem looked at the twitching black mess that now seemed to be swarming high onto the walls overhead.

"I– I don't know."

"You must trust me. They are *not* there. Come."

Ann took another step forward and pulled the unwilling boys with her. Cleo shrieked. Jem looked down at Ann's determined face and suddenly felt ashamed.

"I believe you. Come on, Tolly, we must do as Ann says."

Jem took a step forward, so that he was level with Ann.

"Walk with me," said Ann again, and this time even Tolly took a step forward.

"I think I'm going to be sick," he groaned as they walked grimly towards Tapwick.

"Believe," whispered Ann, as, in unison, they stepped into the carpet of insects.

As their feet touched the ground the swarm vanished. Just a few feet ahead, Tapwick's candle flickered and the tufty hairs sticking up from the man's wig began to jitter.

"Into positions, quickly," yelled Ann. Snatching the candle from Jem's hand, she blew the little flame out and tossed it over the bannister into the darkness, before heading back towards her room.

Tolly and Cleo raced off into the gloom and Jem

scudded into position behind the bent little steward.

Tapwick's frozen foot quivered and then it came down to make contact with the floorboards. He continued to scuttle along the corridor and down the stairs as if nothing at all had happened. Jem followed. When they reached the hallway, the steward turned his parchmenty face up to Jem and scowled.

"Ptolemy will take you to the bridge but no further, mind. He's needed back here."

Tapwick raised his nose to sniff the air. "I can smell you and that monkey, boy. Where are you? There's work to be done."

"There's no one here but you and I, sir," Jem said hurriedly. Tolly and Cleo clearly hadn't made it back in time.

The man took a step forward and his boot crunched down on the small candle that Ann had flung over the bannister just a minute earlier. He bent down.

"And what do we have here, then?" he said, picking up the candle in his skeletal fingers and raising it to his nose. He turned his sightless eyes on Jem.

"I can smell *your* fingers on this candle, boy. Now, why should that be?"

Tapwick started to sway excitedly from side to side

and for a second Jem was oddly reminded of Count Cazalon's revolting pet raven. He thought quickly.

"I found it on the stairs earlier, sir, when you took me up to the count's room. I– I put it in my pocket because I like to read at night, but there are never enough candles at Ludlow House. It must have fallen out through a hole."

"So you're a thief, are you?"

Tapwick seemed to be enjoying this.

"No. Not at all. I just thought it wouldn't be needed. You told me that yourself earlier, sir. You know all the ways here without need of light."

"Indeed I do, boy," said Tapwick, thoughtfully turning the candle beneath his nostrils. Then the man leaned in so close that Jem almost choked at the stench of his foul breath.

"But if I ever find that you have been trying to trick me, I'll make sure that you know all about the ways here, too. And some of 'em aren't too hospitable, if you get my meaning."

The man began to giggle at some private joke and little bubbles of spittle appeared at the corners of his lips.

Tapwick wiped his mouth and raised his own candle. "Are you there, moor?"

There was a chirp from Cleo as Tolly stepped into the yellow candlelight and winked at Jem.

"So you've finally deigned to join us, have you?" said the blind man, sniffing hard. "You're to take him to the bridge and no further."

Tapwick shoved Jem towards the doorway and then raised his hand to smell the candle again. The man's nose creased and wrinkled as he snuffled.

His sightless eyes closed and he opened his mouth as if to speak, then stopped himself, muttering something that sounded like, "No. Not possible – she can't have done."

Tapwick shuffled over to the doors and grappled with the huge bolt.

"Be off with you," he called as the boys – and the monkey – gratefully tumbled down the crumbling steps and into the fading light of a February afternoon.

As the great double doors creaked and juddered to a close behind them it sounded as if the house was muttering to itself.

꛰ ☰ ꛷

Jem trudged along behind Tolly, lost in thought. It was getting dark now – the icy streets were treacherous and it was colder than ever. Tolly had wrapped Cleo into the thick folds of his chequered cloak. She was perched on the boy's shoulder with her head peeking out next to his. Jem could just see the end of her long white-tipped tail swishing under the red and white material.

Occasionally, Tolly spoke into Jem's mind, urging him to keep up, but the boys didn't talk until they turned into a broad street leading down to the river where shops and brightly lit taverns were thronged with noisy customers.

They crunched past a baker's shop where a man was clearing snow-dusted currant buns from the wooden shelf outside his window. Jem realised that he was ravenous.

He felt for the two coins in his pocket. He knew he would have to use the bridge going back. He didn't want to skidder across the frozen river – and the dead girl – in the dark.

Jem turned the coins in his fingers and looked at his companions' hungry faces.

He heard Tolly's voice in his head. *"If you are thinking about the buns – and I hope you are – the bridge toll is a penny, you'll still be able to pay your way."*

Decision made, Jem handed over a coin and

bought four currant buns. Pocketing the treats, the boys slid off down the street towards the southern entrance to the bridge. Fire lamps were now burning at the gateway and a long queue of carts, carriages and people waited to return to the city.

Jem tapped Tolly on the shoulder and pointed down to a sheltered stone archway set into the riverbank. The archway faced onto a small platform, used by boat traders to load and receive goods, and it was deserted apart from the glowing embers of a fire that someone had lit there earlier, when the river itself had been a bustling marketplace.

"Come on," said Jem, "we can warm ourselves while we eat."

"And perhaps you can answer some questions," he added, meaningfully.

The boys picked their way down a short flight of ice-crusted steps to the privacy and shelter of the archway.

"That was fast thinking with Tapwick and the candle back there," said Tolly aloud, arranging his cloak to sit cross-legged in front of the small fire.

"I'm used to it. Pig Face is always trying to catch me out in the kitchens. And there's Wormald, too. You met him, remember?"

Tolly snorted. "It would be hard to forget him!"

Jem reached into his pocket for the buns and handed one to Tolly.

"Right. I think you owe me some answers," he said, decisively, tearing off a curranty morsel and offering it Cleo.

"For a start, who is Count Cazalon and what does he want of me? You two seem so sure that I'm in some sort of danger from him. Why?"

Tolly sighed. "I'll tell you as much as we know, Jem, but I'm not sure it will help."

"Well, you can at least try me," Jem snapped. "After all, I thought it was you two who needed *me*!"

Tolly caught his meaning.

"No, it's not that we don't trust you. It's just that we don't know what he's up to. Even Ann, with all her gifts, can't make out his intentions."

"That's another thing," said Jem through a mouthful of currants. "I don't want to be rude, but who *is* Ann anyway?... And for that matter, who are *you*?"

Tolly looked uncomfortable. "Look, I know this is all confusing and difficult, but, please, you must trust us."

He frowned and huddled Cleo against his side.

"So many stories." The words were spoken softly, more to himself than to Jem.

Then he looked up and smiled sadly.

"I'll tell you my story and then you can make up your own mind about me. But I think I'll need another one of these first."

Tolly tore a bun in two and offered half to Cleo. He began to speak, but his voice seemed to come from somewhere very far away.

"Once, I had a father, a mother and a baby sister. My father was a good man, a great and powerful man, and my mother was kind and beautiful. We lived in the most wonderful city. Our home was by a wide green river and we were happy. Then traders came. They pretended to be our friends, but they were liars – they tricked us all. They invited our people to a great festival outside the walls by the river. Everyone was so excited. We trusted our new friends and wanted to impress them so we dressed in our finest clothes and brought all our richest goods to trade. But they didn't want our goods. They wanted us."

Tolly paused and took a deep breath before continuing.

"When we arrived at the water, five huge black barges were waiting for us. Instead of trade goods, our *friends* had weapons and we were bound, herded on board and trapped below the decks. Those who fought back were killed. The only people left behind the red earth walls of the city were the old and the sick. Everyone wanted to be at the festival."

Tolly shuddered. Jem saw that his friend was pulling the remains of the bun in his hands into tiny, tiny pieces.

"We sailed up the river for days, perhaps weeks, all of us crushed together in the dark and filth of the barges. At first we talked, sometimes we sang, but eventually we fell silent. All apart from the smallest children… I remember my little sister crying in the dark and my mother trying to comfort her. Some people became very sick. For a long time I was chained to a dead man, Jem. Can you imagine what that was like?"

Jem shook his head.

"My father was so angry. He promised us that when we stood on the ground in the open air again, he would call up a storm and destroy the traders and their boats.

"Then, one day, the doors were thrown open and blinding light flooded into our prison. We were dragged from the barges and forced to line up on a long stone quay. I'd always thought my beautiful home was the biggest place in the world, but the city where we now found ourselves was huge. It was called Alexandria, in the place your people know as *Egypt*. So many people, so many buildings, so much noise… We were terrified."

Tolly looked deep into the fire, as if he could see the scene he was describing flickering in the flames.

"Only my father was strong and brave. He began the chant to call up the storm he had promised, but the traders knew of his power. They made him kneel in the dust and the sand on the riverbank. They whipped him… and then they cut out his tongue."

Tolly stopped.

Horrified by what he had heard, Jem reached over to touch his friend's shoulder. Tolly tensed and a single tear rolled down his cheek.

"It was the first time I heard a voice in my head. My father spoke to me that day, after they ripped out his tongue. As he lay in the dust, I heard his voice telling me to be strong, telling me to protect my mother and sister."

He took another deep breath. Jem knew Tolly was trying not to cry, so he looked away.

"I never saw my father again after that day.

The women and children were separated from the men and were taken in chains to the marketplace. We were sold like animals, right there on the quay. My mother fought to keep me with her, but the traders knew a strong boy was more valuable when sold alone.

"Sometimes, at night, in my dreams, I hear her calling out my true name, just as she did when I was dragged away from her and my sister."

Tolly looked straight at Jem. "On the day that Count Cazalon bought me, I had seen six great floods – so, in your world, I was six years old."

Jem didn't know what to say. Tolly's words made him feel ashamed of ever feeling sorry for himself. Wormald and Pig Face were nothing compared to this. At least he had a mother who loved him, sometimes.

After a moment he stammered, "And your mother, did you ever see her again?"

Tolly shook his head.

"That day on the quayside was the last time I saw my family. Within three days Cazalon boarded a ship for London and I was part of his baggage – as was Cleo here."

Tolly fondled the monkey's ears – she had crept

into his lap as he spoke. Her head was now poking out of the front of his cloak and she was peering up at him anxiously. "I don't know what I would have done without her company during the voyage. And since."

"I am so sorry, Tolly," whispered Jem.

Tolly stared into the flames. "It was a long time ago."

The boys sat in silence.

Across the river, thousands of lights were now twinkling from the houses. Tolly pointed at the thin sliver of new moon that was now apparent in the inky sky above St Paul's.

"You must go home, Jem. You'll get in trouble and I will be missed at Malfurneaux Place."

"But there's so much more I need to know," Jem protested. "What about Count Cazalon, who is he?"

Tolly laughed grimly. "My master is a collector. He was in Egypt buying mummia. Do you know what that is?"

"I do now. I've got a pouch of it here for the duchess." Jem patted his pocket.

Tolly looked alarmed.

"You must be careful, Jem. Mummia is a most powerful medicinal and magical powder. It is said to prolong life and restore youth, but it is dangerous.

Very dangerous. Never touch it directly."

Jem felt for the pouch in his pocket and carefully tested the string that tied it. It was sealed.

"What does Cazalon do with it – with the mum… mummia?" he asked Tolly.

"He dissolves it in wine and drinks it every day."

"That's exactly what he says the duchess must do. It must taste disgusting."

Tolly smiled.

"As you must have noticed, my master does not live like other men. His interests are… singular. If something is strange or contrary or *other* – he must have it. I think that's why he took Ann into his household."

Jem nodded. The white-haired girl was certainly strange.

"What happened to Ann's parents, Tolly?"

"Her mother and grandmother were hanged as witches. The Metcalfs were a wealthy family with a fine house and acres of land. Ann believes her grandmother was accused by a jealous neighbour.

"The old woman was taken and tortured and then Ann's mother was arrested, too. Ann was just a few years old at the time and was therefore deemed innocent."

Here Tolly paused and added with a wry smile, "But as you have seen, she *is* a witch. One day she might be a very powerful one – although she needs to practise more."

He grinned mischievously. "A couple of weeks ago she tried to turn herself into a bird, but it went a bit wrong. She had feathers for eyelashes for several hours afterwards. But you mustn't tell her I told you about it."

Jem stared at his friend. Witchcraft was evil, a crime punishable by death. What if Ann was in league with the Devil?

Tolly held up a hand to stop Jem's racing thoughts.

"Jem, there are many sorts of magic. When I read the images in your mind and speak silently to you, is that not a wonder? It is not evil.

"Ann has inherited great powers, but she is a good soul and a good friend to me. And to you too, now, I think?"

Jem was quiet for a moment. Even if witchcraft was a crime, he knew deep down that Ann was a good person. He thought about her mother and grandmother and shivered. What if someone accused Ann of witchcraft? Would she be hanged too? The thought was horrible and upsetting in a way that Jem couldn't begin to understand.

Tolly smiled.

"Although Malfurneaux Place is not a... comfortable home, at least Ann is safe there. She believes that one of the reasons Cazalon paid the courts to become her guardian was because he wanted the Metcalf family possessions that would come with her, and most particularly, the books belonging to Ann's mother and grandmother. Now, their grimoires are part of his library."

"Their what?" Jem was lost, again.

"A grimoire is a book of spells. Ann's family has practised magic for generations so their books are especially powerful."

"But hang on," Jem pressed his friend, "what did you mean about *one of the reasons* he paid to be her guardian? Weren't the grimoires enough? Why else does Cazalon want her?" Jem fixed his eyes on Tolly's. "There's more, isn't there... What aren't you telling me?"

Tolly suddenly looked fearful. He stood up, and pulled his cloak around him, making sure that Cleo was covered by its folds.

"Enough stories for today. I must go back now or there will be hell to pay."

He smiled, but there was something about his words that made Jem feel anxious.

"Wait. I have to know more. Why does Cazalon want *me*?"

"That's something we need to find out. We are certain you are the jade boy, but we don't know any more than that," said Tolly, stamping on the embers of the little fire. "Now, you must go too, before the bridge closes for the night."

Tolly ducked out from the beneath the shelter of the arch and began to climb the icy steps. At the top, without turning back, he raised his right arm in salute. In his head Jem heard the words, "*Thank you for the food, Jem. We'll meet again soon.*"

As Jem made his own way back to the bridge, snow began to fall again thick and fast. He joined the long queue of people waiting to pay the toll for crossing on foot.

Jem's mind was swimming with questions as slippery and quick as a shoal of a thousand fish, but one thought kept bobbing to the surface – if the count was a collector, as both Ann and Tolly had said, why did he want to add him, ordinary Jem Green, to his collection?

CHAPTER TEN

Sarah and the duchess were waiting anxiously for him in the small blue salon. His mother's face was pinched and her eyes were pink, as if she'd been crying.

"Where have you been?" she demanded as he stood shivering in front of the bright little fire.

"I– I got lost."

Jem glanced uncertainly at the duchess. She gave a quick nod.

"As I told you earlier, it is entirely my fault. I ran out of red thread for the slippers I have been making for His Grace. I sent Jem out to buy some more. Forgive me, Sarah, it was foolish on such a day as this, but I was impatient to finish."

The duchess looked at Jem and gave a tight smile.

"And now he is safely back with us," she continued briskly. "Sarah, would you go and make sure that Jem's bed is warmed tonight and that a fire burns in his room? It is the least I can do to make amends."

Sarah looked suspiciously from Jem to the duchess and was clearly about to make a comment, when the duchess continued, "Perhaps you could also ask one of the kitchen maids to warm a posset of hot milk and brandy for our prodigal son here."

She turned to look at Sarah. "While you arrange matters I shall keep Jem here with me by the fire. He is chilled to the marrow."

Jem shuddered, remembering that Cazalon had used those very words earlier.

Sarah bristled a little at the duchess's order, but rustled into action. As she passed Jem, she laid a soft hand on his face and bent to whisper, "Don't ever frighten me like that again, do you hear me, Jemmy? Never again."

She hadn't called him 'Jemmy' for a long time. He felt guilty about lying to her.

When they were alone, the duchess patted the stool beside her chair and invited him to sit by her. Her brown eyes were twinkling with nervous excitement.

"Now, I think you must have something for me?"

Jem felt for the pouch of mummia in the pocket of his jacket and handed it to the duchess.

She looked disappointed.

"Is that all? It is a very small quantity."

Jem shifted uncomfortably.

"He says, er… that is to say, the *count* says, that you are to take one spoonful in a glass of wine each day. But no more. Just the one, ma'am, he was most specific."

The Duchess of Bellingdon seemed to weigh the pouch in her hand for a moment.

"Why, it is more valuable than tea. I shall have to lock it away."

She looked shrewdly at Jem.

"Do you know what this is, boy?"

Jem looked at his feet. The snow was beginning to melt from his boots into a little puddle on the floor.

"Um… he said it was a– a… medicine, ma'am."

The duchess clapped her hands and laughed.

"Indeed it is. Indeed it is – a most extraordinary and *secret* medicine. Do you understand?"

She stared meaningfully at Jem and he nodded. Satisfied, the duchess patted the pouch in her lap and smiled broadly.

"Thank you, Jem. That will be all for today. You must rest now as I can see that my little *errand* has tired you." It was true – Jem's eyelids were drooping as he huddled on the stool. He was fighting hard to stay awake. The duchess rose from her chair and rang a tiny silver bell. Then she carried the mummia over to her desk, unlocked a drawer and placed the pouch among her papers and writing things. All the while, she hummed a merry tune.

Then the door to the small salon opened and one of the maids entered, holding a steaming posset. The tantalising aroma of honey, brandy and nutmeg wafted into the room and, despite everything, all Jem could think about was his warm bed in the attic.

⚜ ⚛ ⚜

Over a month had passed since that terrifying visit to Malfurneaux Place and Jem was back to his usual drudgery. A bout of winter fever was burning through the kitchen and today he was hard at work on the tasks usually tackled by at least three other scullion boys. Pig Face had already beaten him twice: once for falling behind and the second time for trying to explain that he was doing enough work for four.

Jem scrubbed at the globules of fat stuck to the metal of a grease-covered pan. The water in the trough in front of him was ice cold.

Sometimes, he wondered if the whole thing had been a nightmare, but on the odd occasion when he was above stairs and came across the duchess, she would smile at him and whisper that her *medicine* was agreeing with her.

And that's when he was reminded that it was all horribly real – and when he found himself worrying about Tolly, Ann and Cleo in that dark and terrible house.

At least the duchess seemed happier. *Even if mummia is disgusting stuff,* Jem thought, *it is certainly doing her some good.*

From petty servants' quarrels to the discovery of a whole side of spoiled ham in the lower pantry, nothing seemed to bother her.

Jem was glad to see the duchess happy, and his mother seemed to have caught her mistress's high spirits. There had been several times recently when Sarah had laughed and joked with him just as she had when he was still a small child, and once, he had even heard her speak of his father.

He was carrying a pitcher of sweet wine to the duchess and was just outside the door to the blue room when he heard Sarah say, "He is so alike to his father in manner that it takes my breath away. Sometimes I can't look at him because the likeness is so strong."

"Yes. I often see it, too," came the duchess's reply

through the half-open door. "Something in the way Jem stands – and, of course, the face he makes when he is angry."

The women looked up from their sewing as Jem entered the room. "There. Do you see it now?" said the duchess and Jem saw them exchange a meaningful look. He scowled. They didn't know he had heard their words. Once again, it seemed that everyone was at liberty to discuss his father except him.

"The shame of it," one of the kitchen maids had hissed, when she thought Jem wasn't around. "Forced to raise *his* child in her own home – and she as barren as a mule." The maid had laughed, cruelly. But when Tobias the footman raised an eyebrow and indicated that Jem was standing behind her, she'd just covered her mouth with her hands and scuttled off.

Jem loved his mother, but he was also angry with her. Why did she never mention his father? Was it possible that the servants' chatter was true?

Was the Duke of Bellingdon his father?

It was the first time he had let himself pay any attention to the servants' idle gossip and it made him feel shabby and sick at heart. In truth, the man had never shown him any particular affection, but his wife, childless Mary, had once treated him like her own son. Jem knew that she had been his mother's close friend for many years, but was *he* the secret lurking at their heart of their friendship?

But if the duke really was his father then why was he treated so badly himself?

Jem winced. His hands were like blocks of ice in the water and he couldn't feel his fingers. He leaned against the trough and tried to rub some blood back into them.

"Slacking again, are we?"

Thwack!

The blow caught him across the shoulders. Wormald stood just behind him, his malevolent grey eyes alight with pleasure. The steward flexed the jagged cane between his fingers.

Jem looked desperately around the kitchen, there was no one else in the room. Wormald took a step closer.

"And don't think your hoity-toity mother will come running to save you, boy. She's upstairs planning the Easter feast with the duchess. We are completely alone."

The steward smiled unpleasantly. "And even if there were other people here, no one would raise a hand to help you. You've no friends, lad."

Thwack!

The second blow caught Jem's arm. But just as the steward was about to lift his cane again, he gasped and clutched his stomach. The air was suddenly filled with the most potent and appalling smell of rotting cabbage laced with bad egg. Seconds later a gigantic rumbling rippled from the man's breeches.

Wormald hopped from foot to foot for a couple of seconds making little grunting noises, then, with a face as grey as his hair, he doubled in two and scuttled like a crab to the yard door.

Jem let out a long breath and grinned broadly.

Wormald was wrong. He did have friends.

✄ ⚊ ✄

Easter came, and, as usual, Sarah presented Jem with a gift – a fine new linen shirt she had made in secret. He gave her an egg on which he had carefully painted the image of a leaping hare. He couldn't buy her a proper gift, but she seemed delighted.

As was customary on Easter Sunday, the whole household, right down to the lowliest kitchen spitboys, went to the service at St Paul's – the greatest and oldest of the City's churches.

Inside, it was dark and shadowy and even the

decorations of bright spring flowers failed to banish the gloom. The Duke and Duchess of Bellingdon sat in their own crested box pew near the altar and the servants stood at the back of the congregation with the city commoners. Jem and Sarah positioned themselves somewhere midway, between the rabble and the richly dressed aristocrats, wealthy city merchants, aldermen and judges.

Jem's new shirt was stiff and scratchy, and the band of material he wore round his neck to cover the ugly birthmark felt hot and uncomfortable as it rubbed against the starched linen collar. He fidgeted moodily and stared up at the soaring arches of the ceiling above to try and stretch his itching throat.

The sermon was long and very dull. The fat little preacher had a high-pitched squeaky voice, but what was even worse was that he couldn't sound the letter 'r' properly.

"We must all stwive to wemember," quavered the cleric, "that evil wears many faces and will twy to twick us. Do not take the wong woad, for only the wighteous may find eternal west in the heavenly wealm."

Jem stifled a snigger and his mother prodded him with her elbow. He managed to control his laughter until the little man finally concluded by shouting out the triumphant words, "Wejoice! Wejoice for He is Wisen!" Jem's shoulders started to rock, but the more he tried to control himself the funnier it seemed. He buried his chin into the collar of his coat as hot tears of unexploded mirth started to stream from his eyes. Covering his mouth with his hands, he pretended to be coughing, as he tried to convert the wild bubbling sound that was building up within his chest into something more acceptable. He could feel Sarah's angry eyes boring into him. "I think you had better go outside, right now!" she hissed, and Jem gratefully turned to push his way through the people standing in front of the west door.

The press of bodies was thick here and the crowd reeked of sweat – and worse. Jem was relieved to burst out into the fresh air and bright spring sunlight, where he threw back his head and finally allowed the huge guffaws that had been bottled up inside to erupt.

"I am glad that you seem to find the rituals of the church as ridiculous as I do, Jeremy." The sibilant voice was unmistakable. Jem spun round and found himself staring into the glinting black eyes of Count Cazalon. The man was dressed in a black cloak that reached to his ankles and his curled periwig was white as snow. His red-painted lips curved into a smile.

"It is always so pleasant when friends find something new to bind them together, is it not, Jeremy?" Jem took a step back and looked about, the City streets were deserted. Everyone was attending the service.

"I– I had to leave because I was coughing and didn't want cause a disturbance," he said weakly, aware that Cazalon had been watching him.

"Well, well, that is certainly a most irksome affliction: perhaps I can offer you something for it – a soothing lozenge, perhaps?"

He reached forward and Jem saw a pouch in his hand.

"Do take one of these, Jeremy. I find them most efficacious for congestive problems."

Out of nowhere, Ann's warning about not taking food from the count rang clear and true in his mind.

"No!" He shouted.

Cazalon's eyes narrowed.

"I– I mean, no… no thank you," Jem stuttered. "I do not think it will be necessary, sir."

The boy took another step back. Cazalon slowly detached himself from the ancient blackened wall against which he had been leaning and stalked towards Jem, supporting himself on his twisted staff.

"You disappoint me, Jeremy. And it is always so rude to reject a friend's offer of help."

There was anger in Cazalon's expression, but his voice was controlled.

"I shall cast my sweetmeats to the pigeons here instead then."

He reached into the pouch and threw a handful of red sugared balls into the midst of a nearby knot of cooing grey birds. Immediately they fell upon the offering.

"It is no matter. I shall forgive your unkindness. Now, I have a private message for the duchess and I wish you to convey it to her."

Jem looked at his feet and shuffled uncomfortably.

"Look at me, boy," Cazalon commanded and Jem raised his face. The count was staring at him intently, and the tip of his tongue appeared briefly in the middle of his painted lips, like that of a snake testing the air.

"Tell her that I will bring a new supply *very* soon."

Jem nodded. He tried to look away but found that he couldn't. He was also horribly aware of a familiar itching, prickling feeling beneath his scalp.

But this time it was more powerful, as if something with hundreds of slimy tentacles was probing his thoughts.

Remembering Ann's advice about concentrating on a strong memory or a desire, Jem thought hard about the huge feast waiting back at Ludlow House. Christmas Eve and Easter Sunday were special occasions when the whole household ate together.

It wasn't difficult, he could almost taste the succulent roasted lamb and there were rows of pigeon pies waiting in the pantry. Jem smiled at the thought.

An odd expression crossed Cazalon's face. He turned and looked up at the vast, looming bulk of St Paul's behind them. After a moment he sighed.

"Such an ugly building, don't you agree, Jeremy?"

The boy didn't know what to say. St Paul's was a constant landmark in the city and in his life.

He glanced about, trying to find an appropriate answer and his eyes fell upon the bodies of three dead pigeons – the ones that had fought earlier over Cazalon's lozenges.

Jem's eyes widened in horror and the count followed his gaze. He smiled cruelly.

"Such horrible, greedy scavengers, aren't they. Fit only for *a pie* I would say, wouldn't you?"

Cazalon stared at him and once again Jem was aware of the probing, flickering sensation inside his mind. But before the count could delve any further, a great peal of bells sounded from the lofty square tower behind them, breaking his gaze.

The service was over.

CHAPTER ELEVEN

Jem had found that his appetite for the Easter feast had vanished.

The entire household had gathered together at a long table in the great hall of Ludlow House, but despite the platters of delicious meats, pies, syllabubs and pastries, Jem hadn't been able to eat. He'd asked his mother if he could be excused and had slipped from the hall.

Now, one thought kept chasing around his head – what would have happened if he had taken one of Cazalon's lozenges? Would he be dead too, like the pigeons?

"Ah Jem! This is where you are hiding."

The curtain to the window seat where he sat, lost in thought, twitched aside. It was the duchess. Her eyes were bright and her skin shone, but as Jem looked up he also saw that she was breathing very quickly. Her pearl drop earrings quivered on their pins as her body trembled.

He stood and bowed, but the duchess smiled, settled herself down and patted the padded wooden seat next to her.

"Now, Jem," she began, "I need to speak to you very privately and this is just the place." She smoothed out her skirts. "I find that my supply of *medicine* is running rather low, so I shall need to you to make another visit to my dear friend the count." The smile disappeared and her eyes grew hard. "Of course, you do understand, Jem, that this is a very... delicate matter. You shall not speak of it to anyone. Not even your mother." She gripped his hand so tightly that it began to hurt.

Jem shuddered. The last thing he wanted to do was to go back to Malfurneaux Place. For days after that first visit, the infernal house kept appearing in his dreams. Jem would find himself lost in a labyrinth of dark door-lined corridors and every time a door opened, it would reveal another room of hideous things.

He gulped. "I– I don't think that will be necessary, Ma'am. I– I... met the count at the cathedral this morning. He told me that he will bring you a new supply of the m– m– medicine."

The duchess dropped his hand.

"When?" she hissed. "When is he coming?"

For a moment her face looked strained and old, as if a veil of creased muslin had fallen over her features.

Jem stared and then, aware that he was being rude, he looked down. He cleared his throat.

"Um… Count Cazalon said it would be very soon, ma'am. That's all I know."

"Good," the duchess snapped. "You may leave me now."

She waved her hand and turned to stare out over the formal gardens beneath the window. Jem backed away as swiftly as was polite. It wasn't just that the duchess looked different – when she waved her hand he had caught a faint waft of the sweetly putrid smell he had come to associate with Cazalon.

✵ ⚎ ✵

Two days later, Count Cazalon called at Ludlow House.

Tolly and Cleo were with him as usual, but this time he was also accompanied by two men.

One was tall and ancient with a mottled, slab like face that resembled an old cheese. The other was a thin and rather nervous young man with pale, watery eyes and a receding chin. He looked very like a fish.

The odd party arrived just as Jem was crossing the gallery above the hall on an errand for Wormald. He ducked behind a huge ornamental vase to listen.

The duke came to greet them himself. He seemed eager and excited.

Jem watched as Cazalon, who today was dressed entirely in black, including his wig, introduced the other visitors.

"Your Grace, it is my pleasure to present the Marquis of Kilheron," the count said, as the younger man stepped forward and swept a low bow. "And, of course, you already know Lord Avebury, here."

The older man nodded at the duke. The movement was slow and deliberate, as if his head and neck were made from stone.

A loud knock echoed through the entry hall and the footman swung back the massive carved doors to reveal a very fat red-faced man puffing on the doorstep.

"I'm not late, am I? Never does to be tardy in business. Now, what I always say to the wife is—"

"And this is the fifth member of our little club," Cazalon interrupted. "May I present Alderman Pinchbeck, whose fame as a merchant already stretches from the Indies to His Majesty's new colonies in the west."

Pinchbeck lumbered forward and clasped the duke's hand. His shabby grease-marked frock coat gave no clue to the fact that he was known to be one of the richest men in the city and his broad accent suggested that the place of his birth was not within the finer districts of London.

The other men eyed the alderman disdainfully and acknowledged his presence with the barest inclination of their heads. Members of the nobility did not like to mix with the merchant classes – even when those merchants were extremely wealthy.

"To business!" exclaimed Bellingdon. "I have ordered refreshments and a fire to be set in my rooms so we shall not be disturbed."

Cazalon raised his gloved hand.

"I wonder, Your Grace, if my servant here might provide some amusement for the duchess while we are otherwise occupied? The monkey is vastly entertaining and I thought that the lady…'

"An excellent suggestion," beamed Bellingdon. "It will do her good. Between ourselves, gentlemen, my wife has been acting most strangely these last few days. You know how women take on so."

He laughed and the other men smirked in agreement. The young marquis made a noise like a donkey.

"So," Cazalon continued, "perhaps after Ptolemy

has carried these plans to the gallery, young Master Green – who I see is polishing the vase on the balcony above – might convey him and my monkey to your good lady?"

Jem reddened and stepped out from behind the vase. How had Cazalon known he was there?

Now that he had a clear view of the floor below, Jem could see that Tolly was carrying four great rolls of paper and several more were stacked at his feet.

Bellingdon looked up.

"Well, boy? Do as my guest asks."

Unwilling to meet Cazalon's gaze, Jem bowed his head and descended the wide oak staircase to the floor below.

"Pick them up and follow us," said the duke, pointing down at the scrolls.

As Jem bent to gather them together, Cleo, who was nestled on his friend's shoulder, let out a welcoming chirrup. Jem looked up and caught the expression of warning on Tolly's face.

Bellingdon led the way across the black and white marble tiles of the hall. Up ahead, a footman opened a set of double doors. The duke allowed his guests to enter the room first, then he followed, leaving the boys staggering after him with the scrolls.

"You may leave them there and then go," said the duke without looking at Jem and Tolly, indicating the table at the centre of the room. "Oh, and take the moor and the animal to the duchess," he added to Jem.

The boys shuffled over to the table and gratefully allowed the heavy scrolls to roll from their arms.

Jem bowed to the duke's guests and led the way from the room, passing a gilded buffet table that groaned with pies, tarts, tiny roasted larks, marchpane fruits, custards and pitchers of wine. It was obvious that Bellingdon had ordered that no expense should be spared to impress his guests.

The centrepiece of the display was a pineapple, but Jem knew that no one would taste this exotic morsel. It had been specially hired for the occasion at great cost.

Jem's stomach rumbled and Tolly shot him a quick smile.

As the doors closed behind them, Jem tried to communicate silently, but his question was met by a sharp, "*No, not here.*"

The trio headed back across the hall and were halfway up the great staircase on the way to the duchess's salon when Tolly spoke into Jem's mind.

"*We should be safe now. I can't feel him any more –
there's enough distance between us.*"

Jem didn't need to ask who Tolly meant.

Tolly continued, "*Ann warned me that we must not
communicate when we are near him. Because Cazalon
has your blood, he can enter your mind and listen. But,
the greater the space between you, the less he will be able
to hear.*"

"*But what about you and Ann?*" Jem thought.

"*We found out long ago that he can't hear us. Ann
thinks it's because of our own gifts – her magic, and
my ability to read and speak into minds. He foolishly
assumes that I can't think for myself, because I don't talk.
Cazalon regards me as a pet, like Cleo here, and I intend
to keep it that way.*"

Tolly scratched Cleo's nose affectionately and the
little monkey caught his finger and hugged it.

"Now, we need to find out what they're doing in
that room. Is there any way we can get near enough
to hear them without being seen?"

"But what about the duchess? The duke said
I was to take you to her…" Jem was uneasy.

"There's plenty of time for that. It's more important
to find out what they're up to – if we can."

Jem thought for a moment and remembered that

the massive fireplace in the duke's meeting room was connected to a smaller fireplace in a bedroom directly above it. The bedroom was grand, but hardly ever used because the sun never shone through its windows and it was always cold. Once, years ago, Jem had squeezed himself into the deep recess of its fireplace while playing a game of hide and seek with his mother, and had been surprised to hear, very clearly, the sound of two housemaids grumbling about their duties coming up the chimney from the room below.

"*Follow me,*" he thought, and led the way up a second flight of stairs.

Easing the door open, the boys and the monkey crept into the gloomy bedroom. The dark velvet hangings on the monumental four-poster bed that stood opposite the window were dusty, and despite its size and grandeur, the room had the air of somewhere sealed up and forgotten.

"Over here," whispered Jem. The boys tiptoed across to the fireplace and ducked inside, under the carved stone opening. At the back, a vent connected with a main flue that ran from the room below, up into the huge brick chimney on the roof above.

"*We must be very quiet and still here – and so must Cleo,*" thought Jem.

Tolly smiled. "*She knows that already.*"

Tolly reached up to his red silk turban and eased a familiar jewel from the folds.

"Ann!" Jem asked in an excited whisper.

Tolly placed the jewelled scarab beetle on the hearth stones just outside the fireplace. Within a few seconds the transformation began as before. The boys shielded their eyes as the plume of purple smoke coiled itself into a glowing human shape. Once again there was a soft, sad musical noise and Jem caught the scent of violets. When he looked up Ann stood there, brushing glittering dust from the folds of her ragged dress.

"Hello again."

She grinned at Jem and bent down to join them. "Budge up then," she whispered as she crammed herself into the little gap between them. Cleo jumped from Tolly's shoulder to settle in Ann's lap.

Carefully and silently, they folded themselves into comfortable positions in the cramped soot-blackened space. Already they could hear echoes from the room below, but, as they sat in perfect silence, they began to hear almost every word quite distinctly.

"Do help yourself to another pie, Kilheron. My cook is one of the finest in London."

This was the duke. They heard footsteps – presumably the young marquis – walking over to the buffet.

"Excellent. They really are most awfully good."

Kilheron's voice was high and thin.

Jem's empty stomach made a small growling noise like a hungry kitten. He looked down guiltily.

"Never mind the food, Bellingdon. We are here to discuss the matter of London." This was another voice. It was deep, dry and resonant. Jem thought of Lord Avebury. Tolly nodded.

The duke's eager voice came again.

"Indeed, indeed. And so we shall, my lords."

There was a cough and the duke added, "My lords *and* Alderman Pinchbeck… Now, I feel that perhaps Count Cazalon is the man who can best explain our business proposal."

The children heard a rustling noise. It sounded as if someone was limping to the fireplace while dragging a swathe of material behind them.

"My dear friends," the sing-song voice was unmistakeably Cazalon's, "we are gathered here today because we love this great city."

There was a murmur of assent.

"And we love our king, too, do we not?"

The murmur became a clamor of agreement.

"God save His Majesty," called out Kilheron.

Cazalon continued. "Then what better service could we offer him than to embark on a project to create a great new city that is fit for our most gracious monarch?"

There was a moment of silence below, then Cazalon's voice came again, "London has become a sewer, an abomination, a pit of squalor and pestilence. Only last year we carried the diseased bodies of our citizens from their houses and buried them, by the thousand, in lime pits beyond the walls."

More murmurs of assent below. Jem shivered as he recalled the events of the previous summer, when plague had stalked the city, claiming victims wherever it found them. Old, young, rich, poor – all were equal in the shadow of the Great Sickness. Most of the duke's household had moved out of London to Pridhow, the Bellingdon country estate in Herefordshire, but reports came daily of the suffering and horror.

Four of the servants who had stayed behind to mind Ludlow House had unwisely visited family in the narrow, fetid streets of the city and never returned. Little Simeon the pot boy had lost both his parents, which was why Jem always looked out for him.

When the worst of the sickness was over and the household returned from Pridhow, one of the younger footmen who had stayed on in London took great pleasure in describing the sight of the plague carts that rolled past the windows of Ludlow House.

"Piled with corpses they was – sometimes stacked seven or eight deep. And the stench! You've never smelled the like of it. But d'ya know what the worst thing was, Jemmy boy?"

Jem had swallowed and shaken his head. "The very worst thing of all was that some of 'em was still a-twitchin' and a-moanin'."

Jem looked across at Tolly, but his friend's eyes were closed to Jem's thoughts as he concentrated on the room below.

From below, a leaden voice cut into Cazalon's speech. It was Avebury.

"Who can assure us that the plague will not return this year?" he asked, although it was more like a statement. The heavy voice continued.

"The streets are a stinking disgrace and the poor who infest the city are like vermin. They and their diseased houses should be wiped from the face of the earth so that we may build a new and godly city in the place of this swamp of sin."

"A new Thebes," said Cazalon softly. Tolly's eyes snapped open and he stared at Ann.

She nodded, whispering, "You're right, Tolly, the ancient city of Thebes…" Then she looked at Jem and added, "The library at Malfurneaux Place is full of manuscripts from this place, but we can't work out why it is so important to him…"

"Steady now."

This was clearly Alderman Pinchbeck, his tone was stronger and less respectful. "You say that London must be cleansed and built anew. That's all very well, but how can this be? The plague didn't kill everyone. What will you do with the citizens, magic them away?" The alderman snorted.

"I cannot invest in a whimsy. I'm sure your plans are very pretty, my lord, but how can we build a new city here when one already stands beside the Thames? Answer me that."

There was a long silence and then Cazalon spoke.

"I believe that an element of… *sacrifice* will be necessary to help us achieve our vision."

The rustling noise from below indicated that Cazalon was moving away from the fireplace.

Then his voice came again, more distantly, but still audible.

"Look at my plans, gentlemen. Do you not marvel at the beautiful city that London will become?"

There was a crackling sound as if stiff parchment was being unfurled.

Cazalon spoke again.

"Here, Lord Avebury, is a magnificent square that will bear your name. George, this sweeping and generous avenue at the heart of our new London shall be Bellingdon Street, and we will build you a fine new house just here. Kilheron, do you mark that grand crescent? It is yours.

"And finally, Alderman Pinchbeck, I have set aside a park for you."

There was a general murmur from below. The men were examining the plans.

"And what is this?" The weedy piping voice belonged to Kilheron.

"That is the new cathedral' Cazalon replied casually.

There was a pause and then Kilheron continued, "But it is the most extraordinary shape, sir. Why, it looks like a star. Yes, that's it – a star with five points. I've never seen a church like that before."

Cazalon's reply was smooth and measured. "Gentlemen, this is a new London. We shall be the masters here, free to create whatever we like – to build to the limits of our imagination and beyond. We shall create a phoenix from the ashes."

"Do you mean to burn the old city to the ground? What about the people?"

This was Pinchbeck. He sounded outraged.

Cazalon's reply was chilling. "How else are we to achieve our goal? Have we not already agreed that the poor and their contaminated buildings must make way for our wonderful city? One great fire will purge London and clear the ground."

"But what of the king?" demanded Kilheron. "It is his city. This is madness. Indeed, sirs, it is treason."

There was a long silence below as Kilheron's words hung in the air.

Then Cazalon began to speak again and Jem noticed that his voice had taken on a quality that was almost rhythmic, like a chant.

"George, Duke of Bellingdon, as the founder of the company that will build our new city, you will become one of the greatest and richest men of the realm, rich enough to buy any beautiful object or trinket that you desire... Matthew, Marquis of

Kilheron, after we have reduced old London to a pile of smoking cinders, you will reveal our brilliant designs to the king. His new city will be the envy of every monarch and he will be grateful. You will be known far and wide as his most loyal and trusted servant, not to mention one of his closest and dearest friends at court… Edward, Lord Avebury, you will be praised as a great and saintly benefactor to the poor. The new, purified city that your money will help us build anew will be renowned as the most perfect and godly place in Europe."

There was silence below and then Alderman Pinchbeck spoke.

"And what's in it for me? Burning down the city doesn't make good business sense. That's what I say. What could possibly be in it for me?"

Cazalon answered, slowly and deliberately, as if talking to a small child.

"My dear friend, I urge you to take a moment to weigh up the advantages here. When old London and its filthy streets are purged, to whom will the king turn…? Why, he will need men about him who have a plan. Men who are quick and clever, and ready to invest. There is a great opportunity here for those who are prepared. And fortunes to be made as a new city rises from the ash. It makes *perfect* business sense, Alderman."

Kilheron cut in eagerly.

"Indeed, I see now this is no treason. For we shall build a new London to the *glory* of His Majesty. A city that is at last fit for our most gracious monarch."

"A city where the ungodly and the corrupt shall find no sanctuary."

The dreary, ponderous voice was Avebury's.

"A city where you shall be *enobled*, Alderman. You shall choose any title you like and pass it on to your line."

This last was Cazalon.

There was another long pause in the room below. Then the sound of footsteps and the rustle of paper. After a moment, Alderman Pinchbeck spoke again.

"And this park here will be named after me?"

Struggling to contain his disgust, Jem looked at Tolly and Ann. The girl's eyes were huge in the shadows.

Unable to stop himself, Jem gripped Tolly's arm. The other boy's eyes snapped open.

"These men want to murder people," Jem hissed. "We have to find a way to stop them."

Tolly put his finger to his lips and shook his head violently.

Suddenly there was a crackling noise directly beneath them and Cleo leapt from Ann's lap to Tolly's shoulder.

A voice echoed in the chimney. "I hope you don't mind, George. You know how, after my travels, I am most susceptible to cold. I have lit the fire. Why look, it is blazing... like old London will." The voice was Cazalon's.

CHAPTER TWELVE

Thick black smoke began to rise through the vent at the back of the fireplace.

Cleo made little gasping noises and buried her head in Ann's lap. The children covered their mouths and noses with their hands and stumbled out of the fireplace and into the room.

As they struggled for breath, they sat down on the heavily draped four-poster. A cloud of dust rose into the air from the velvet coverlet, which made them cough even more.

"Do you think he knew we were there?" wheezed Jem.

"I'm not sure." Ann's eyes were streaming. "It's possible he might have heard you speaking just now. He is sensitive to the smallest of sounds… But it's also true that he is a cold soul and could have simply wanted the fire lit. As he told the duke, he lived abroad for many years before returning to Europe."

Tolly stroked Cleo's head. The monkey's button-black eyes were watering and her shoulders were heaving as her tiny lungs battled to clear the smoke.

"Where is the count actually from?" asked Jem.

The other children exchanged grim looks before Ann answered.

"We don't know. I don't think anyone does. His title is a very old one. He has estates in the far south-west of France. But in all the days since he became my guardian, he has never gone there."

Jem scowled.

"Well, I wish he was there now. I wish he was a thousand miles away. I can't quite believe what we've just heard. They were plotting the destruction of London as if they were discussing a business transaction."

"That's what it is to them," said Tolly.

Jem shook his head.

"No. That can't be right. The duke is a vain, greedy man, but I've never thought of him as evil. And Alderman Pinchbeck, too – he was worried about the people, at least to start with. Listening to them just now, it was almost as if they were all under a spell – as if Cazalon had blinded them to reality."

"But that's exactly what was happening!" said Ann excitedly. "Remember the way he spoke to them. It sounded more like a chant, didn't it? He was using a rhythm charm to shape the pattern of their thoughts.

I've read about them. They only work if the person listening is already open to the suggestions being made. Now, what else did the book say…?"

She looked up into the dark canopy overhead and her forehead wrinkled.

"Ah! I have it! *To charm a thought as if it were a serpent you must unlock desire. Find the key to a man's soul before you turn it to your will.*"

Tolly grinned at Jem.

"She's good, isn't she? She remembers every word she reads. It's amazing!"

Ann ignored him. "Don't you see? He found their weaknesses and tempted them. That's why they all fell under his spell. The duke is greedy, Kilheron wants to be the king's greatest friend, Avebury wants to be famous as a pious benefactor and Pinchbeck is desperate to be a nobleman."

She shook her head. "It is totally ingenious!"

"And totally evil," said Jem.

The children sat in silence for a moment before Jem spoke again. "I'll admit, I was scared of Cazalon before today. But now it sounds as if everyone in London should fear him too."

Tolly shifted on the coverlet. "Jem's right. We must tell someone. This is too big and too dangerous."

"You won't want to hear this again," said Ann quietly as she stroked Cleo's rounded back, "but I still believe that you are at the heart of all this, Jem. My guardian is obsessed by you. You are the *jade boy* and the key to Cazalon's plans, not those spellbound fools."

"There you go again with this jade boy business," said Jem, infuriated. "How can you be so sure of any of this? What do you know that you're not telling me? If my life is in danger – along with everyone else's, I might add – then we have to tell someone and make it all stop, now."

Ann rolled her eyes. "And who would we tell? Who would believe our word against some of the greatest lords in the land, Jem? Think – who could we go to? Who would believe that the daughter of an executed witch, a mute servant, a kitchen boy and a monkey have discovered a plot to destroy all of London?"

She was silent for a second and then started to undo the ties of one ragged lace cuff. She rolled the loose fabric back up to her elbow and showed Jem the underside of her thin white arm. He gasped in horror.

Ann's delicate skin was criss-crossed by a series of deep scars – some old and healed, some fresh, livid and crusted with blood. When she looked up again, her eyes were full of fear and pain.

"*This* is how I can be sure that my guardian is obsessed by you, Jem. When he took me in it was not just because he wanted the books belonging to my family and not just because I was a prize to add to his collection." She gave a deep sigh. "He wanted me because I am the only living link to my mother. She was the last fully initiated witch from a magical bloodline that stretches back for hundreds of years. My guardian can communicate with her and is forcing her to give up her secrets."

Jem dragged his eyes away from the vicious scars. He was struggling to make sense of Ann's words.

"But Tolly said your mother is d… d… That she had died?"

Ann nodded. "Cazalon is able to talk to her in the dead lands by building the blood bridge. It is one of the most dangerous and darkest acts of old magic. Only a madman would attempt it. They say that each time you cross the bridge you leave a fragment of your soul behind. He uses my blood to make the bridge, Jem."

"But what happens? What does he… How…?"

Jem looked from Tolly to Ann and faltered.

The world had grown darker than he had ever imagined possible.

Ann smiled bleakly. "I am glad to say that I remember very little from the times it happens. But often, afterwards, I hear the echo of my mother's voice. Her words are faint, like the furthest ripples on the surface of a pond when you've thrown a pebble, but she always says the same thing... *You must seek the boy of Jade.*"

"And that's how you knew about me?" asked Jem.

Ann nodded again. "Cazalon must have heard it too, and more besides – she has to tell him what she knows because he has me in his power. But I know those seven words were meant for me. And now, we've found you."

"Unfortunately, Cazalon has too," added Tolly.

Suddenly Cleo leapt into the air and clung to one of the bed hangings. Chattering with fright, she scrambled up into the gloomy fabric canopy above.

"Someone is coming," whispered Tolly.

Jem thought fast and reached out to the heavy curtains around the bed, pulling them tight shut so that the children were enveloped in a velvet box thick with musty dimness. Immediately Tolly started to tremble.

"I– I can't breathe," he stammered. His eyes were huge in the gloom.

"It's fine, Tolly. You are safe. We are here." Ann said soothingly, and reached over to take the frightened boy's hand. "It's the confined space, Jem," she whispered. "Tolly told you about the barge?"

Ann squeezed Tolly's hand.

"I can't be found here. Jem, look after him. Both of you, shield your eyes."

Jem was aware of a now-familiar pulsing in the air. He closed his eyes and looked away as Ann transformed – then quickly bent forward to scoop up the little jewelled scarab beetle. As Jem slipped the beetle into his pocket, the bed curtains were ripped apart.

CHAPTER THIRTEEN

Wormald glared at the boys. Loose hairs sprang free from the greasy grey rats' tails that hung to his starched white collar. It was probably the echo of Ann's magic in the air, but the stray hairs seemed to dance around the steward's long thin face, crackling with dangerous energy.

"So, this is where you've been hiding."

Wormald's eyes hardened as he caught sight of the monkey crouched behind the crest of feathers on the top of the bed.

"You're supposed to be with the duchess, aren't you? And now the duke and one of his visitors are in her chambers, wondering where you are…"

The steward smiled unpleasantly. "I am to take you straight to them. Call that disgusting animal down and follow me."

Jem saw anger flash across Tolly's face as he looked up at the canopy and simply stretched out an arm. Cleo chattered nervously and clambered down one of the bedposts. When she was half way down she jumped onto Tolly's shoulder. Wormald turned to leave the room, and behind his back, the monkey leaned forward and bared her teeth at his retreating form.

The boys followed the steward down the great staircase and along the passage to the duchess's blue salon. The door was open and they could hear laughter and the murmur of conversation. Wormald pushed them roughly through the door and stepped into the room behind them. He farted, coughing loudly to cover the sound.

"I found them, sir. They were hiding in the north bedroom."

Bellingdon and Cazalon turned towards them – they were the duchess's only visitors, the other men had gone.

"Thank you, Wormald."

The duke flicked a lazy hand of dismissal in the direction of the steward. Wormald pretended not to notice. He was looking forward to seeing Jem punished.

The duke turned to Jem. He was angry. "I told you to take the moor and this animal to the duchess, didn't I? Where have you been?"

The question made Jem redden and look at his feet. He began to stammer a reply, but Cazalon cut in smoothly.

"Ah, George, come now. Boys will be boys, will they not? I imagine they have been plotting some game together. Isn't that so, Master Green? Although I cannot imagine that my dumb servant is the most entertaining of playfellows."

The man's dark eyes lingered on Jem's face and once again he felt that odd, creeping, prickling sensation beneath his scalp.

Jem bit his lip. What was it Ann had said about blocking Cazalon from his mind...? A strong thought? Or was it a happy thought? Jem fought to remember.

Then a sound caught his attention. Out in the stable yard below, one of the grooms was exercising Achilles, the duke's magnificent chestnut horse. Jem could hear the sound of hooves clattering across the cobbles.

He had always admired the graceful animal. He would give anything to ride such a beautiful, powerful creature. He imagined the horse's sweet leathery smell and thought about galloping at lightning speed. The harder Jem concentrated on Achilles, the less he felt the peculiar sensation of someone, or something, rifling through his mind.

Cazalon continued to stare at him, then the

man inclined his head and twisted his lips into a half smile.

"Well, no harm done. And now, dear lady, a little later than expected, may I present my pets to you."

He turned to the duchess, who was sitting by the fire. Her face was eager and alert.

"This is my servant Ptolemy and this monkey is Cleopatra. They are named for Egypt, where I bought them. Do you not think them most decorative?"

"Oh, but they are charming," laughed the duchess. "What do they do?"

Jem felt uncomfortable for his friend and looked up to find that Cazalon was staring at him once again. An odd expression crossed the man's face, then he turned to the duchess and replied.

"The boy is an idiot mute, my lady. His function is largely ornamental, but the monkey here…" the count snapped his fingers and Cleo leapt from Tolly's shoulder, scampering over to where Cazalon stood, "…is vastly amusing."

Cleo cowered at Cazalon's feet. Her eyes were huge and her little body trembled.

The man snapped his fingers again and Cleo jerked upright on her hind legs as if she was held by invisible strings. Her black eyes were wide and frightened and she made a faint, high-pitched keening noise. Slowly, she stretched her paws out on either side of her body and then she began to spin on the spot, moving faster and faster until she was just a tiny spinning blur of black and white fur.

Cazalon made a chopping movement with his hand and instantly she stopped. For a moment Cleo seemed to be suspended in mid-air, she was panting heavily and her head hung limply from her shoulders.

Tolly immediately took a step towards her, but Cazalon raised his hand again and snapped his fingers. The little monkey now began to spin in the other direction, this time even more quickly than before. And as she spun she began to zig-zag crazily across the Turkish carpet like a child's spinning top, bumping into chair and table legs that sent her whirling off in new directions.

The duke and duchess laughed.

Cazalon clapped his hands and Cleo stopped instantly, falling into a crumpled, lifeless heap at Tolly's feet. The boy knelt down and gently gathered her body into his arms, rocking her backwards and forwards with his head bent low.

The duchess laughed again.

"Is it all right?" she asked.

"It will be," Cazalon said. "It is a mere trick, madam, no more than an illusion."

"That's a clever show, my friend," said the duke, warily eyeing the boy cradling the monkey. "I wondered if the little beast might break something."

Cazalon walked stiffly across the room to the dresser that stood against the wall behind Jem. He bent to pour himself a goblet of wine from a pitcher and as he did so he leaned very close to Jem.

"And that, Jeremy," he whispered, "is another taste of what I can do to those who defy me."

Cleo stirred in Tolly's arms and made a sound like a little bird. The boy looked up and Jem saw that along with relief, his friend's eyes were filled with tears.

"Oh, bravo! Bravo!" cried the duchess. She stood up and clapped her hands.

"You are so clever, dear count," she continued. "You always bring us such interesting things."

Cazalon's strange eyes glittered and he made a small bow to the woman.

"Ah yes. Forgive me, my lady. I had almost forgotten."

Cazalon turned to the duke. "George, I have some pleasant news and some disappointing news for you. The pleasant news is that the exquisite book you asked me to find for you has arrived from my dealer in Paris. The disappointing news is that I have quite forgotten to bring it with me. I am sure, given the excitement of our business today, you will understand?"

The duke smiled broadly. "That is quite understandable. But I must have the volume as soon as possible. Is the condition good? And the... engravings," he shot a furtive look at the duchess. "Are they... in order?"

Cazalon grinned and his painted lips parted to reveal the pointed tip of a black tongue. "I assure you that everything is of the finest quality. If we were not both expected at court tomorrow I could bring it to you, but as it is I fear that you will have to wait."

Cazalon stared significantly at the duchess before continuing. "Something of such great value cannot be carried across town by anyone except the most trusted servant."

"But of course. I have the solution, George!"

The duchess's voice was high and careless. "Why not send young Jem?

Wormald coughed and peeled himself from the wall where he had been trying to make himself invisible. He had been waiting to see Jem punished, but now it looked as if the boy was to be trusted with a special task.

"Ahem… if I may, my lady, the lad here is mostly a kitchen boy. If I might be permitted, ma'am, I should be the one to go."

The duchess's eyes narrowed. She would not be thwarted. Cazalon had made it clear – Jem and no one else was to collect her new supply of mummia.

"Nonsense, Wormald. You have too many important duties to be spared. Jem here is ideal. That seems to be an excellent solution, do you not think, George?"

The duchess's anxious question was aimed at the duke, who was now helping himself to an orange from the platter of fruits displayed on the side table. But as she spoke she glanced meaningfully at Cazalon, who inclined his head.

"You may do as you wish with the boy." Bellingdon spoke though a mouthful of pulpy orange flesh and spat out a pip, before adding, "But I'll not have my book carried on the open streets. You'll have to send a coach for the lad, Cazalon. My grooms would never find the way in that maze across the river."

Cazalon's thin scarlet lips curved into a taut smile.

"Oh, I think that can be arranged very easily," he said softly.

With that the count clicked his fingers and Tolly, who was still cradling Cleo, stood and bowed to the duke and duchess. Cazalon brushed a speck of dust from his cloak, threw the long trailing tendrils of his black wig back over his shoulders and stalked towards the door. Tolly followed. As the dark boy passed close, Jem managed to slip the scarab jewel into his pocket.

From the hallway Cazalon's voice came again. "I shall send my carriage for the Green boy at the tenth hour."

CHAPTER FOURTEEN

When he opened his eyes next morning, Jem's first plan was to feign sickness. The thought of going back to Malfurneaux Place made his blood run cold.

Then, as he lay there in the attic wondering what sort of illness would sound most convincing, the horrors of the day before began to worm their way into his mind. He shuddered at the thought of the vicious scars on Ann's arm. Then he remembered the terrible conversation they had overheard from the fireplace, and the men, talking as if they had been infected by Cazalon's evil.

But most horrific of all was the way Cazalon had controlled Cleo, sending her fragile little body jerking, spinning and bumping across the rug like a toy.

"I enjoy games, Master Green." Jem recalled the count's words with a shiver.

But this wasn't a game, it was real – and Cazalon was playing with people's lives.

Jem sat up straight and pushed a mass of black hair back from his forehead.

He'd suddenly realised that his fear of Count

Cazalon, although strong, was now eclipsed by something sharper and fiercer... hatred.

He burned with the desire to fight Cazalon and defeat him – and all at once, it seemed very clear that the only way to do that was to find out exactly what the count was up to.

There was no alternative: Jem had to go along with Cazalon's plans.

For now.

The boy slipped out of bed and splashed cold water on his face. Then he gathered his clothing from the floor and dressed, noting with dismay that the sleeves of his jerkin now stopped just below his elbow.

Outside the city, churches jangled the discordant six o'clock chime – the clanging lasted for a couple of minutes as each church kept its own time. Jem walked over to the little attic window and threw it open to take deep gulps of fresh sharp air. He'd need all his wits about him today.

The smoky haze above the city shimmered and danced. He stared out across the jumble of old rooftops and twisted brick chimneys that glowed golden red in the early morning sun. For a second it almost seemed as if London was burning.

Jem clenched his fists. It couldn't happen. He wouldn't let it – they wouldn't let it.

In a window opposite he saw a man carrying a small boy in his arms. The man was showing the child a couple of pigeons building a nest on a nearby parapet. He set the little lad on his shoulders and held his legs so that the boy could get a better view.

Jem wondered if his own father would have played with him like that. Perhaps he would have carried him through the city on a pair of broad shoulders and...

"Your father is alive."

Ann's words cut through his thoughts. Jem froze. What if his father was right here in the city – the city that Cazalon intended to burn to the ground?

"I will protect you," he whispered, into the shimmering air.

⬧ ⚏ ⬧

As Jem waited in the hall of Ludlow House for Cazalon's carriage, he kicked his heels impatiently against the oak panelling, earning himself a clout from Wormald, who was crossing the hall carrying a steaming bowl of lavender-scented water to the duke's bedchamber.

"Think yourself lucky do you, pot boy?" he hissed. "Perhaps your high and mighty new friend will give you and your hoity-toity mother a home when the duke tires of you. We'll be well rid of the pair of you."

The tufts on top of the steward's head quivered with righteous indignation as he turned his back on the boy and headed to the staircase.

The single hand on the golden hall clock reached the tenth hour and a jingling chime echoed across the marble tiles. At exactly the same moment, there were three loud knocks and one of the footmen opened the double doors to reveal Tapwick standing on the broad steps outside.

The brim of a large floppy hat hung low over the little man's eyes and he carried a whip instead of a stick. "I've come for the boy," he grunted, indicating a monstrous black coach that waited behind him. Four gigantic horses were in harness, also black and each one sporting a red plume. The horses struck at the ground of the little courtyard, anxious to be on the move.

From the hallway, Jem could see that the coach bore a strange painted crest. A central pyramid topped by an elongated eye was flanked on either side by a man with the head of a bird and something like a cross with a loop on the top. Jem gulped as he realised there was no other coachman waiting. Other than small, blind Tapwick.

Jem took a deep breath and walked out into the sunlight.

Tapwick opened the coach door and a small curved red step clattered down. The door revealed an interior that was dark and red as an open mouth – even the step looked like a long, lolling tongue.

Jem shuddered, despite the sunshine, and climbed inside. The door slammed behind him. Seconds later, there was a wild shout from above and the coach jolted forward, rocking and rumbling out of the courtyard and into the busy road.

Jem was thrown back into the threadbare upholstery of the crimson seats. Steadying himself against the padded seat back, he tried not to think about Tapwick's milky sightless eyes and the speed at which they were travelling.

The coach was old and heavy. It smelled musty and Jem recognised the faintest trace of the stench he associated with Cazalon: something overpoweringly sweet and floral, laced with the fetid scent of decay. He wrinkled his nose and looked around.

There was just one small window in the door,

making the interior dark and oppressive. A little gilt vase fixed to the wall behind him contained two dead and faded roses, some of their brown desiccated petals were scattered on the tattered seat.

He thought he heard a sound above and looked up. The coach roof was tented with fraying red fabric that was caught up in a central knot over his head. The knot was held in the jaws of a snarling dog's head carved in blackened wood. The eyes of this animal, a long-muzzled hound, seemed to be watching him.

"Horrible, isn't it?"

Jem started.

"Not sure which is worse," the high-pitched voice continued, "that dog thing up there or the awful smell! I'm down here by the way, just by your left hand."

He looked down and saw a small white mouse on the seat beside him. It was standing on its hind legs, resting its two front paws on the fold of his coat pocket, and it was looking up at him with eyes that gleamed like bright little emeralds.

"Er… is that you, Ann?" Jem coughed, feeling suddenly very self-conscious about talking to a mouse.

"Well, of course it is, Jem. Who did you think it was, Oliver Cromwell?"

The mouse's voice was irritated. Now it definitely sounded like Ann.

"Tapwick and my guardian have no idea what I've been up to – I've been trying different animals. I had quite a success as a cat, but I got left with a tail for several hours afterwards, which made sitting down extremely uncomfortable."

Jem tried not to laugh as Ann continued. "So far, the smaller the creature, the easier the transformation, but for some reason I seem to be much better at objects – like the scarab brooch. Oh, by the way, thank you for passing me back to Tolly yesterday. That was quick thinking."

"How's Cleo?"

"She'll recover, but her right paw is twisted. Tolly thinks it might be broken—"

The coach lurched on a street rut and the mouse rolled to the far side of the seat, getting caught up in some ragged cobweb-like upholstery.

"Blast!" Jem heard an infuriated squeak. "Could you pop me into your pocket or something, please. The way Tapwick drives this thing I wouldn't be surprised if we had an accident."

Jem leaned across and gently freed the mouse from the netted shreds of fabric. He carefully placed her in his coat pocket. Ann peeked out, her nose and whiskers twitching.

"Did you know that there are marchpane crumbs in here?" she asked.

Jem grinned, remembering the sweetmeats he'd stolen a couple of days earlier from the kitchen, from right under Pig Face's very snout. "You certainly don't miss anything, do you?"

"That's the thing about being a mouse. They are always incredibly hungry."

She burrowed down into his pocket and appeared a couple of seconds later with sugar on her whiskers. "That's better. Now, I expect you're wondering why I'm here?"

"I'm certainly glad that you are," Jem replied. "Look, I've been thinking… After yesterday… Ann – we need to find out as much as possible about what Cazalon's up to."

The mouse nodded.

"You're so certain about this jade boy stuff being the real key to his plans, but the only thing we have to go on is the fact that you think it's me."

The mouse nodded again and her tail whipped from side to side.

"So, we need more information," Jem continued.

"And the only way to get that is for me to go back to Malfurneaux Place. It was very clear that he wanted me to go back and we need to know why. Don't worry. I'll be on my guard this time."

He stopped for a moment.

"Ann, what you said about my father being alive. I have to know, please…"

The mouse stared up at him and blinked.

"Please."

The mouse gave a little sigh. "There's not much to say. I'm sorry, Jem. When I held your hand that first time, I saw and felt lots of things about you. But I pick up the details so fast that everything gets confused. I can't tell you anything more about your father, other than the fact that he is alive and that he is near."

His father was near? Then he really was in danger! Jem's stomach clenched tight as an oyster.

Ann continued. "There are so many secrets threaded around you, Jem. They're in a knot – and it's too tight and complicated for me to unravel. I'm sorry."

"Is it the duke?" he blurted out. He couldn't stop himself.

The mouse flicked her tail contemptuously and

made a noise that sounded like a squeak of disgust.

"No, it can't be. I'm absolutely certain of that. How on earth could you imagine that a vile man like that would be your father?"

Jem fell silent for a moment. He was surprised to feel a mixture of relief and disappointment. But if the duke wasn't his father...

"Listen," Ann's voice was high and sharp. "If I knew any more I'd tell you, Jem. Isn't it enough for now to know that your father is alive and that he is here in London?"

She twitched her whiskers before adding, "Oh, and you will know him before your thirteenth birthday. That's the only other thing I can tell you."

"Ann! Why didn't you tell me this before?! My birthday's less than six months away!" Jem was filled with panic. "London could be burned to a cinder in that time. What if we can't stop it? I might never meet my own f– fa...'

He faltered. He knew it sounded selfish to be thinking of himself when a whole city full of fathers, mothers and children was on the brink of destruction.

"I– I'm sorry. I just wanted to know." He reached down and gently gathered the little creature from his pocket, lifting her up in his cupped hands so that she was just below his chin. He stared into her brilliant-green eyes. "I won't ask any more. I promise."

Ann made a noise that sounded like a sneeze and began to groom her sugary whiskers vigorously.

"Er, excuse me," she said after several seconds. "It's really hard not to do mouse things. Anyway, what you really need to know now, Jem, is that I've found a way to barricade your mind from my guardian. That's why I'm here."

"But Cazalon won't be there today, will he?" said Jem hopefully. "He's supposed to be at court with the duke. I thought it might be a chance for me to look round Malfurneaux Place and pick up some clues."

"Of course he's going to be there, Jem. He's waiting for you!" Ann sounded exasperated. "That's why I came to help you. I know what to do to block him."

"Does it work – have you tried it?"

Ann shook her head. "I don't need to. He can't read my thoughts – he's never been able to. He can't read Tolly, either. It infuriates him. Actually, I think it's one of the things he's been asking my mother about but…'

Ann fell silent and Jem saw a series of tremors run through the fur of her tiny white back. He tentatively put out a finger and gently stroked the little creature until she seemed to calm.

She looked up from Jem's cupped palm. "To close your mind against Cazalon you need to inscribe an ancient symbol on your skin in a place where he cannot see it. The symbol is known as the Eye of Ra. Do you know it?"

"I– I don't think so," Jem said, thinking back to any books from the duke's library that he might have read.

"Well, the important thing is that I know, so I can describe it to you. But what can we use to draw it on you?"

The coach jolted again and Jem was thrown forward. Ann tumbled from his hands, but Jem deftly caught the little white animal before she hit the ground, gently closing his hands about her to keep her safe.

"Thank you!" The words came from within the cage of his fingers.

Outside, the street seemed to have narrowed. People thronged about the coach, their curious faces pressed against the pane of the small window. The rank smell of a thousand emptied middens thickened the air… They were crossing the Thames at London Bridge.

"We must be quick, Jem, find something sharp."

He gently set Ann down on the seat and scoured the interior of the coach, but couldn't see anything that might do. Standing, he tried to prise loose a sliver of the blackened woodwork that formed the dog head, but it was hard as iron. He slumped back into the moth-nibbled seat, careful not to crush the mouse.

"There's nothing," he said dejectedly.

"There is another way," said Ann, after a moment. "But it might hurt. I– I could… um, well, that is to say, I could gnaw the Eye of Ra into the sole of your foot?"

"But that's horrible." Jem winced at the thought.

"Well, you come up with another plan then," came the indignant reply.

Jem sighed and bent down to unlace his shoe. "This had better work," he said grimly.

"And your feet had better be clean!"

When she had finished, Jem was left with a sore patch on his heel the size of a sovereign. The Eye of Ra was a circle containing a triangle, and in the centre of the triangle, Ann's sharp rodent teeth had incised an eye.

The mouse stood back on the crimson seat and surveyed her work. "That should do. It's not pretty, but as long as you keep it hidden he won't be able to open your mind. Did I hurt you?"

"Not really," Jem lied.

It had actually been incredibly painful and now it stung. He held his foot and bent it round so that he could see the still-bleeding mark more easily. Even through the blood, he noticed that it was very like the symbol on the door of the coach.

"What does it mean?" he asked.

"The Eye of Ra is an ancient symbol of protection," Ann replied. "I found it in one of my grandmother's books."

The coach lurched sharply as it came to a standstill. Ann's mouse nose quivered.

"We're here. Tapwick's gone to open the stable gate, but he'll be back in a moment.

"Quickly, hide me in your pocket so that we can go into the house together. I need to be back in my room before Tapwick comes to check on me."

"What about Cazalon, won't he know you're missing?"

The mouse appeared to sneeze again, but Jem realised that this was really a chuckle.

"That's the one good thing. He despises me so much that he only ever bothers to visit me once a week – and then only to speak to my mother. He… came to me two days ago…"

The mouse quivered, then added more certainly, "I won't see him again for some time now. I am sure of it. And there is one more thing you should know, Jem…" The mouse stared up at him intently, "Every time he makes the blood bridge, my guardian takes a terrible risk. It leaves him exhausted. Over the last few months he seems to have aged terribly. Tolly says he sometimes sleeps for days. I think he is growing weaker. Perhaps we can use that?"

Jem nodded slowly. "But if he can read my mind he'll always be one step ahead of us."

The mouse flicked her tail. "Well, now that you are protected, he won't be…" The coach rumbled forward again. "Quick! Hide me!'

Jem scooped Ann into his pocket.

"Jem, when we are inside, you must give me to Tolly," said Ann, her voice muffled now. "And be on your guard. You must take great care when you are with my guardian. Remember what I said about food and clothing. Be sure not to kneel to him either. You must not give him more power over you."

The door jerked open and Tapwick's hatless head leaned into the compartment.

"You! Out! Master's waiting."

The man's bristle-packed nose wrinkled and his sightless eyes rolled from side to side as he inhaled the air inside the carriage.

"Must do something about those damned mice," he muttered to himself.

CHAPTER FIFTEEN

Tapwick led the way from a crumbling stable block round to the courtyard in front of Malfurneaux Place. Despite the sunshine, the silent monument-lined courtyard was filled with shadows. As they passed under the broken arch into the smaller yard directly in front of the house, Jem experienced the same unnerving feeling as he had on his previous visit – that the building itself was alive. And watching him. Tapwick scuttled up four broad steps to the huge double doors and fumbled in the pocket of his tattered coat. The key he produced resembled the odd design painted on the side of Cazalon's coach – a sort of cross with a looped head.

Jem looked up and shuddered when he saw that in the centre of each door the wood was carved to form the shape of a woman's head. He hadn't seen her last time. The woman's mouth was open wide, exposing the savage points of finely carved teeth. Instead of hair, her face was surrounded by a mane of snakes, each one separate, expertly executed and twisting in a different direction.

"Medusa!" he gasped, remembering a book from the duke's library that included the legend of Perseus. No wonder just one look at this hideous creature could turn a man to stone.

"Pretty, ain't she?" Tapwick snickered, reaching up to stroke the points of the woman's teeth as he fitted the key in the lock.

The face split in two and the door swung into the blackness of the hallway.

"I suppose you'll be wanting some light, then? Ptolemy! Here!"

A light appeared at the far end of a corridor to the left. A short time later, Tolly arrived, carrying a long candle. He smiled, but Jem noticed that his friend's right eye was swollen and inflamed – the injury clearly visible, even though he wore his red turban low on his forehead. Cazalon had obviously beaten him for his disobedience yesterday.

"Give him the candle and be off," said Tapwick.

Jem took the candle and gently placed the little white mouse into his friend's hands, mouthing the word 'Ann' as he did so. He made a questioning face and indicated the injured eye. Tolly nodded, then tried to give an encouraging smile before he stepped back into the darkness.

"*Be careful, Jem.*" The words were spoken softly into his mind.

"Now boy," Tapwick pushed Jem towards a huge carved staircase in the middle of the hall. "The master is waiting. You are to climb the stairs. You'll know when you've got there. Up!'

The steward spun on his heels and scuttled across the hallway until the sound of his clacking footsteps faded to nothing. Jem swallowed hard and looked up. It was the same staircase, and was in the same place as his previous visit, but now there were no landings, no galleries and no crossings like last time, just hundreds and hundreds of stairs marching up into the black.

He began to climb.

Every thirty steps or so, the stairposts were topped by towering oak statues. The figures – male and female – were clad in robes or armour. All of them were blindfolded... but Jem sensed that, somehow, they knew he was there.

A rustling noise in the darkness beyond the heavy balustrade to the left made him stop dead. He raised his candle.

"Wh– who's there?" he whispered. "Tolly...?"

Silence.

Jem took a deep gulp of musty air and carried on. He had climbed another fifty steps when he heard the shuffling again, much nearer this time. He froze.

Now he could hear hoarse, rasping breaths directly behind him. Brandishing the candle like a dagger, he whirled round.

There was no one there.

The candle flame wavered and Jem caught sight of something glistening on one of the dark bulbous spindles of the staircase. As he looked around he realised with horror that all of the spindles above and below were now moving and glinting. Sheeny black snakes as thick as a man's arm curled around every one of them, making it look as if the whole staircase was undulating and moving steadily upwards of its own accord.

Jem turned very slowly and raised the candle higher. The air was instantly filled with a dry rustling sound as if thousands of scales scraped and rubbed against each other.

For a moment he was paralysed, then Jem remembered Ann's words when the carpet of insects was swarming around Tapwick's feet.

"*The house is playing tricks on us. If we truly believe they are not there, they won't be.*"

He gritted his teeth, held the candle at arm's length in front of him, so that light illuminated even more of the writhing bodies, and stepped upwards.

Immediately there was a hissing noise.

"There is nothing here," he said out loud. "I– I don't believe in you."

He took another step upwards.

"You do not exist!" he called out again, surprised that his voice sounded much more brave and certain than he felt. It was only the slightest shaking of the candle in his hand that gave the game away. As he spoke, dollops of wax spattered across the stair, one of them catching the flicking tip of a serpent's tail.

There was a sizzling noise, then a terrible echoing shriek and Jem was alone once more in silence.

His heart was pounding, but he felt a small sense of victory. He had outwitted Malfurneaux Place.

Taking care to stay at the centre of the stairs, just in case, he started to climb again, concentrating hard on the flame to block out the thought of anything following behind him in the darkness.

After a minute he came to a step that was much broader and deeper than the others. The stairs ahead carried on upwards, but to the right there was an arched door... and it was open.

Jem raised the candle and peered in. He was confused – should he keep going up or was this where he was supposed to stop?

What had Tapwick said? "You'll know when you've got there…"

Jem took a deep breath, pushed his hair back from his eyes and stepped into the room.

It was dark and smelled very like a rotting pork carcass that Pig Face had once thrown out of the larder. As his eyes became accustomed to the gloom he noticed that the deserted chamber had a high ceiling crossed by tapering arches that fanned out above his head like skeletal fingers.

He held the candle higher and the bobbing flame was instantly reflected in hundreds of glass jars that squatted on rows of shelves, lining the entire wall to the left of the door.

Cautiously, Jem moved closer for a better look. As he did so, the wooden floorboards groaned beneath his feet. The first jar he came to appeared to be filled with something rounded and grey. The thing was suspended in a yellowy liquid – its surface glistened where the light picked out dimpled folds of fat or flesh. Jem couldn't make out what it was.

He held the candle to the next jar and was

immediately revolted to see that it contained a pale knotted jumble of limbs and hoofs. It was a tiny lamb. Its waxy skin was mottled and wrinkled, but that wasn't what then made Jem step back in shock.

The creature in the jar had two heads. One of them had its mouth open and Jem saw a long black tongue protruding into the liquid in which the dead animal was suspended.

Moving along the shelves, he realised that every jar contained a lifeless creature – creatures that seemed to be wrong or distorted in some horrible, pitiable way. A featherless bird the size of a cat appeared to have three sets of bony wing stumps erupting down its back. A naked rat with a grotesquely over-sized head seemed to scrabble in desperation at the glass walls encasing its lifeless body. At the end of the row, a domed jar contained the head of a calf. Dead-white flesh frayed from the animal's skull and peeled upwards into the cloudy liquid around it. Jem was revolted to see that the calf had been born without eyes – or even a space for them.

He heard a clinking noise behind and spun around.

At first he thought nothing had changed, but then he noticed that the first jar he'd looked at seemed to have shifted. Now it was balanced precariously over the edge of the shelf. He moved along the row and held the candle close to the glass. Suddenly, the lumpy grey mass seemed to ripple. In the middle of the jar, the flesh puckered tight and then something round and dark like a mouth, with rows and rows of sharp, tiny teeth, opened and closed.

Jem bit back a yelp of disgust and backed away.

The house was playing with him, again.

Every fibre of Jem's being was yelling at him to get out, to get away, but a small, insistent voice in his head reminded him of his vow to find out as much about Cazalon as he could. He was hesitating, when he heard another faint sound from the other end of the room – not clinking this time, but something soft and regular.

He stepped cautiously towards the sound. Soon the weak light from the candle revealed two large wooden chests against the far wall. The noise seemed to come from the chest on the left.

Jem slowly lifted its lid and looked down into the open box. At first he couldn't understand what he saw.

In the middle of the chest a large, shaggy hound was suspended on a network of metal spikes and pins. Glass tubes connected to the animal's body snaked out to a series of flasks and vials that were balanced on a ledge running around the inside of the chest. The tubes were full of moving liquid.

As Jem looked he realised with horror that the hound's skull had been opened like a box. Something like a large, moist, lumpy walnut was positioned on a small glass tray just above the gaping wound and this grey object was also connected to the creature by a second, finer array of glass tubes and pipes. Jem felt as if he was going to be sick.

The soft rhythmic noise came from the right of the box. Now Jem saw that the creature's heart had also been removed from its body. The organ was still twitching and beating on a second glass tray.

This was appalling. The poor, poor creature.

Jem's hand began to shake so much that he dropped the candle into the chest. The flame sputtered and dimmed and Jem knew that he had to retrieve it before it died and left him in total darkness.

Fighting back his revulsion, he reached carefully into the chest. As he caught hold of the candle his hand brushed against some of the liquid-filled tubes connected to the animal's body. Immediately the hound shuddered and whimpered in pain.

Jem felt tears pricking his eyes.

'The master's toys' – that's what Tapwick had called the poor mutilated creatures he'd seen on his first visit to Malfurneaux Place. But these were not toys and this was certainly not a game that Jem wanted to play. Rubbing his hand roughly over his eyes, Jem raised the candle over the second box. This time he saw a cat.

The animal appeared to be curled up and asleep, and there were no organs removed, but as he looked closer he realised that it was dead. Its fur was matted and patchy, and maggots wriggled in the rotting flesh. The cat was the source of the vile smell in the room.

Jem wondered what Cazalon had done to this poor creature. His hand trembled again, but this time, instead of dropping the candle, he managed to hold tight.

A few drops of hot wax fell onto the little corpse below.

The cat opened its eyes and stared up at Jem. It blinked twice, and continued to stare.

Jem reeled away and bent double as his stomach lurched and heaved. He dropped the candle and it rolled across the floor, guttering and spluttering as wax flicked across the boards. He had never seen anything so cruel. What kind of a man could be capable of such brutality?

"Ah, here you are, Jeremy."

The count stood in the open doorway, casting a shadow across the room that reached the tips of Jem's shoes.

"You have kept me waiting so long that I decided to come and find you. I see that you are admiring my… experiments."

CHAPTER SIXTEEN

Cazalon leaned heavily on his black staff and took a halting step forward. His long black robe rustled and Jem now saw that the blue plait that grew from the centre of the man's shaven head was so long that it trailed across the threshold behind him.

The count smiled.

"They say that sorcery is dead, Jeremy. In these enlightened days science is the new magic – and as I have such a thirst for knowledge, how could I resist the opportunity to make some scientific enquiries of my own?"

Cazalon gestured at the boxes. The room was stifling, but he still wore gloves. "My particular interest, Jeremy, is the nature of life itself. More specifically I am fascinated by the existence of the soul. Where do you think it resides? In the brain… or in the heart?"

Jem didn't answer, but he thought about the poor hound in the first of the count's chests. So that's what he was trying to do!

Cazalon sighed. "It has been a most disappointing test, to be frank. But the other one, the little cat there, is much more interesting. I managed to hypnotise the creature on the very point of death, Jeremy. Imagine that? Now its soul, its spirit, its ba – as I believe some ancients might have called it – is captured in that rotting carcass. It cannot depart – I have created a sort of immortality. I think you will agree that it is quite an achievement?"

He paused for a moment and stared intently at Jem. His slanted eyes narrowed. "In fact, the cat has been such a success that I am hoping to perform my next experiment on a higher animal... possibly a monkey, or perhaps a mute?"

Jem's stomach churned again. It was all he could do to stop himself from actually throwing up.

Cazalon smiled more broadly than ever. His red lips stretched and curved across his angular face and the chalk-white paint on his skin crackled. "Enough of this. Come!"

He swept from the room and although Jem tried to resist, he felt compelled to follow. It was as if the count were drawing him along on an invisible leash.

Beyond the door a broad passage now led from the opposite side of the step. Jem was certain it hadn't been there before.

The passage glowed with light from hundreds of

red candles caught in clawlike hands that sprouted from the walls. Between the twisted hands, the walls were lined with paintings. Men and women dressed in the most fantastic costumes stared down at him. Although he tried not to look too closely at any of them, Jem couldn't help pausing in front of a huge portrait of a woman in a dress made from glittering black material that looked like thousands of beetle wings stitched together.

Jem's gaze was drawn to the woman's face. Her left eye was covered by a jewelled patch with delicate ribbon ties that crossed her forehead and disappeared into a mane of russet hair. Her right eye was golden and oddly alive. She was beautiful, but this wasn't the soft, fair beauty of his mother. This woman was proud and triumphant. Jem felt as if a cold draught had blown on the nape of his neck, but he couldn't help staring at her.

Folds of glinting fabric swirled at the woman's feet and, fascinated, Jem felt that if he put out a hand he would be able to feel each brittle fibre of material. He was just reaching out when he noticed that the woman's foot was revealed by a parting in her skirts. The foot was the gnarled and blackened talon of a huge bird.

Jem sprang back in shock. Tearing his eyes from the picture, he forced himself to carry on along the corridor, almost certain that behind him he could hear the sound of laughter.

At the far end, the passage turned sharply to the right. A little way ahead of him Cazalon was leaning back against the wall and staring up at another painting.

"Come and stand by me, Jeremy."

The count continued to contemplate the portrait. Jem looked up and immediately recognised Ann. She was dressed entirely in silver with a thick curl of her luminous white hair caught up in a jewel shaped like a crescent moon. In her left hand she carried a pair of fine gloves and, when Jem looked more closely, he noticed that the cuffs were embroidered with a coiled serpent.

Cazalon turned to look at him.

"What do you think of her?" The count's eyes seemed to be boring into him.

Jem suddenly realised he mustn't give away that he already knew Ann.

"I– I... She's very, er... pretty, sir."

The man continued to stare and Jem felt the most tremendously painful burning sensation in his heel where the nibbled Eye of Ra was hidden. The sensation strengthened and it was all Jem could do to stop himself crying out.

A look of fury crossed Cazalon's face. Just as they had before, the man's eyes blackened completely, so that the iris and pupil appeared to bleed into the white. Then, just as quickly, the count's expression changed, assembling itself into something more pleasant.

"She is Elizabeth Metcalf, the mother of my ward, Ann."

He stared intently at Jem, his eyes flickering over the boy's face as if searching for something. After a moment he continued. "This portrait was commissioned on the eve of her thirteenth birthday – a very significant age for Metcalf girls, as it marked the time when they came into their... inheritance, shall we say?"

Jem nodded, unsure what to say.

Cazalon smiled. "It was painted in 1643 – not a happy time for people like Elizabeth. I believe that the Eastern parts of this land were not always hospitable to families like the Metcalfs. You'll note the gloves. A symbolic gift I imagine. The serpent represents wisdom, and Elizabeth was on the verge of inheriting a wisdom that most would never have in their entire lifetime, never mind as a thirteen year old."

Jem looked up at the painting. Ann and her mother were identical.

"Remind me," Cazalon's voice was smooth and lazy, as if he didn't really care about Jem's answer. "How old are you, Jeremy?"

"I will be thirteen this year, sir."

Jem remembered their first meeting, when the count had asked the same question.

Cazalon continued to gaze at the painting. "Such an interesting number, thirteen," he said after a moment. "A number of endings and of beginnings. The end of childhood and the beginning of manhood, Jeremy."

He looked closely at the boy before continuing.

"Thirteen lunar cycles in a year, thirteen signs of the true zodiac. The thirteenth rune of the Norse alphabet is called Eiwaz, and it represents the point of balance between the light and the dark, between life and death. And, of course, there were thirteen present at the Last Supper. Now, why do you think that is?"

"I– I have no idea, sir."

"Then I shall enlighten you. Thirteen is a number of power, a number of magic and a number of... completion. When is your thirteenth birthday?"

"September, sir."

"Ah yes. Now I remember. The date again?"

Cazalon continued to sound bored, but Jem sensed that the man was actually intensely interested. He wondered why.

"September the fourth, sir."

Cazalon smiled. He looked back at Elizabeth's portrait for a moment. "My ward will celebrate her own thirteenth birthday next year. They are most alike – do you not think so?"

Jem winced as a red hot pain from his heel shot up through his leg. It was a warning.

"I– I cannot tell, sir."

"Of course. How forgetful of me. You have not been introduced."

Cazalon laughed and then clasped Jem's shoulder. As his grip tightened, the burning pain from Jem's heel became so acute that he thought he might actually faint.

Suddenly Cazalon let go and stepped back. He stared at his gloved hand and then back at Jem. For a second he looked confused. The count tightened his hand into a fist and turned away so that Jem could not see his face. After a moment he said hoarsely, "Come."

He limped away up the corridor, his cloak rippling behind him like a stream of black water. Jem followed, the pain in his heel now easing, until they reached a pair of massive double doors that seemed to be formed from cast metal.

Cazalon clapped his hands twice and the doors swung back soundlessly to reveal the most extraordinary room that Jem had ever seen. Or heard.

CHAPTER SEVENTEEN

The first thing Jem noticed was the noise – thousands of voices seemed to be talking, singing and chanting. Just occasionally he thought he caught snatches of sobbing, too – and something that sounded like wailing.

Despite himself, Jem couldn't help letting out an exclamation of wonder.

This was clearly the library of Malfurneaux Place, but it was the most stupendous library Jem had ever seen. The duke was proud of his much-admired collection of books at Ludlow House, but that paled into insignificance compared to this room. If you could call it a room.

Jem found himself standing on a broad gallery that ran around five book-lined walls. He took a couple of steps forward, to peer over the polished rail in front of him, and saw that above and below, as far as he could see, rows and rows of books and rolls of parchment were ranked on shelves around similar galleries, all connected by a single spiralling staircase that appeared to have no bottom and no top.

Around the walls, hundreds of candles shed a cold light that was tinged with purple.

He peered down into the well of the library and felt a prickling sensation in the back of his legs and a fluttering in the pit of his stomach as he realised that he was so high up he couldn't see the floor.

Dizzy and slightly nauseous, Jem shrank back from the rail and leaned against the solid shelves behind him. The babble of noise continued to fill the air and Jem looked about to see where it was coming from.

Cazalon regarded him narrowly from the other side of the gallery and smiled at his confusion. He raised his hands, clapped slowly three times and the sounds ceased immediately.

Jem was even more confused. He took a step forward and nervously looked over the rail again, then up at the galleries overhead, but there was no one else in the room.

"My children can be so noisy." Cazalon stared expectantly across at him. Now Jem was completely thrown.

"Er… your children? Where are they, sir?"

"They are everywhere. Look about you, Jeremy." The man made a sweeping gesture to the bookshelves.

"These are my children – thousand upon thousand of them. And I care for them well."

Dumbfounded, Jem looked at the count and then at the books around him.

Cazalon grinned.

"I should explain to you, boy, that I have made it my life's work to collect the unusual and the extraordinary, and these volumes are most certainly that."

He turned to stroke the spine of a particularly thick and ancient leather-bound tome on the shelf behind him, before continuing softly, "*Magnificata Trismegistus* – do you know what that is, Jeremy?"

Jem shook his head.

"It is one of the most powerful and ancient books of magic ever written. This, I believe, is the last copy in the world. I found it, several years ago now, in one of the monasteries despoiled by that fat king of yours – he was a most disagreeable and odious man, so very… pungent. I couldn't bear to be near him for long. Henry, wasn't it? The eighth monarch of this grim little country to bear that name I believe?"

Utterly bewildered, Jem stared across the gallery.

Had Cazalon just implied that he'd actually known King Henry the Eighth? That was impossible

– Henry had been dead for more than a hundred years.

Cazalon continued. "Always grubbling about for gold and silver, when, of course, the treasure was right under his nose in the monastery libraries. But that's always the way, I find. From Babylon to Rome and from Jerusalem to Constantinople, the barbarians always miss the real prize. Knowledge."

He stopped for a moment and ran a hand over the volumes on the shelf below the *Magnificata*. "Even in my own beloved Thebes…" He trailed off, then turned to face Jem. "These are books of magic, mathematics, medicine, astrology, astronomy and philosophy taken from every corner of the known world and from every civilisation since the dawn of recorded time. I have travelled the earth in search of knowledge and the power that knowledge can bring. These books are my children, Jeremy Green… and my insurance."

He raised his hands and the noise began again, building and building until Jem had to cover his ears. Cazalon laughed, clapped three times again and the room fell instantly silent.

"When books contain such power they develop a life of their own. I suppose you might even call it a soul." Cazalon sounded the last word with a bitter hiss.

"Some of the souls here are children of light and some of them…" he pulled down a large, ragged black volume that appeared to be covered with spots of mould, "are the sons and daughters of darkness."

He began to leaf through the stained pages and didn't look up as he spoke again.

"Now, to the errand that brought you here. Would you please fetch me the book just behind your left foot."

Jem looked down and saw a single volume on the bottom shelf near his foot.

"Yes, that's right, the red one. It is for the duke. Bring it to me."

Jem bent down to retrieve the book. Although it was small, it was incredibly heavy. He tried to lift it with both hands, but it wouldn't budge.

"I haven't got all the time in the world, boy!"

Jem got down on his knees and tugged hard. Suddenly the book shot out of the shelf and into his hands.

"Perfect. Now hand it to me."

The voice was suddenly very close. Too close. The Eye of Ra burned on his heel but the warning was too late.

Jem twisted round and was horrified to find that somehow, he was kneeling at Cazalon's feet.

A harsh cry came from somewhere high above and Jem heard a swooshing sound like the beating of huge wings. He looked up and saw a distant white blur spiralling down towards them. The shape grew larger and larger until Jem recognised the horrible form of Osiris.

With a loud 'kraak', the raven settled on Cazalon's shoulder. The air around the count shimmered and wrinkled, and Jem had the strangest impression that the man and the bird were one. Cazalon seemed to grow even taller and his outline pulsed in the eerie purple light. A pair of distorted wings unfurled from his cloak and his face lengthened and blurred so that, for a second, Jem felt that he was in the presence of a gigantic bird.

Jem clamped his eyes shut, shook his head and looked again.

Osiris was sitting on the count's shoulder.

As he had when Cazalon took the bloody bandage from Jem, the raven performed a vile head-bobbing dance of victory. His ghastly beak was wide open and his pink eyes locked onto Jem's.

"Thank you, Jeremy." Cazalon's slanted eyes

returned to normal again, although they glinted with unmistakable triumph.

Jem's heart stopped. Ann had specifically warned him to be on his guard, but now he had been tricked again into fulfilling another the rites of binding.

"You must not kneel to him," she had said.

He felt sick and scared, but forced himself to stand up so that he was almost on eye level with Cazalon.

The count began to laugh and the noise whirled around the gallery and library. Jem clenched his fists and blood pumped through his body. More than anything he wanted to destroy this man. But how?

"You certainly have spirit," Cazalon smirked. "It is most impressive for the bastard son of a k... kitchen hand."

Jem took a step forward. His fear was forgotten, replaced by fury.

"How dare you! My father was not a kitchen hand, he was a soldier."

"Was he now? And how do you know this, Jeremy? What, pray, has your pretty mother told you about your father?"

Cazalon waited for a reply that never came, before continuing.

"So, we can deduce, can we not, Jeremy, that the

reason your mother never mentions your father is that she has something to be ashamed of? And every time she looks at you she is reminded of her shame."

Jem lashed out, but his hand passed through nothing but shadow.

From the far side of the gallery, Cazalon clutched the rail to steady himself and laughed. Osiris took flight across the library to join him.

"Such a fine and brave young man. If I did not have another purpose in mind for you, Jeremy, I would be tempted to find a place for you here. You would be a pretty toy. Perhaps I could play the father you have never known."

At these words all the fight suddenly seemed to evaporate from Jem and he crumpled against the shelves. The count obviously knew everything about him and his life; how could Jem possibly imagine that he could defeat this monster?

Cazalon regarded him with a calculating gaze and after a moment he spoke in a bored tone. "Now to other matters. The duchess will be expecting her medicine."

He limped over to a large golden box that stood upright on the gallery behind him. The box was taller than the count and painted to resemble a man.

"Do you know what this is, boy?"

Jem stared at his feet. He would not answer. Cazalon smiled.

"Well, despite your bad manners, I shall tell you. It is a sarcophagus made for a dead Egyptian king. It is nearly three thousand years old… as is the body inside it."

Jem's eyes widened as Cazalon swung back the painted front of the sarcophagus to reveal a shrivelled, blackened corpse. Tattered grey wrappings hung loosely from its head, revealing a grinning skull covered with shreds of tight, parchment-thin skin. The mummy's eye sockets were huge and empty.

With one quick movement, Cazalon wrenched the mummy's left arm from the bandages and Jem heard a sickening crack. He watched, revolted, as the count took a small knife from his sleeve and began to scrape little strips of dust-dry, powdery flesh from the arm of the mummy into a leather pouch.

When he was finished, Cazalon dropped the filled pouch to Osiris, who caught it in his beak. The raven flew across the gallery and deposited the pouch at Jem's feet. Osiris clung to the rail and bobbed his head for a moment before flying back to his grinning master.

"I think that is all for today, Jeremy. You will now take my treasures back to your master and mistress. I trust the duchess has made it most clear that you are not to speak of her medicine?"

Jem gave a curt nod.

"Good. And I have a message for her. This new supply is particularly fresh and potent. It is most important that she uses no more than a pinch of powder each day. Is that understood?"

Jem nodded again.

"There is enough in that pouch to last for more than two months. I am travelling to Paris on business tomorrow, so she must make that quantity last through the summer. You will tell her that."

Jem gave another small, surly nod.

"Excellent. You may go now, Jeremy."

The great doors to the library swung soundlessly open. Tapwick was waiting in the candlelit passageway.

"Don't forget the duke's new treasure." Cazalon hurled the small red book across the gallery. It fell open at Jem's feet, revealing a lurid image. Jem blushed, closed the book hurriedly and stuffed it into his pocket.

Cazalon laughed, but the laugh turned into a cough,

and he gripped the rail to steady himself. Suddenly he looked terribly old. He fell silent, staring across at Jem. His lips curved into a smile, but it did not reach his eyes.

"You will leave me now, boy, and you will return to Ludlow House immediately. There will be no time for... exploring today. The duke will want to examine his book."

With a weary flick of his hand, Cazalon dismissed him and turned his back. Jem saw the count's hand quiver as he reached for a roll of paper on a high shelf.

"Go boy. Tapwick will be waiting for you."

The great library doors swung back and Jem stepped into the odd light of the passage.

As the doors closed behind him, two things blazed like brilliant fireworks through his mind. By kneeling to Cazalon he had completed yet another of the rites of binding, and the count had talked about performing his terrible experiments on Tolly and Cleo.

He had to tell his friends, as soon as possible.

CHAPTER EIGHTEEN

Ludlow House was quiet as Jem crossed the hall.

"Jem!" Sarah's voice came from above. He looked up and saw his mother leaning over the first gallery. She propped the bolt of cloth she was carrying against the rail and hurried down. "How did you fare with Count Cazalon?" she asked eagerly.

Jem thought about the man's taunt, "Every time she looks at you, she is reminded of her shame."

He couldn't meet her eyes. "It was fine, mother," he grunted.

"I hope you acquitted yourself well. He has connections that could be very useful to a boy like you."

Jem gritted his teeth and spoke without thinking first. "And what exactly does that mean, mother? What sort of a boy am I?"

Sarah froze. Her face set hard into a pale mask.

Jem shuffled his feet and looked at the floor. After an uncomfortably long silence, he continued, "I think you'll find I did exactly what the count wanted, mother... and I have the book for the duke."

"Then you must take it to his room immediately," came the duchess's voice from above. "Immediately!"

She rustled down the staircase. "I know exactly the place where His Grace will expect to find it, Jem. Come."

Sarah made to accompany them, but the duchess raised her hand. "I left my needlepurse in my bedchamber. Would you bring it to me in the blue salon?"

An odd expression crossed Sarah's face as she looked from Jem to the duchess, but she nodded curtly, dipped the faintest of curtseys and turned towards the stairs.

The duchess led Jem directly to her salon. When they were alone together she gripped his arm.

"Give it to me."

Jem felt in the pocket of his coat and handed her the leather pouch full of mummia.

She looked disappointed. "But there is even less here than before. This is not enough. I must have more!"

Jem looked up. The duchess's eyes were gleaming with a feverish brilliance and her skin looked tight and sallow. Purple bruises bloomed beneath her eyes. Far from looking youthful, today she looked old and sick. The duchess noticed his stare and took a step back.

"You will have to go back for more."

"No!" Jem almost yelped the word, before adding, "I… that is… he, the count, said that this is a very potent supply. It will be more than enough. You must not take more than a single pinch of the mu… medicine in a glass of wine. He ordered me to tell you that."

The duchess looked suspiciously at the little bag and weighed it in her hand.

"Well, we shall see." Her eyes narrowed. "I can always send you to collect more, Jem."

Jem shook his head. "I am very sorry, ma'am, but the count is travelling to Paris. He is leaving tomorrow. He said that you must make that quantity last through the summer. It is very fresh, my lady. You must be careful not to use too much."

The duchess looked furious. She turned her back on Jem and studied her face in a little gilt mirror on the wall. After a moment she spoke.

"Very well. You may go."

She waved a hand and didn't look back as Jem bowed and left the room.

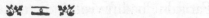

London basked in unusually warm sunshine. Fat red roses glowed in the gardens at Ludlow House – but their fragrance was swamped by the stench from the household middens and open drains in the city's streets.

The duke gave an order that all the windows should be shut against the horrible smell that smothered the city like the folds of a soiled cloak. But even that, along with huge bowls of dried lavender, spices and flower petals placed about the rooms, could not keep out the throat-gagging stink.

London was not a healthy place in the summer months. Usually, the duke's household moved to his country estate, Pridhow, where the air was pure, but this year it soon became apparent that the annual journey to Herefordshire would not take place.

A part of Jem was disappointed. He loved the green rolling hills around Pridhow and this year, more than ever, he longed to be far away from the city.

But when he thought of Tolly, Ann and Cleo and of the plot to reduce London to a heap of smouldering ash, he was almost glad to stay.

At least one thing was clear – Cazalon was in Paris. He hadn't visited the duke for weeks now.

Jem thought about his friends constantly – if only he'd been able to see them again before leaving Malfurneaux Place that last time. Had Cazalon taken them away with him? And if so, was he yet experimenting on Cleo or Tolly? And what about Ann? Had he opened the blood bridge again? In his darkest moments, Jem found himself wondering if his friends were actually still alive.

Worst of all, there was no way he could slip away to find out. The duke had given strict orders that no one should leave Ludlow House unless they had his permission. It was never discussed above or below stairs, but everyone knew he was worried about the plague – they all were.

Wormald watched over the servants like a gaoler and took great pleasure in making sure that Jem's days were filled with exhausting menial chores that started at dawn and lasted until sunset.

Bellingdon himself was often away from Ludlow House for days at a time and even when he was at home he spent hours locked away in his study with Lord Avebury, Alderman Pinchbeck and the Marquis of Kilheron.

Mysterious letters arrived from Paris, too. These were collected at the door by the duke himself and he would rush off to his chamber to read them in private. He paid little attention to the duchess.

As the days became hotter and longer, the Duchess of Bellingdon spent more time in her rooms with only Sarah for company. The servants gossiped that her ladyship didn't bother to change from her morning wrap. Some of them whispered that she was gravely ill and Jem noticed that his mother often seemed preoccupied.

Then, one morning, he took a bowl of scented lavender water up to the blue salon and was surprised to find the duchess neatly dressed and sitting at her writing desk. The curtains were partly drawn against the light.

"Ah, Jem," she exclaimed as he entered the room. "I believe that you are assisting with the inventory this morning?"

Jem nodded. The annual inventory of all household items took place each summer before the move to Pridhow. This year it was still taking place despite the fact that they were staying in London.

"Then you will need this list of the silver. Give it to Wormald."

She held out a sheet of paper covered with lines of writing and numbers. Jem went over to take it, but as he got closer he noticed in the thin light that – unusually – the duchess's face was heavily painted. Her lips and cheeks were coloured red and even though her skin was covered in chalk-white powder, it could not conceal the mottled lumpy patches that stretched from her right eyebrow across her eyelid and down to her chin.

The air around the duchess was thick and sweet – as if she had recently doused herself with a floral cologne, but Jem also recognised another scent. It was not the stench from the streets outside, it came from the woman sitting before him – something old, something musty, something rotten… Something very like Count Cazalon.

Aware that he was staring at her, the duchess turned her face away. "That will be all, Jem," she snapped.

CHAPTER NINETEEN

The first cases arrived from Paris at the end of July.

Jem and the kitchen scullions were called up from the kitchen one broiling afternoon to assist the footman and several of the grooms, who were struggling to lift twelve huge black boxes from a massive wagon in the courtyard.

The duke watched from the first landing of the main staircase in the hallway as the sweating servants heaved the delivery into the house. The cases were so large that they almost covered the entire chequered floor.

When the last of them was hauled over the threshold, the duke spoke. "Take them all to the great gallery and leave them there. Do not open them or attempt to look inside. When you have completed this task, the gallery will be locked. From this day on, no one, I repeat no one, will be permitted to enter. Do you understand me?"

His gaze swept over the servants and over the boxes once again. "Now, go to it."

Without another word, the duke returned to his chambers.

The servants muttered and grumbled as they heaved the enormous cases across the tiles. When all the boxes were moved to the great gallery, Wormald made a show of locking the doors.

"You all heard His Grace," he said, his cold eyes scanning the exhausted men and boys. "No one is to enter that room."

He placed the enormous, clinking ring of keys for Ludlow House in his pocket and patted it twice. "Because it is such a hot day, the duke has decreed that you may take refreshment in the kitchens. Ten minutes... and no longer, mind. There's cordial and ice set ready for you all."

"What d'you make of all that then?" Tobias the footman was sitting at the end of the long trestle table next to Jem.

Jem shrugged and wiped beads of perspiration from his forehead. "I'm not sure. It all seems very strange."

He glugged the cup of iced cordial gratefully, before adding, "What could make them so heavy?"

Tobias snorted, "An' there was I thinkin' that what with you an' him, bein'... you know? He might have let somethin' slip."

Jem bristled, "What do you mean, Toby? Me and the duke being what, exactly?"

But Tobias just laughed unpleasantly and another of the footmen joined in.

"Perhaps he's bought some toys for you. Or perhaps they're presents for his mistress, your mother. What d'ya think, gypsy brat… or perhaps I should say Your graceling?"

Jem felt himself go red. The birthmark on his neck began to itch. More than anything he wanted to hit the smirking footmen, but he knew that was exactly what they wanted him to do.

He simply stood, turned his back on them and walked to the far end of the kitchen where he stared out of the small window onto the herb garden.

It wasn't true, Jem thought furiously, the duke wasn't his father. Ann had said so, hadn't she?

But she had also said that his father was here somewhere in the city – a city that the duke and his cronies intended to burn to the ground.

"You will know him before your thirteenth birthday."

Jem gripped the edge of the little water trough used for pot scrubbing in front of the window. He had the bleakest, emptiest feeling that time was running out for so many things. And there was nothing he could do about it.

He felt a tug on his sleeve and looked down to see Simeon standing next to him.

The small boy smiled shyly.

"Don't take any notice, Jem. They just like to see you get angry, that's all. And being cooped up here for the summer has made them all bored and scratchy. They bait each other, too... and me."

Jem looked out onto the dusty garden and sighed. "Do you think about your father, Sim?" he asked.

"All the time," said the boy, quietly. "And me mother."

Jem squeezed the boy's thin shoulder. "I'm sorry. They were good people."

They were quiet for a moment. On the window sill just in front of them sat a small glass bowl full of crystallised fruits and sugared flowers.

Pig Face had clearly been busy again.

"Try one. They're really good," whispered Sim. "I've had three, but don't tell Wormald."

Jem's mouth began to water as he looked at the dish. He checked that no one was paying attention, chose a fat sugared strawberry and crammed it into his mouth. It was a small sweet revenge and it was delicious. He licked the crystals from his lips and reached for another two, handing one to Sim.

Thwack!

Wormald's thin cane came swishing down on the back of Jem's hand.

"No you don't, you thieving little toerags. Those sweetmeats are for the duchess. Arrived today they did from Count Cazalon in Paris."

The rites of binding!

Instantly, the delicious taste turned to something bitter. Jem's mouth seemed to burn, his tongue and lips felt as if they were scraped raw and scalded. He choked and tried to spit out the half-chewed strawberry, but it was too late.

The burning in his mouth and throat made it difficult to breathe. For a while Jem struggled like a gasping fish out of water, his body wracked by spasms as he fought to gulp air into his lungs.

Simeon raced to fetch a tankard of water, but Jem couldn't swallow a drop. The serving lad's eyes became huge with concern as Jem bent double, clutching his heaving stomach. Even Wormald seemed anxious rather than angry when Jem vomited on the flagstones.

The steward eyed Cazalon's sweetmeats

suspiciously and tipped them swiftly into a little slop bucket in the corner.

Eventually Jem managed to calm himself. But, after taking one look at his shivering body, wraithlike face and watering eyes, Sarah, who had been called down to the kitchens to deal with her ailing son, demanded that he should rest.

Reluctantly Wormald agreed, but only after one of the maids whispered loudly that the sickness might be the start of something contagious.

Jem's duties were cancelled for the rest of the day, and Sarah helped her son from the kitchen, supporting him up the stairs to his truckle bed in the attic.

But instead of getting better, Jem grew worse. His body burned with fever and his bedding became so sodden with sweat that it had to be changed on the hour. He became delirious and babbled incoherently about fires and white ravens. For two days and two nights Sarah tended to him while the servants whispered fearfully that the plague had returned to London.

On the third morning the fever broke and by evening that day Jem was sitting upright in bed asking for food.

"You must be feeling better." Sarah smiled fondly at Jem, but she had huge black circles under her eyes. She fussed over the covers, then bustled off to fetch some milk, bread and honey. Jem lay back and stared at a cobweb hanging from a ceiling beam.

Despite his exhaustion, his anger at the ways Cazalon had tricked him burned sharp in his mind. Jem counted on his hand:

He had crossed a barrier of salt at the man's invitation.

He had given him his own blood.

He had knelt before him.

… And now he had eaten his food.

Jem had unwittingly done four of the five things that Ann had expressly warned him against. All that remained was for him to offer Cazalon an article of his clothing.

He remembered her words, "*Once you have tricked a person into fulfilling the five rites you have complete power over them. You will be able to make them do exactly what you want. They will become your creature.*"

Jem hammered a clenched fist down onto the blanket. He stared furiously at his hand, the stupid, greedy hand that had taken the strawberry from the bowl.

Cazalon had outwitted him at every turn, but Jem was determined he wouldn't let him do it again.

CHAPTER TWENTY

Scritch, scratch…

The noise came from over to the left. At first Jem ignored it. There were always mice or rats scuttling around in the eaves and behind the walls of an old building like Ludlow House. But the noise came again, and this time it sounded more like tapping on the window. He sat up and was surprised and delighted to see the tiny black and white form of Cleo huddled against the panes.

Jem weakly pushed back the bedcovers and walked over to open the window – although it was hot outside, the window was closed in an attempt to keep out the evil miasma of the streets. Everyone knew that plague was carried on the air.

Cleo chattered softly as she leapt into the room. Jumping onto his shoulder, she stroked his ear and nuzzled his neck for a moment before feeling into her little red jerkin. A roll of paper fell to the floor and the monkey dropped lightly from his shoulder to stand beside it. She looked up at him and nudged the roll across the boards in Jem's direction.

As she did so, Jem noticed that her right paw was oddly clenched and seemed to twist inwards. He bent to collect the paper and stroked her.

"How could Cazalon do that to you, Cleo?" he whispered angrily as he unrolled the paper.

The message was brief.

"Meet us at the back gate tomorrow at the fourth hour after noon. A & T"

Jem's heart leapt.

He read the message again. Ann and Tolly were here in London after all – but why hadn't he heard from them until now?

He looked down at the monkey, who was staring back up at him intently. Her task completed, Cleo gave one more brief, soft, friendly chirp and jumped back onto the windowledge. With a flick of her tail she was gone, and Jem leaned out to watch as she expertly negotiated the brick ledges and foliage all the way back down to ground level. When she reached a clump of nettle bushes at the bottom, she disappeared from view.

As instructed, just as the city church bells sounded the fourth hour after noon, Jem was waiting at the back gate to Ludlow House. It had been easy to persuade his mother that he was still too weak for kitchen work, and he had been granted leave to rest in the attic for two more days.

Just before the meeting time, Jem changed into some fresh clothes and sneaked through the maze of servants' passages, out across the stable yard and through the gardens to the back gate, which was overgrown and seldom used. He felt a sharp jolt of happiness and something like relief mixed with gratitude when he saw Tolly and Ann waiting for him on the street.

As he slipped through the ivy-covered gate to join them, a huge grin spread across Tolly's face, and Ann, although thinner and paler than ever, looked equally delighted.

"Jem!" she ran forward and took his hand. "We weren't sure if you'd manage to get away. It's so good to see you."

"Still alive then?" said Tolly, punching Jem's shoulder.

"I was wondering the same about you! I thought Cazalon had taken you to France."

Ann glanced at Tolly and grinned. "He wouldn't take the likes of us with him! He is attending the French court for the entire summer and isn't due back in London until the end of August. We have been left in the tender care of Tapwick. I'm sure you can imagine what that's been like…"

She arched an eyebrow before continuing, "He also placed a sealing charm about Malfurneaux Place and the streets beyond to make sure that we couldn't go anywhere."

"But you're here?" Jem looked questioningly between them.

Tolly smiled even more broadly. "As you know, Ann is very resourceful."

He spoke aloud. Today, instead of the rich and colourful clothes he usually wore, he was dressed in a loose white shirt and dark breeches. His head was bare, revealing close-cropped, wiry black hair. Cleo popped out from under the folds of Ann's skirt and jumped up to Tolly's shoulder.

"You should try to hide her, Tolly. You'll both draw attention to us," Ann said.

She turned to Jem. "It's taken weeks, but gradually I've been able to stretch the spell. We've managed to go a little further each day, although we couldn't cross the river. But then last week we found a break, a sort of hole in the charm. I think I might have stretched it so far that it's become... frayed at the edge."

"What about Tapwick?" asked Jem.

Ann's eyes glittered. "Oh, he's quite easy to deal with now. He thinks he's so clever, with his prodigiously sensitive nose and all, but, actually, I can freeze him for hours on end – or make him fall asleep. He never seems to notice. Or if he does, he won't say anything to Cazalon because he knows he'll be punished."

She looked at the busy street around them. Carriages rocked by and people jostled past – some of them stared openly at Tolly, but the colour of his skin wasn't so much of a novelty on the teeming streets of London as the monkey on his shoulder.

"These poor people have no idea what danger they are in." She shivered.

It was as if February had suddenly returned. The warm glow of happiness Jem felt on seeing them again evaporated in an instant.

"I– I've got so much to tell you." His words tumbled out in a torrent. "I've done something really stupid and I think that Cazalon means to experiment on Cleo and perhaps you too, Tolly. I mean, I can't be sure, but I saw these terrible—"

Ann stopped him with a frown as a man slowed beside them to stare at Cleo.

"We must find somewhere we can talk properly, somewhere people won't pay attention to us," Ann hissed.

Jem thought hard for a moment and remembered a conversation he'd once overheard between Tobias and one of the other footmen who'd committed a minor offence and wanted to lay low somewhere Wormald would be unlikely to find him.

"Best place for that, my friend, is a tavern. You'll find all sorts in there and no one asks questions. No one cares if you're a servant or a prentice boy. As long as you've coin in your breeches you can lose yourself in a London ale house for a couple of hours – and very nice it is, too."

Feeling rather grown-up, Jem repeated Tobias's suggestion, but he was still a bit surprised when Ann nodded enthusiastically.

"Yes, that would be perfect. Lots of noise, lots of people. The best place to hide is always in a crowd! As long as Cleo stays hidden they'll be too interested in the ale to notice us."

"But we can't just sit there," said Tolly. "We need money to pay for bread and ale at least. And we don't have any."

Ann bent down and picked up a handful of grey pebbles, slipping them into her pocket. "We do now," she grinned broadly, showing the little gap between her front teeth.

❦ ⚎ ❧

The Jack in the Green was a tavern in a narrow lane quite close to St Paul's and several streets away from Ludlow House.

The children liked the look of the place immediately. It was busy, but not too busy. Several travellers with trunks and bags were in the doorway, waiting for coaches, and three of the young servers who bustled between the trestles on the rush-strewn floor were about the same age as Jem.

Ann took the lead. Sweeping into the smoky tavern, she made for a partly private booth formed by two tall-backed benches at the far end of the room. She beckoned Tolly and Jem to join to her.

When the landlady, a fat, grease-spattered woman with a red face and thick meaty arms, bustled up to them with a threatening look on her face, Ann played the lady to perfection, telling her that she was waiting for her father who was up from the country on city business. She even asked about the possibility of taking a room for the night and accommodation for her servants, airily indicating Tolly and Jem.

The woman seemed delighted to have a young lady of quality in her inn and was even happier when Ann displayed four bright coins from her pocket and ordered a jug of small beer, bread and a platter of meat.

"That was impressive," said Jem when the woman had gone. "Although I'm not sure about the bit when you described me as your servant!"

Tolly laughed. "Me neither – but it seemed to do the trick."

Ann sighed in exasperation, then checked the room around them before leaning forward to whisper urgently. "Tolly, please try to keep Cleo's head down!"

Then she turned to Jem. "Right, tell us everything. Try not to leave anything out. Even small details could be important."

Once he started, Jem found it difficult to stop. Ann and Tolly listened intently.

When he described Cazalon's experiments on

the dog and the cat, his friends were horrified.

"The cruelty… Those poor creatures."

Ann's voice was a cracked whisper and her huge eyes brimmed with glassy tears. "We often hear strange noises, sometimes the most pitiful shrieks and cries, but whenever Tolly goes to find out where they are coming from it's… it's as if the house seems to fold in upon itself to hide its secrets."

Tolly nodded grimly. "And from what you've just told us, Jem, it sounds as if it was a good thing I didn't blunder in on one of his experiments. Did he really say that he was thinking of doing that to Cleo and me?"

Jem nodded miserably.

Tolly put a protective arm around Cleo and huddled her closer. The little group fell silent for a moment, then Ann pushed her white hair back from her face and reached across the table to squeeze Tolly's hand.

"Go on, Jem."

He began to describe the library, but Ann stopped him. "Yes, yes. I know all about it. I've been there, remember? It's one of the only parts of Malfurneaux Place where I can move about quite freely. I think it holds so many books belonging to my family that

I am… I don't know… protected perhaps? It's as if the house doesn't notice me among so many other Metcalf things."

"But don't you think it's… odd? The library I mean?" asked Jem.

"Well, of course I do!" she retorted. "But this is Malfurneaux Place, remember? I would have thought that you of all people would appreciate that it's not like Ludlow House… or anywhere else."

She stopped and tapped the table irritably, staring at her long elegant fingers, but when she looked up again and caught sight of Jem's face her voice softened.

"I– I'm sorry. I didn't mean to be so abrupt. I do know this must all be very strange for you."

Tolly nodded solemnly. "It's as I told you, Jem. We've lived with it for so long now that we've ceased to notice how very peculiar it is to someone from… outside."

Ann smiled. "Just ignore me. Go on. Please."

When Jem described the fresh mummia and how Cazalon obtained it, Ann gasped in shock at the news that the sarcophagus did indeed contain a mummy. She was so fascinated she took a stub of charcoal and a little notebook from the folds of her skirt and began to scribble, stopping Jem every now and then to get him to repeat things.

He only faltered when he described the moment in the library when he had been tricked into kneeling.

"Oh Jem, you should have been on your guard." Ann threw the little charcoal stub down in frustration. But she was absolutely furious seconds later, when he admitted that he'd eaten Cazalon's food too, slamming the notebook down so hard that several people in the tavern turned to look at them.

"But I warned you!"

"I know. It's just that he caught me out. Both times he managed to trick me. He cheated, he…" Jem slumped miserably into the seat.

It was probably a good thing that the proprietor reappeared at that point carrying a jug and three pewter tankards. The trio were quiet as they filled the tankards and sipped the ale. It was thin and weak, but always safer to drink than the city's putrid water.

"I hardly dare to ask this question." Ann's voice was tinged with sarcasm. "But you are quite sure that you haven't given him any of your clothing, aren't you?"

Jem nodded glumly. "That's the one rule left, isn't it?"

"Rite, Jem. The word is rite." She was still angry. "You have willingly completed four of the five rites of binding. There is just one more rite to go before he will be able to control you completely. Do you understand what this means? You will become his creature. Cazalon will be able to command everything that you say or do."

"But why would he want that?" Jem looked into the bottom of his tankard as if he might find an answer there. "I don't understand. Why on earth does he want power over me? What use am I? This doesn't make any sense."

They were all silent.

After a moment, Ann sighed.

She looked across the table. Her expression was unreadable. "Do you know what an androtheos is?"

"What do you think?" It was his turn to snap.

Ignoring his sulky tone, Ann continued, "The night before he went to France, my guardian communicated with my mother." She flinched, before continuing, "I didn't expect him to come to my chamber as he had made the blood bridge just days before."

She broke off and loosened the ties on her cuff. Rolling her sleeve to the elbow, she exposed the soft scarred skin of the underside of her arm. A new wound stretched from her wrist to her elbow. It was vicious, deep and jagged and only just beginning to heal. Jem's throat tightened.

"He did that?"

Ann nodded, unable to continue. Tolly spoke instead. "It bled for hours, Jem. I thought it wouldn't stop. I– I thought she might..."

Tolly bit his lip and looked down.

Ann rolled back her sleeve and retied the cuff. She sat upright on the bench and shook her head as if trying to clear her mind. "When he made the bridge last time, one word – androtheos – kept ringing in my mind for hours afterwards. My mother planted it there for a reason. I heard it again and again, like an echo."

She flicked through her little notebook. "I looked it up in the library. It appears in some Roman accounts of Caesar's invasion of Britain. Apparently, the great emperor was terrified of our primitive pagan ways."

She smiled tightly. "Ah, here it is. The book was damaged and the page was stained. I couldn't read it all because some of the words were missing, but this is what I was able to copy and translate.

" 'Androtheos: the man reborn as a god. In ancient

tradition the druids of Britain were said to derive their great power from the Androtheos of their making and their choice. A willing human sacrifice was necessary for the arch-druid to achieve this transformation.'"

She looked up at the boys. "I think there was more about finding the right person and the qualities that person should possess. And there was something about awakening the place of sacrifice, but I couldn't read it all because the page was badly stained."

Ann looked back at her notes. "This is how it finished: 'The druid priests believed that if all this was properly achieved at the appointed place, then all the powers of a god would be granted to their Androtheos.'"

She looked up at Jem and Tolly. "I believe that Cazalon intends to make himself the Androtheos. But who will be his willing human sacrifice?"

She paused for a moment and then, quietly, she answered her own question. "I think it must be you, Jem. Why else would Cazalon have sought the boy of jade for so long unless he needed him for some very particular reason... I think Cazalon is trying to bind you so he can control your mind and make you a *willing* sacrifice."

Jem clenched his fists. He would let Cazalon do nothing of the kind.

The children sat in baffled, fearful silence. When the trencher of bread and cold meats arrived, none of them felt hungry. It was now early evening and the tavern was becoming noisy and busy. Tolly looked towards the door where a group of rowdy young men were jostling one of the serving girls. His eyes narrowed. "It's getting late, Ann. We must go."

He tucked the reluctant Cleo deeper into the folds of his shirt.

"You're right. I'm certain Tapwick's still sleeping, but we must be there when he wakes." Ann stood and put the four shiny coins on the table. As she rose, a ripple of white hair fell back over her shoulders.

Several men stared at her as the little party picked its way through the tavern. They were still several yards from the door when there was a furious shout.

"Oi! You three! Pay me in pebbles, would ya?"

Jem turned to see the tavern keeper lumbering towards them. Her face was red and as she pushed through the crowd she started to roll her greasy sleeves up to her elbows.

"Hold it right there, you thieving vagabonds. Stop them!"

"Run!" Jem yelled at Tolly and Ann, who were ahead of him. "I'll give you a chance to get clear."

"But Jem, what about you?" Ann's voice was full of panic.

"Just go – and don't look back." He leapt up onto a long trestle table and let out a loud mocking whistle. Everyone in the alehouse turned to look at the boy on the table and Jem was relieved to see that the momentary distraction gave Tolly, Cleo and Ann the chance to slip through the door up ahead.

He looked at the hostile faces staring at him and took a deep breath. Now what?

He felt excitement and fear flood through him as he made a snap decision.

"Good evening gentlemen," he shouted, then grinned, bowed and began to race along the table top, jumping easily from table to table and kicking out at the foam-topped tankards in front of the customers. He felt as if he was flying. He revelled in the fact that he moved so fast and leapt so nimbly that no one was able to stop him. Men who weren't dabbing at their ale-spattered clothes and sodden wigs tried to grab his feet, but he was too quick for them.

Jem had never felt so elated. After years of taking orders in the kitchens and being at everyone's beck and call it was as if something in him had been set free.

But when he reached the end of the next trestle table, a group of city men were waiting for him. A rotund alderman with tiny piglike eyes removed his wig, wiped his sweating pate with it and rubbed his hands in anticipation.

"You've had it now, my lad." He started to clamber up onto a bench beside the table so that he could catch hold of the boy, but Jem launched himself into the air and grabbed hold of a metal hoop hanging from chains attached to a beam running across the ceiling. If he could clear just a few feet more he'd almost be at the door.

The hoop held several metal cups set with stinking tallow candles and as Jem swung out over the men at the end of the table, greasy dollops of thick yellow wax rained down on them.

The fat alderman yelped as the hot wax splatted on his bald head and he toppled from the bench, knocking over several of his comrades who floundered around in the damp rushes.

When he had sailed clear, Jem dropped to the floor and darted to the door. The sound of angry shouts rang in his ears as he sprinted down the street.

Bumping and blundering into finely dressed gentlemen, scented ladies, merchants, traders and beggars, Jem ran and ran until it felt as if his heart would burst, and then he ran some more.

When he couldn't go another step, he staggered into an alleyway and collapsed, choking and gasping for air as he leaned against a stone wall.

After a minute he slid down to a sitting position and rested his head on his knees. His damp curly hair flopped down over his face.

"Ah, here he is!"

Jem heard the sound of clapping and looked up to see Ann and Tolly beaming down at him.

"That was brilliant!" said Tolly, offering a hand to pull Jem to his feet. Cleo was perched on his shoulder. She chattered with excitement and performed a little salute with her good paw.

"That was quite a performance," said Ann. "We might have ended up in prison tonight if it hadn't been for you. I'm sorry – I hoped my spell on the pebbles would last longer than that!"

Jem performed another elaborate bow. "It was nothing," he grinned. "Actually, I really rather enjoyed it!"

The evening was bright and warm as the trio made

their way back to Cheapside, where they would go their separate ways. A man carrying a large square parcel pushed past as they turned into a cobbled side street.

"That reminds me! I forgot to mention the cases," said Jem. "Huge wooden cases for the duke have been delivered to Ludlow House from Paris. We're not allowed to open them."

"They must have come from the count," said Tolly.

Jem nodded. "They're all being kept in a locked room and no one is allowed to go in."

"Can you get in there, Jem?" asked Ann. "Whatever's inside those boxes it's obviously something important – and you are the only one of us who can find out what it is. I can give you a charm to—"

"No. I won't need that," Jem cut in quickly. He felt funny at the thought of being turned into something strange, and besides, now he thought about it, he did know how to get in. "I think I know a way. But, er, thank you."

Ann stared at him speculatively. "As you wish. I suggest that we meet again as soon as possible and then you can tell us what you've found."

"As soon as possible? But what about the plot?

What about London?" demanded Jem, also thinking *What about my father?*, but deciding to keep that to himself. "We might be running out of time. We don't even know what they are actually going to do or when they are going to do it."

Tolly looked at him intently. An odd expression flickered over his features, before he replied. "Look, we know the count isn't due to return to London until the end of August and that's still weeks away – we can be very sure that nothing is going to happen without him. There's still time, Jem."

Ann nodded. "And we can't risk raising Tapwick's suspicions, so I dare not send him into a long sleep again for several days. But we promise we will send Cleo with a message about another meeting as soon we can."

Without allowing Jem chance to reply, she continued decisively, "Whatever the day, we will meet at the same hour, at the back gate to Ludlow House. Come on, Tolly, we really must go back. Keep Cleo hidden!"

The children walked together to Cheapside. It was still thronged with people. Dust thrown up by horses and carriage wheels filled the air. Cracked-voiced street-sellers carrying broad trays that swung on leather straps from their necks still tried to attract customers.

A booming voice sounded suddenly from somewhere above them. "Ann! Ann Metcalf. Where the devil have you been?"

A huge hand came down and gripped the girl's shoulder.

CHAPTER TWENTY-ONE

Jem looked up in panic. A dark, broad-shouldered man was leaning down from a covered wagon above them. Ann shrieked and twisted, trying to free herself from the man's grip. She tried to bite at his stubby fingers, but could not get away.

"She always fought like a tiger, this one." The booming voice rang out again, but this time, with a chuckle.

"Calm yourself, girl," the man said, releasing Ann from his grip. "It's me, Gabriel. Gabriel Jericho."

"Gabriel! You frightened the life out of me! What on earth are you doing here?" said Ann, finally managing to free herself from his hand. She stood in the street with her hand on one hip, staring indignantly up at him.

Gabriel leaned back on the wooden plank that formed the driving seat and handed the reins to a ruddy-faced boy sitting next to him. Turning to someone behind him in the depths of the wagon he called out.

"Peg, lass. Pass me out a handful of the bills."

A skinny hand appeared through the flap, thrusting a sheaf of papers at him.

The man leaned over again and handed the children a sheet each.

It was a playbill:

Gabriel Jericho

Proudly Presents His Theatrical Circus of

stupefying splendour. For one season

only in the City of London, before

travelling to the capitals of Europe.

Commanded to Perform at Court by

his Moste Gracious Majesty,

King Charles the second.

"What do you think of that then, my lady?"

Ann smiled broadly. "I think it shows that your

well-deserved fame has spread far and wide – even to the very highest persons in society." She laughed, adding, "So, you are to perform before the king himself?"

Gabriel nodded. "But not until the first weekend of September, mind. We've been asked to perform at His Majesty's end-of-summer revels, no less. Before that we thought we'd set up camp in the fields just beyond the northern wall. Reckon we can make a pretty penny from the city folk in the long evenings."

He pointed with his whip to a dozen or so brightly painted covered wagons halted in a long line behind him, blocking the road. Behind them came of row of heavy flat carts carrying huge rectangular boxes covered with oil skins.

"And how did the king come to hear of you?" Ann asked.

Gabriel shifted his large frame on the narrow seat. "Well, that's something of a long story. Let's just say that one of my young actresses has done rather well for herself and is now in a position to do me a bit of good. You might call it a very… personal recommendation."

Ann grinned and clapped her hands. "Bravo! The king will love you, I know it!" There was a wistful note to her voice as she continued, "It's wonderful to see you."

The man's eyes crinkled with affection, but then a shadow crossed his face. "And you, little one? How goes it? After your mother and grandmother..." He stopped and then continued, quieter this time. "We looked everywhere for you. Asked in all the towns and villages from Colchester to Norwich and no one knew where you were. It was as if you'd been spirited away."

Ann looked at her feet. When she looked up again her eyes were brimming with tears. "That's a long story too, Gabriel. Not one for the street."

The man nodded and bent to put a hand to her shoulder. "In your own time, my love," he said. "You come and find us at the Spital Fields and we'll speak. You'll find some familiar faces here, lass."

He looked at Jem and Tolly properly for the first time. "These your friends then?"

At that moment Cleo stuck her nose out of Tolly's shirt. She sniffed the air suspiciously and looked down the road at the wagons and carts before leaping deftly onto the boy's head, where she balanced delicately, craning her neck for a better look at the procession.

Gabriel gave a huge laugh of surprise. "A moor and a monkey? Well, I never. There's always a place for you two in my troupe, lad – just you remember that."

The city church bells began to ring out. It was six. Gabriel frowned and looked back at the wagons, before turning to Ann again. "We'd best be off, lass. They close the Bishop's Gate at seven, and we'll be fined if we end up locked inside the city. You come and find us."

It was definitely time to move on. The odd procession was blocking the road and angry voices could be heard calling out in complaint from the rear.

The man cracked his whip and the cart rumbled forward.

"Wait! Wait!" Ann ran until she was level with him again. "Take us with you."

Jem and Tolly exchanged astonished glances.

Gabriel reined back the horses and Ann continued in a rush. "You said there was a place for Tolly and Cleo here in your troupe?"

The big man nodded. "He's a fine-looking lad and the monkey is a little beauty. We could work them into the act with no trouble. And you don't need to ask for yourself – your mother was a dear friend, it's the least I can do, to look out for her beloved daughter."

Ann turned excitedly to Tolly, her eyes were sparkling. "Don't you see? We don't have to go back to Malfurneaux Place at all, Tolly. Jericho will give us a home. We will become players and we will be safe among friends. Cazalon won't ever be able to experiment on you or Cleo, or… well, you know…" She rubbed at her arm before continuing, "and with Jem's help we can still stop the plot against the city."

Tolly looked confused. "But what about your things, your mother's books? Perhaps we should collect them and then…"

"There's no need," Ann smiled. "Everything I've ever cared for in that hideous house is here on the street with me now. We can be free at last and we can make a new home with Gabriel here." She grinned shyly up at the man on the wagon. "It's… it's all right, isn't it?" she asked.

He laughed and simply offered her his huge hand to pull her up beside him. "And you lad, too. Up you come," he added, shifting on the seat to make extra space for Tolly. "What's the monkey's name, then?" he asked as the boy clambered aboard.

"She's called Cleo," said Tolly. He frowned for

a moment and then asked, "Sir, that smell. Do you… are there any… lions with you?"

Gabriel slapped his thigh and his huge booming laugh echoed across the street.

"Indeed there are, lad. And you're a sharp one to notice it. I've got two of them under wraps in the last wagon there."

He pointed back with his whip. "But I don't like to let people see them until they've put money in my pocket. How did you know?"

"It was the smell," Tolly said. "When I was small my father gave me a lion cub as a pet. I recognised the scent, immediately." Tolly sounded happier than Jem had ever heard him.

More angry yells reminded them all that they were blocking the way. Gabriel twitched the reins and his wagon jolted forward again.

"What about you, young sir? You coming too?" He smiled warmly at Jem.

The boy shook his head sadly. "I can't. But I'll come and find you all soon," he called as the wagons rumbled away.

Ann and Tolly leaned out over the side and looked back. Their faces shone with excitement.

"It's up to you now, Jem," Ann called back. "If we

can fit all the pieces of this puzzle together, then we'll see the whole picture. Find out what's in those boxes…"

She and Tolly waved until the wagons reached the end of the street and turned left in a cloud of dust. The thought that his friends would never again have to face the horrors of Malfurneaux Place made Jem smile. He turned and headed in the opposite direction.

But as he entered the street leading to Ludlow House he didn't notice the huge white bird that circled overhead. The raven performed another lazy circuit of the sky before flapping its enormous wings and soaring off to the south.

CHAPTER TWENTY-TWO

When Jem returned to Ludlow House later that evening he tried to sneak up the back stairs to the attic, but Sarah caught him just as he was turning into the passage leading to his room.

"I don't know what's got into you," she said. "I believed you were ill so I made excuses for you. But now I find that you've been gadding about for hours on end, going Lord knows where. If I find that you are bringing shame on me, Jem, I'll... I'll..."

"What will you do?" Jem was tired and he spoke angrily and thoughtlessly. "I sometimes wonder why you speak so much of shame, mother. It's not me who has anything to hide."

Sarah blushed and turned away. Then she spun round again and slapped him across the face. "Don't ever speak to me like that again! Do you understand, Jem. Never again."

He brought a hand to his stinging cheek. Sarah had never struck him before. The blow hadn't been that painful, but the realisation that his careless words had wounded her hurt him a great deal.

The pair of them stood in silence for a moment, then Sarah turned and walked away.

"Mother... I..." Jem called out, but Sarah didn't look back.

She didn't speak to him again for several days after that. Jem felt as if he'd lost his only ally in Ludlow House, and Wormald, who sensed the rift between them, lost no opportunity to make the boy's life even more miserable than it was already. As Jem scraped out the servants' stinking, fly-blown middens one sticky afternoon, he gloomily wondered what horrible task the steward might set for him next. He had heard that there were a couple of maggot-riddled sides of pork in the cellar meat locker that would need seeing to. Even though they were salted, the hot weather had made them go bad. Jem shuddered at the thought of handling the slimy, stinking meat. Wormald was clearly saving up all the worst chores for him.

Over the next week, more mysterious boxes from Paris arrived at Ludlow House – all of them were large, all of them were heavy and, as before, all of them were locked away inside the great gallery.

Then, on Sunday, the duke informed the kitchens and the servants that they were to prepare a lavish feast for some special guests. The event would take place in two days' time and no expense was to be spared.

After producing a list of the wines, tarts, meats and puddings that he required, the duke disappeared alone into the great gallery for hours. Sounds of thumping and banging – and occasional hammering – could be heard from behind the doors, as if heavy objects were being moved about.

Over the next two days, there never seemed to be a chance for Jem to put his plan into action. Wormald kept finding evermore disgusting tasks for him to do and anyway, Bellingdon was always locked inside the gallery with the boxes.

Usually so conscious of his elegant dress and cleanliness, the duke – when he appeared at all – looked hot and dishevelled. His magnificent, tightly curled golden wig hung in lank, sweaty rats' tails down his back. He worked non-stop alone in the gallery, and then, on the morning of the feast, the servants awoke to find the hallway filled with splintered wood and broken boxes.

The Duke of Bellingdon had clearly finished his unpacking.

The feast was to be laid out in the antechamber leading to the great gallery. Four places were set at the table and the duke gave orders that everything should be ready for noon. The household had risen early. Throughout the morning, elaborate cold dishes were prepared and Pig Face sweated even more than usual over a side of beef that was turning slowly on a spit set across the largest hearth in the kitchen.

Jem was called to carry the silver service up from the locked vaults beneath the kitchens. As he passed a row of glistening raspberry tarts lined up on a dresser in the antechamber, his stomach rumbled, but not with hunger, with anxiety. He had told Ann that he knew a way to get into the locked room, but now he felt sick at the thought that the time had come to put his plan into action.

Wormald was already in the chamber, busy arranging each polished item in the place settings with the precision of a watchmaker. The dining table stood opposite a pair of locked doors that led directly into the great gallery.

Following the duke's instructions, no one, not even Wormald, had entered that room since the day when the first boxes arrived from Paris. After lecturing the servants, the steward had taken the gallery key from the great metal ring at his waist and handed it to the duke himself. But, as Jem knew, one other person possessed a copy of every key to every door in Ludlow House...

His mother.

Jem left the goblets on the dresser, then hurried to the kitchen and filled a pitcher of water. He carried it to the duchess's bedchamber, where he knew the women were together. The duchess hadn't been seen by anyone but Sarah for days. He knocked twice.

"Enter."

His mother looked up from the book in her lap. The curtains were drawn and the only light came from a small candle burning on the table beside her. The air was foul. The smell immediately reminded Jem of Cazalon, but here, the stench was almost overpowering. His mother looked pale and strained. "What is it?" she said.

"I– I have brought you both some fresh water. And I– I wanted to apologise," Jem stammered, feeling guilty as the lie popped out of his mouth. True, he did want to apologise, but that wasn't why he was here.

Sarah's expression softened. "I am sorry too, Jem. You're a good lad, but there are some things I..."

She broke off as a soft moaning noise came from the heavily curtained bed. The duchess was stirring. Sarah took the pitcher from Jem and poured a glass of water. She placed the pitcher by the candle and took the glass over to the bed, pushing back the hangings a little to offer the drink.

"It is the mirror, Sarah."

Jem heard the duchess speak, but he couldn't see her. The woman's voice was hoarse and breathless. "The mirror cannot be right, it must be cracked. The medicine should make me younger... It is not working, I must have more. Make him bring me more."

"Hush," Sarah soothed, and just for a second Jem caught sight of the duchess's hand as she reached for the glass. He blinked and looked again but it was gone. Was it the poor light, or had he really seen something that looked like a scaly claw?

"Jem!" His mother's voice was sharp. "Fill this again."

She handed him the glass and he went over to the table where the pitcher stood. Just as he had hoped, Sarah's ring of keys stood next to the pitcher. Quietly and carefully he picked up the ring and slipped it into his pocket.

"The water, please, Jem."

He filled the glass and moved towards the bed. Sarah prevented him from coming too close. She smiled sadly. "Thank you. That was a thoughtful thing to do. I think you should go now. The duchess is tired."

Jem nodded and turned to leave.

"Jemmy," his mother's voice was pleading. "Don't tell anyone how sick she is, please."

He nodded but didn't turn back, stepping swiftly and gratefully out of the horrible, clammy room.

As he raced down the back stairs his heart was pounding. He would worry about getting the ring of keys back to Sarah later, but for now he was more concerned about finding the right key for the gallery and getting into the locked room without being seen. Wormald was fiddling with the last touches to the elaborate table decorations when he returned to the antechamber. Two maids and a footman were plumping cushions and arranging the hangings. The buffet table groaned with food and the room looked magnificent.

The steward surveyed the table, nodded to himself and clapped his hands.

"Out!" he called. The bustling stopped and

Wormald ushered them all from the room, closing the door behind him. There was less than a quarter of an hour to go before the guests arrived.

As they returned to the servants' quarters, Jem stopped dead. "Sir! Mr Wormald," he called out.

The stringy man turned to look at him. "What do you want?"

"I've left a tray on the floor, sir, by the table. I brought up the goblets on it and forgot to collect it."

The grey tufts on the steward's head quivered and his eyes glinted. Wormald smiled unpleasantly. "Then you had better go and collect it."

"Sorry, sir. I'll go now."

"And to teach you to be more careful in future, you will not be permitted to dine on the leftovers with the rest of the servants this evening."

Jem nodded sullenly and retraced his steps to the now-empty antechamber. As he crossed the entry hall, the hand of the golden clock showed that it was now perilously close to noon. He closed the antechamber doors behind him, took out Sarah's ring of keys and crossed to the doors of the great gallery. Bending to the lock, his hands shook as he tried a succession of the keys on the large metal ring. Just as he heard a great booming knock on Ludlow

House's great front doors, a little clicking sound told him that, at last, he had the right one. Turning the handle gently, Jem pushed open the door and crept into the locked room.

He was astonished at what he saw.

CHAPTER
TWENTY-THREE

The great panelled gallery was filled with model buildings, each constructed from dark shining wood. In all, there were about twenty of them ranged from one end of the room to the other. Elegant town houses, mansions, sweeping terraces, stable blocks, palaces and ornamented archways – the models were exquisitely made and precise in every detail. The air was golden with motes of dust and the room smelled of wood and varnish.

At the far end stood a model that was much larger than the others, almost as tall as Jem himself. Intrigued, Jem walked towards it, uncertain what it could be.

The dark wood building was shaped like a five-pointed star and was set on a raised platform with steps leading up to it. On every side the star was flanked by rows of severe columns that were topped by carved decorations that reminded Jem of ferns. The fronds fanned out to support a flat roof at the centre of which stood a huge dome made from black glass.

The models reminded him of the ones he had seen on top of the chests at Malfurneaux Place. With its columns and steps, this one looked a little like a Greek temple, but at the same time, it was not like anything he had ever seen in any of the duke's books. The sound of conversation came from the closed doors to the antechamber behind him. The duke's guests had obviously assembled. Thinking quickly, Jem tiptoed over to the door, counting along the ring of keys to find the right one as he went and locked the door softly again from his own side. It gave a tiny click, but no one seemed to notice the sound.

The duke was giving final instructions to Wormald. "We are not to be disturbed. On no account is anyone to enter this room. Do you understand? Leave us now."

Jem heard the sound of a door closing. There was a pause before the duke began again. "Gentlemen, you are all welcome to my house on this most auspicious of days."

"Well, if everything goes to plan, this won't be your house for much longer, George."

The braying voice belonged to the Marquis of Kilheron, and his comment provoked much amusement in the room beyond.

Kilheron continued excitedly, "Indeed, sirs, I believe we shall all soon be living like princes. George, I cannot wait a moment longer, let us see the new London."

Jem looked again at the strange model with its black polished points, shadowy colonnades and opaque glass dome, and shuddered. He'd suddenly remembered the conversation they'd overhead from the chimney. What had Cazalon said when the young marquis questioned the plans? "We shall be the masters here, free to create whatever we like; to build to the limits of our imagination and beyond."

Now Jem realised what these models were. They were buildings for the new London. They showed the city that Cazalon, Bellingdon and the other conspirators intended to construct when they had burned the old one to the ground.

"Patience," replied the duke. "Before I reveal the bones of our city, there are matters to be settled."

There was a thumping noise as if someone had slammed their fist on the table, then Alderman Pinchbeck spoke. "Well, I don't know about you, my lords, but I'm not handing over a penny until I've seen what I'm buying."

Heavy footsteps came towards the doors leading into the gallery. The handles turned and the locked doors shook. Jem sprang back.

"Come now, Your Grace, let the dog see the rabbit." Alderman Pinchbeck bellowed.

The doors shook again.

Terrified, Jem looked about for a hiding place. As he was desperately scanning the room he heard the duke's voice. "Very well, Alderman. I understand your concern, but I assure you that you will not be disappointed."

Jem fled to the far end of the gallery, intending to crouch behind the huge model on the raised platform. But as he slipped into the space behind the furthest points of the star he noticed a small gap in the wood. The model was so large that it had been assembled from different sections and each point was separate. Jem pushed gently on one of the column-lined sides and the gap widened enough to allow him to squeeze inside.

He shifted forward into the hollow at the centre of the model until he was standing, slightly stooped, just beneath the dark glass dome. The air inside was thick with the smell of varnish and tiny flecks of sawdust settled on his head and shoulders.

It was not a moment too soon. The double doors were thrown back and the duke's party entered the room. Although the glass was completely black from the outside looking in, Jem's view through the dome was clear as day. Through the glass, he saw Alderman Pinchbeck's corpulent body first, followed by Lord Avebury, Kilheron and finally the Duke of Bellingdon himself.

Today Bellingdon was dressed more magnificently than ever before. His golden wig tumbled over a red embroidered frock coat, a ruffle of bright white lace foamed at his neck and his pointed shoes were tied with loops of crimson ribbon. Jem was reminded of a cockerel.

For a moment there was an awed silence. Then all the visitors broke into spontaneous applause.

"Bravo!" shouted Kilheron. "They are magnificent. Which is mine?"

The duke took Kilheron's arm and led him over to a model of a fine mansion with long windows and a sweeping double stairway leading to a central door.

"Marvellous. It fair takes my breath away," said the marquis, stroking the wooden roof.

There was a coughing noise and the duke turned to Pinchbeck, who was scanning the room greedily.

"Alderman, your house is over there."

The duke pointed at a particularly grand model that was as tall as it was broad. "And this is the great archway that will lead to Pinchbeck Park," he continued, walking over to a highly decorated archway, designed, no doubt, to straddle a road. "The Pinchbeck Triumph will stand more than seventy feet high," the duke added.

Through the glass, Jem could see the Alderman's beady eyes widen in surprise and pleasure. Pinchbeck rubbed his hands together.

"Well, that looks most satisfactory. Most satisfactory indeed," he said.

The duke continued his tour of the models and soon he was standing just a few feet away from Jem's hiding place. "And this is Cazalon's new cathedral, gentlemen. What do you make of it?"

Cazalon's cathedral? Of course! Jem realised with a start what his hiding place was.

Lord Avebury stalked towards the model. Jem was sure that he could not be seen through the glass, but he ducked lower, just in case. His breathing became fast and shallow and his heart began to thump so loudly that he was certain the men gathering around the model could hear it.

Avebury's eyes narrowed as he took in the odd shape, the columns, the steps and the dome. At last he spoke.

"It is an abomination!"

The duke sidled up to him. "But do you not think it is interesting, Avebury? A building like this will be the talk of every capital in Europe. Cazalon has employed the finest architects on our behalf. That is why he has been in Paris these last weeks. He has commissioned these models to show us the new London. They are mere shadows of the real city we will build. And this magnificent construction will be our new cathedral."

Avebury's flat, slablike face was grim. "It is ungodly," he replied. "I knew the man was fascinated by the pagan temples of the past, but I did not think he would make one for himself. Cazalon once told me that he believes St Paul's to have been built over a Roman temple. And now I see he means to build that ancient heathen monstrosity anew."

The room was silent as the other men watched this exchange.

After a moment, Bellingdon clasped Avebury's right arm. "We are all engaged in the work of the Lord, Richard," he said. "When we cleanse the city with flames we will serve the righteous and sweep the sinful away with the ashes. This is holy work."

"And work that will delight and glorify our king," interrupted Kilheron. "Remember, Avebury, we will surely be rewarded on earth as well as in heaven."

The duke continued softly, "Why not allow Cazalon this folly, this artistic extravagance, when he has asked for so little? Even now he is in France raising the monies for our scheme, so that when London burns we will be ready. He has been tireless in his quest to help us build our great new capital – and this," the duke tapped the model, "is all he asks in return."

Avebury grunted. "And that's another thing that worries me, George. Why would a Frenchman want to help us?"

Bellingdon laughed uneasily. "French, you say? No, that's not right. Cazalon has spent a great deal of time in France, true, but he has estates and ancient titles here in England – and land in the Indies and the Americas, too. He is a man of the world, Richard. One of a new breed – and we are fortunate to be his friends. Now, come and look at your house over here. It has a fountain."

Bellingdon placed an arm around Avebury's

shoulders and guided him over to one of the most imposing models in the room. The duke pointed out its various features and after a short while, Avebury seemed almost happy.

Kilheron and Pinchbeck stayed close to the model where Jem was hiding.

"And what do you think of it, Alderman?" asked Kilheron quietly.

Pinchbeck puffed out his cheeks. "Avebury is right, it is an abomination. But that's a small price to pay when there's money to be made."

"And titles to be bought?" There was note of scorn in Kilheron's voice, but the Alderman had turned away and was already lumbering back up the room towards the duke and Avebury.

"I suppose you'll be wanting this then?" Pinchbeck called to Bellingdon and produced a leather pouch from the folds of his coat. "All in gold, as requested."

The duke smiled as all his visitors produced similar fat pouches that chinked with coins. "I believe you will find that your investment today pays rich dividends," he said. "When old London is burned to a crisp, the king will be grateful and generous to those who are ready to help him."

His words were met by nods and grunts of approval.

Inside the model, Jem shuddered. These greedy conspirators thought only of themselves, they didn't care at all about the thousands of people in the city.

Would his own father be burned to a crisp before Jem had even found him?

"Now, to the plan," said the duke, and he collected several rolls of paper from a desk. "Do you all have enough men to set the fires?" he asked, handing a roll to each conspirator.

Kilheron sniggered. "It was easy to find the right fellows for the task. London is full of ruffians and cutpurses. Poor rogues will do anything for ready coin."

Pinchbeck didn't sound so happy. "I've done as you asked, but to my mind this is all getting very expensive. I like to strike a deal as much as the next merchant, but so much outlay without immediate return – well, that's a risk. And maybe a poor one?"

The duke's reply was cold and formal. "You speak like a mere Alderman, sir. You'll find it's been a small price to pay when you and future generations of Pinchbecks add a title to their name. We must all make sacrifices – I am prepared for my own house to burn."

Jem froze. What about his mother and little Sim, and all the other inhabitants of Ludlow House? He'd never imagined that the duke meant to harm his own property and his own people. These men were discussing the destruction of everything he knew as easily as if they were bartering for a pig.

"Now, gentlemen," the duke spoke again. "If you would unroll the papers I have just given you and place them together on the floor here, we shall discuss the instructions I have received from our friend in Paris."

The men unfurled the rolls and placed them on the rug. The duke pushed the papers together so that they formed one large sheet, then stood back. "My dear fellow!" Kilheron exclaimed, "A plan of the whole city! And we each seem to have a different section."

"Good, Matthew – you are quite right." The duke looked down. "The count has split the City of London into four equal parts. Each of us is to be responsible for a quarter. The ruffians we have employed will set fires at each point throughout the city marked with a red cross, so – here, here, here and... here."

The duke pointed at the map and the conspirators bent closer.

"I shall take the north," Bellingdon continued, "Avebury, you will take the south, Alderman Pinchbeck the east, and Kilheron, you have the west."

Avebury looked up. "And what's that star at the centre?"

The duke chuckled, but it was a nervous sound. "That, dear friend, is Count Cazalon's concern. He has stipulated that he and he alone is to be responsible for the streets around St Paul's Cathedral. You will find those places clearly marked on your own maps. That is Cazalon's territory. Are we agreed?"

The men were quiet for a moment, then Pinchbeck muttered, "Well, if that's what he wants. Though, I must say, it all seems very odd."

The duke was sharp. "However strange you think it, Alderman, you will find that Cazalon has been most careful in devising this scheme. Your men are to be ready on the first day of September. Fires are to be lit at midnight across the city in these places."

He pointed at the maps on the carpet. "I have a copy kept somewhere safe so that I can coordinate the plan. But from here on in, it is up to you, and your men, to make sure that everything – every house, every tavern, every merchant's shop – is destroyed. They are to be burned from the face of the earth.

Now, take up your maps gentlemen."

Inside the model, Jem rubbed his eyes as a speck of sawdust settled on his lashes. The first of September was just days away! How could they possibly be stopped in time?

Kilheron piped up. "Why, that is an excellent date, George. How clever to choose the first day of September! We shall all be safe at court with our families and far from the old city, enjoying the king's end-of-summer revels. It is most ingenious."

The duke smiled. "I believe the count chose the date specifically for the convenience of his friends. If you have… concerns in the city, you have a week to make the relevant arrangements, which should be sufficient. And if our henchmen do all that we pay them for, we will not only be safe from the flames but safe from suspicion."

"But what about me and my girls?" said Pinchbeck. "What am I supposed to do, eh? My house and my main business are all within the city walls and people like us don't have an invitation to court."

The duke sighed and pretended to look out of a window. "I am sure that I can find a place at the king's revels for a wealthy man like you, Alderman. Doors can always be opened – for the right price."

Pinchbeck was silent for a moment, then he grumbled. "This is all getting very pricey. The wife and girls will be wanting new dresses for court and it'll cost a pretty penny to ship our goods out of the city at such short notice. I trust this will be worth it, My Lord?"

The duke smiled broadly. "Oh I think you'll be very satisfied, Alderman. Indeed, I trust that we will all be most satisfied."

He walked over to a particularly elegant model that looked more like a palace than a house. "Gentlemen, this will be my home at the heart of the new London. I always wanted a fine house on the banks of the river. When our fire has cleared the diseased scum and the deadwood from those narrow passages down by the Thames, I shall build this house on that very spot. It will be my... reward."

His eyes gleamed as he turned to look at them again. "There is one last thing. You all know that our friend in France can be a little... how can I put this? Eccentric?"

The men chuckled in agreement.

"Count Cazalon has asked that we should sign our names to this contract."

The duke produced a smaller roll of paper from

his coat and untied the red ribbon that bound it. The paper unfurled, and Jem could see that it had a large wax seal hanging from ribbon at the bottom.

"It is a formality, nothing more," Bellingdon continued in a bored voice. "This document merely records our interests as partners of the company that will own the new London."

The duke paused for a moment and then added, "Count Cazalon was most specific on this point. He returns to London this week and when he returns he expects to collect the completed contract from me – a contract we have signed in our blood."

The men shuffled uneasily. Avebury gave a great snort.

"That smacks of devilry. I'll not do it."

Bellingdon gave him a narrow look. "The choice is yours, Edward. You either sign or leave us. But if you choose to leave, I believe things will go very badly for you."

"Is that a threat?"

"It is a statement of fact," the duke replied, fingering the hilt of his sword. "Come, Edward," he said evenly. "We have all walked a long way down this road now. Is a drop of blood too much to ask?"

Avebury snorted again and then gave a curt nod.

"Very well. It seems I have no choice."

The duke produced a small knife and pricked his own thumb. He signed the document with a quill from the desk dipped in a bright drop of his blood. Avebury went next.

Just as the last of them, Kilheron, was scribbling his name on the contract, Jem sneezed.

CHAPTER
TWENTY-FOUR

The men froze. Bellingdon's hand gripped the contract so hard that the paper crackled as he turned to scan the room.

Terrified that he was about to sneeze again, Jem gripped his nose between thumb and forefinger and bent lower in the model. His legs were trembling and he felt as if he might be sick.

It was the sawdust. Inside the hollow, echoing model, the sneeze had seemed incredibly loud. Jem was certain that his hiding place was about to be discovered. Now, every beat of his heart sounded like the tolling of a bell.

In the gallery the men were silent, until Kilheron piped up in a nervous half whisper. "What was that, George?"

Bellingdon's voice was tight with fury. "This room was sealed on my order. I promise you, gentlemen, no one has been in here except me."

"Well, I certainly heard something," said Pinchbeck.

"And I too," said Avebury, adding, "it came from

down there." He pointed at the far end of the gallery where Jem crouched in the model cathedral.

"Then let us investigate," said the duke, drawing his sword and advancing slowly.

The others followed, throwing back their coats to reveal the light swords hanging at their sides.

The men circled the models in the gallery on the right and left flank. As they neared the wooden cathedral, Jem dipped to the floor and tried to fold himself into the smallest shape possible so that he could squeeze into the furthest arm of the star.

He could hear the footsteps coming closer and closer and he could hear the metallic scrape of the men's swords on the walls as they flicked at curtains and hangings.

Heavy boots sounded on the floor right next to his hiding place.

"I think there's something over here, George," a voice hissed.

Every nerve in Jem's body coiled tight as a hangman's noose. Suddenly there was a tearing noise as a tapestry was ripped aside, followed by a huge roar of surprise.

"God's teeth man, it's huge! A monster!" said Avebury.

294

Jem heard the sound of something scratching and skittering on the wooden floor, followed by the sound of running and thumping. The footsteps moved further up the gallery.

"Hit it, George! Use the hilt of your sword," shrieked Kilheron. "It's making for the chimney. Quick, man. Now!"

Jem heard a heavy blow and single high-pitched screech. There was a moment of silence and then the sound of more footsteps.

Pinchbeck spoke. "Well, I've seen some rats in my time, but never a beggar that big. Not even in the grain holds of me ships."

"It's the heat," replied Avebury. "They are living well off the middens this summer."

"Be that as it may, gentleman," the duke interrupted, "but in any case, I believe we have found our spy."

There was a general murmur of agreement before Bellingdon continued, "Come. We shall cement the contract we have signed today with a toast and then we shall dine."

Jem heard the sound of stamping feet as the men marked their approval, then the gradually quietening sound of retreating footsteps.

Inching from his hiding space, he stood up again and peered through the glass. Midway down the gallery, the duke was ushering his guests back into the antechamber where the banquet was set.

As the last man left the gallery, the duke walked over to a cabinet set against the wall. Jem watched as he bent low to feel for something on the far side of the black lacquered doors. A narrow tray shot out from the base between the clawlike feet and the duke placed the contract carefully into this secret compartment, before pushing it back into place. As he straightened up he turned and stared hard at the model cathedral before shrugging his shoulders and following his guests.

The doors closed behind him and Jem heard a click as a key turned to lock the room. His stomach performed a somersault and his head felt as if it might explode with a mixture of fear and relief.

⚔ ⚒ ⚔

The voices grew louder as the afternoon wore on. The duke was entertaining his business partners like royalty.

For now, Jem was trapped. He couldn't leave the gallery until the guests had gone. He shifted uncomfortably, suddenly aware that he needed to relieve himself.

Looking up through the dome he tried to assess the hour from the light in the room. It was, he guessed, late afternoon. The day was hot and inside the model, the air was thick and muggy. Trying to ignore his full bladder, he leaned back against the wooden wall and rested his head on his knees.

※ ⊥ ※

When Jem woke it was dark and his first, panicked thought was that he had been buried alive. Reaching out in the blackness, his hands touched wooden walls and his nostrils were filled with the smell of sawdust. It took him a moment to remember where he was and in a moment more, he was reminded of the urgent need to empty his bladder.

The room was utterly silent. Cautiously, he felt his way to the place where the sections of the model cathedral fitted together and pushed gently until a chink of grey appeared in the dark.

The tall narrow windows of the gallery lit the room with the weak light cast by a half-moon. Jem squeezed through the gap and carefully pushed the section back together to disguise his hiding place.

Around him the bulky black shapes of the models were brooding and almost alive. Their shadows made the gallery dark and menacing.

As he padded past the cabinet he remembered the contract. Every one of the conspirators had signed it in their blood. He had to take it for evidence.

The cabinet was Oriental in design and decorated with twisting golden dragons chasing balls of fire. The pattern gleamed clearly in the thin moonlight. Running his fingers lightly across the cabinet's side, Jem felt that one of the flaming balls was raised a little from the lacquered surface. He pressed the ball and heard a small click as the hidden drawer shot out. Nestling in the drawer was the contract, bound in its red ribbon. But deeper inside the drawer was another, larger, scroll. Jem quickly picked it up and unrolled it to reveal a drawing of the city with a star at its centre. The duke's copy of the fire map! Jem grabbed both scrolls and pushed the drawer shut again before stuffing them both into the torn lining of his jacket.

He walked softly to the doors and brought the ring of keys from his pocket. He found the right key and brought it to the lock.

Carefully he opened the door. The anteroom had

been cleared and returned to normal. Apart from the long table and chairs, nothing remained of the feast. Ludlow House was silent.

Jem locked the doors behind him and headed across the anteroom toward the hall.

"And what do we have here, then?"

He was just at the foot of staircase when he felt cold, bony fingers grip the back of his neck.

Wormald's eyes glowed in the moonlight. He could hardly conceal his delight at catching the boy. He shot out a hand and gripped Jem's ear, twisting it sharply and painfully.

"Sneaking about looking for food at this time of night, eh? I thought I told you that you were barred from partaking of the remnants of the feast with the rest of us. But it seems, as usual, that Master Jeremy Green is too high and mighty to abide by the rules."

It was a lifeline and Jem grasped it. Wormald had no idea what he'd really been up to. He almost felt the duke's papers burn through the lining of his jacket as he pulled himself to together to stammer. "I– I'm sorry Mr Wormald. But I was so hungry. I couldn't help myself."

The steward's eyes narrowed.

"I wonder how hungry you'll feel after a night

locked in the cellar? There are rats the size of cats down there. And then, tomorrow morning we'll ask the duke what he thinks, shall we? He won't take kindly to thievery in his own house."

Much to Wormald's disappointment, the duke didn't seem particularly interested in Jem's midnight raid on the kitchen. He seemed to be afflicted with a headache and was more concerned about positioning a band of linen soaked with cool lavender water across his forehead than listening to the steward's complaints.

"Wormald, I really have no time for these petty household disputes," he muttered. "Punish the boy as you see fit. And you," the duke glanced at Jem. "… should endeavour to curb your greed."

He squeezed the linen strip above the bowl and reapplied it to his temples. "Now go." He flicked a lace-cuffed hand in their direction and closed his eyes.

When they were in the corridor, Wormald smiled maliciously. "Punish the boy as you see fit, eh? Well, Master Green, what I see as fit punishment is for you to clear the blocked drains under the kitchen and then to be locked in the attic for the next two days without food or water – after a beating, of course. Wait here. You, Tobias, watch him for me."

Toby the footman put a hand on Jem's shoulder as Wormald stalked back to the kitchen to fetch his cane.

A door further down the corridor opened and Jem's mother appeared. She bustled past and made a show of ignoring him. Then she stopped and retraced her steps. Leaning close so that Toby couldn't hear her, she brought her lips close to Jem's ear as if she was going to kiss him.

"I know what you did," she hissed.

Jem's eyes widened in amazement. Sarah continued, "Stealing my keys to open the larder! I am ashamed of you."

With that Sarah turned her back on her son and marched away up the corridor. Jem watched miserably as she disappeared into the duchess's rooms.

✄ ⚏ ✄

Jem paced the boards of the attic again. His back stung from Wormald's lashes and his whole body stank after a morning of crawling through the broad drains that led from the kitchen out under the thick old walls of Ludlow House to the open channels of the yard. The drains were clogged with knobs of rotting meat, rancid animal fat and unidentifiable gristly things that Jem didn't like to think about. He'd scraped his way through the filth to clear a fresh escape route for the kitchen slurry and now he was sweaty, rank and desperately thirsty.

The hot stuffy air of the attic made him smell even worse. At first it hadn't been so bad. He'd flicked through a book and then he'd leaned out of the window trying to gulp some fresh clean air into his lungs. He watched the colour fade from London as the red burning ball of the sun set in the west. The jangling chimes of the city churches told him it was nine o'clock. A whole day had passed since he'd hidden in the model!

He had to tell Tolly and Ann what he knew. The men had named the date of the fire, and what's more, the evidence of their crime was still concealed in the lining of his soiled, stinking jacket. He had to escape.

In frustration, Jem thumped his fist down hard on the windowsill and a little part of the ancient brickwork crumbled away, falling to the ground below. He looked down and noticed how fast and how thickly the ivy had grown up the side of the building. No wonder he'd lost sight of Cleo after she'd delivered that message…

That was it! Cleo!

There was a way out of the locked room – but one that would take every ounce of his courage. He would have to climb down the four storeys of Ludlow House, clinging to the ivy like a monkey.

Jem took a deep breath and clambered out through the small window and onto the wide stone parapet that ran around the top of the building. Careful not to look down, he gripped the wall behind him and shuffled along until he came to a corner where the jutting bricks provided some footholds and the ivy grew thick and strong.

His hands were clammy with sweat. Gripping a wrist-thick rope of knotted ivy tendrils, he swung his body round so that he was facing the wall. Still clinging on tight, he lowered his right leg and felt cautiously on the brickwork below for a foothold. The ivy made a cracking noise and moved away from the wall. Jem felt himself sway out. He lunged back at the wall and gripped another stem. This was more secure and at the same time his foot made contact with a groove in the brickwork, but Jem's body suddenly flooded with fear and he froze.

Sweat was pouring from his forehead, his limbs were locked and completely unresponsive, and he was fifty feet above the ground.

CHAPTER
TWENTY-FIVE

Jem closed his eyes and gripped even tighter. His mind was screaming at his body to keep going, but somehow, he couldn't move a muscle. His fingers were beginning to lock and cramp. He knew that it wouldn't be long before his rigid body simply plummeted to the ground.

There was a feather-light touch on his right hand. Jem opened his eyes and saw Cleo swinging from a tendril of ivy. She gave a chirp of encouragement and fixed her warm brown eyes on his.

"That's good... You're doing well. Hold there and breathe slowly. Now, just to your left, by Cleo's tail, down a little, there's another hand hold."

Tolly's encouraging words sounded in Jem's head.

"Don't look down," the voice came again quickly. *"Just concentrate. We'll help you. Cleo can show you the way – just follow her. Look – to your right. Yes, just there, by Cleo's paw. Slooooowly – good! Now move your left leg down a little and in. Yes! Good. We'll soon have you down, Jem."*

The descent was slow and agonising. Jem's arms and legs were shaking so much that he could barely move them, but Cleo stayed close by, making soft encouraging noises and guiding him gently to foot and hand holds. Tolly's voice was patient and when Jem stiffened in panic, his friend's calm instructions helped him to grit his teeth and move on.

"You can jump now."

For the first time, Jem allowed himself to look down and saw that he was just four feet from the ground. With a huge rush of relief he let go and dropped down lightly to where Tolly was waiting for him.

This side of Ludlow House was invisible from the road. The narrow passageway led around to the gardens and it was so rarely used that it was overgrown with nettles.

Tolly grinned and spoke out loud. "You did well. Watch out for the stingers there. I thought you might—" he broke off. "Jem! What on earth is that terrible stink? It's worse than that man Wormald!"

Jem bent double and breathed deeply, he could feel his kneecaps twitching oddly as all the built-up tension drained from his body. At last he straightened up and, pushing a mass of damp, black curls back from his forehead, he grinned. "Thanks, Tolly. If it for wasn't for you and Cleo I'd probably be stuck up there for ever. The height... I don't know what happened... I just couldn't..." Jem faltered, embarrassed.

Tolly shrugged. "Don't be ashamed – we all have our demons. You remember when we hid in the darkness in the four-poster bed? And the fear I couldn't control? Since the days I spent in the boat to Alexandria, in the dark hold, I haven't been able to—" he stopped himself, as if the memory was too painful to recall.

"I'm sorry about the smell," Jem apologised. "I've been cleaning out drains."

Tolly wrinkled his nose in disgust. Now that he was dressed in ordinary clothes, instead of the formal uniform of a rich man's page, he looked younger and less exotic.

"Er... how did you know I was up there on the wall?" Jem asked.

"I shared your mind."

"How does that work? Do you mean you were reading my thoughts?"

Tolly shook his head. "It's not like that. I can't hear words exactly. When I have a– a... bond with someone I sometimes see images and pick up feelings. I suddenly knew you were in trouble yesterday afternoon. I was fetching clean hay for the lions when I sensed your fear – it was so sharp and strong it was almost like a smell. The trail of it led me straight to Ludlow House. I've been waiting here ever since, trying to find a way to reach you, but it was Cleo who got there first." Tolly's eyes glinted with mischief. "But to be honest Jem, the way you stink right now I can't be entirely sure it wasn't that awful smell that led us to you, after all."

Jem grinned as he looked down at his stained clothes. He realised that Tolly must have felt his fear at the very moment when he thought that he was going to be discovered in the model. In a rush he began to tell his friend about everything that had happened, but Tolly stopped him. "You must tell Ann all this too. Save your words and come with me. Are you hungry?"

Jem nodded. He was ravenous as well as thirsty.

"Well, follow me. There's always a good rich stew bubbling on Mr Jericho's campfire – and you can tell us everything while we eat."

With Cleo perched on his shoulder, Tolly led the way along the passage, careful to avoid the clumps of nettles. "You'll have to wash first though," Tolly called back. "I don't think even *I* could eat anything if you're within ten feet of me!"

The boys and the monkey passed through one of London's eastern gates and into the fields beyond the city walls. Gabriel Jericho's theatrical circus was spread across an acre of parched grass – a lively mass of colourful tents, glittering fabrics, fires, torches, wagons and carts. At the centre of the camp was an open ring. A huge, curtained stage erected on poles and scaffolding stood at the far side.

Jem could hear the sound of laughter, conversation and music and, more importantly, he could smell the tempting savoury smell of roasting meat. As they reached the outskirts of the camp a painted woman with an enormous snake draped about her shoulders waved at Tolly and came over to greet them.

"I hope your friend'll be joining us, Tolly?" she grinned. "He's a bit whiffy, but he's the most handsome lad I've ever clapped eyes on... Apart from you, of course."

Tolly laughed and Jem felt his face burn.

"I think that's up to Jem here, Juno." Tolly nudged

Jem's arm, "I know there's a place for him with us, if he wants it."

"Our lion boy is back then?" A deep voice thundered from behind them.

A burly man with thick golden hair, a reddish beard and a fur pelt thrown over his shoulders sauntered over. He grinned and winked at Jem. "Balthazar Sampson, lion tamer, at your service. Your mate here is the talk of the circus. He's a marvel!"

Jem looked at Tolly and raised an eyebrow. Tolly looked delighted. "Come on," the dark boy said, grinning broadly, "I'll show you. It won't take long."

Tolly led the way back over to some torchlit cages at the edge of the field. In the central cage two massive male lions were lolling in the straw. As the boys approached, the animals lifted their heads and sniffed the air. Immediately they sprang to their feet and hurled themselves against the bars, snarling and roaring. The sound was deafening.

Cleo shrieked and leapt from Tolly's shoulder to the roof of the cage, where she kept up a furious chatter.

Tolly smiled. "They can smell the drains on you, Jem. Like the rest of us."

He bent to a small gate in the side of the cage, unhooked the wires that fastened it and stepped inside.

Jem was astonished. "Tolly! No! You'll be eaten alive!"

But Tolly just walked slowly over to the largest crouching lion and held out his hand. He stared intently at the creature and after a moment it licked his hand and nuzzled its enormous head against Tolly's shoulder. The other lion did exactly the same. Within a minute the two animals were sitting meekly on either side of the boy. Then they rolled over and playfully invited him to tickle their tummies.

"He's quite a performer, isn't he?"

This admiring voice belonged to Jericho. He was watching through the bars on the far side of the cage. "In all my years on the road I've never seen anything like it. Those two are usually devils incarnate, but Tolly here has made kittens of them, hasn't he Balthazar?"

"He can make them do anything," the lion tamer nodded. "He's a veritable Daniel – don't know how he does it."

Tolly looked even more delighted. Jem smiled at his friend. Even he wondered how he had done it.

A voice sounded in his head. "*I just asked them politely, Jem. That's all they wanted.*"

The boys laughed at the same moment and the men turned to look at them.

"And I wonder what your secret might be, gypsy prince?" enquired Gabriel shrewdly, his warm brown eyes crinkling with interest.

For the first time ever, Jem didn't mind being called 'gypsy'. The way Jericho said it, the word sounded like something special, something good.

He looked around at the twinkling camp. In just a few minutes he'd felt more at home among Mr Jericho's players that in all the years he'd lived at Ludlow House.

Ludlow House!

He had to tell the others what he knew.

"Er… sir, Mr Jericho," he began quickly. "Where's Ann, please? I need to see her… I…"

"She'll be glad to to see you too, lad. You as well, Tolly. She's been fretting about you and little Cleo since you both disappeared yesterday without saying a word. In the end I had to tell her some cock and bull story about sending you out to the city with playbills, but I could see she didn't believe me. She was quite sharp." The big man pulled a face and winked conspiratorially, "You know how she can be."

Gabriel led the boys and the monkey back to the heart of the camp. Just beyond the stage Jem saw a large, circular tent beautifully decorated with colourful scenes of mythical beings and creatures. One of them was a smiling mermaid and Jem was momentarily reminded of the pedlar girl frozen into the River Thames. This painted mermaid was shimmering and silver and oddly alive. Unlike that poor dead girl in the ice.

"Welcome to my home, boys," said Gabriel, striding towards the tent. They headed round to the door flap, which was lit by flaring braziers. "Ann's over there practising. I thought it might be a good idea to give her something to do."

The showman pointed across the field. A little way off, Ann was standing beneath a tree talking to a man wearing a long coat made of hundreds of different squares of bright material.

She laughed with delight as the man pushed up his sleeves and held out his hands to reveal two small green fires burning brightly in each open palm. He whispered in her ear then made a low bow. Ann blushed and dropped a curtsey.

Then she held out her right hand. At first nothing

happened. Then a tiny blue light seemed to flicker in her palm. The light grew larger and stronger until a glowing ball was hovering there.

Ann pointed at the ball with her other hand and it rose into the air, following the direction of her finger. Slowly she raised the glowing orb higher and higher until it floated over the man's head. Then she clapped her hands and it burst into a shower of sliver sparks and shimmering moths. The man grinned broadly. Looking over to Jericho and the boys, he called out, "She is remarkable. Truly her mother's daughter, Gabriel."

"Jem! Tolly!" Ann came running over as soon as she saw them. "Where have you been, Tolly? And you, little one?" She bent to fondle Cleo's velvety ears. "You've been missing since yesterday. I was beginning to worry." She sounded annoyed and relieved at the same time.

She grinned up at Jem and touched his arm, "It's so good to see you. I've been..." she stopped and wrinkled her nose. "What's that awful smell – you haven't brought that man Wormald with—"

Jem began to gabble. "Ann, I know what they are going to do! There are buildings in the boxes, London's going to burn on the first of September,

Cazalon's going to build himself a hideous cathedral and thousands of people are going to…"

"Slow down. Slow down!" Ann flicked her thick white hair back from her shoulders and began to knot it loosely at the nape of her neck. As her tapering fingers wound the hair into a white ball she scrutinised him closely. "Look at you, Jem, you are exhausted – and famished, no doubt. Come inside. Before you do anything else you need to eat."

It was an order, not a suggestion.

CHAPTER TWENTY-SIX

Inside Gabriel Jericho's tent, small metal lanterns set with coloured glass hung from the ceiling. They cast pools of painted light across a warm inviting space filled with painted hangings, cushions and furs.

At the centre of the tent a cooking pot bubbled merrily over a small fire. The air was filled with the scent of spices and a plume of smoke coiled up to a vent overhead.

Ann bent down to scoop a bowl of rich stew from the pot. "Here, try this." she said, offering the bowl to Jem.

"But I can't eat," he blurted out. "Ann, I know what's in the boxes. I know exactly what they intend to do."

Her eyes sparked with excitement, but she rapped the ladle sharply against the pot. "You need food to feed the brain, Jem Green. You can't do anything on an empty stomach. Eat!"

Gabriel chuckled. "I wouldn't argue with her, lad. And her food's as good as any I've tasted, so get stuck in. You can tell us while we sup."

He took the ladle from Ann's hand and helped himself to a great dollop of the stew. "Smells delicious. You've your grandmother's touch when it comes to recipes, my lass."

He folded himself comfortably into a pile of cushions and began to slurp.

Ann smiled fondly at him and at Tolly, who was already helping himself to a large portion. "These last few days it's been like having a family again, Jem," she said quietly.

He took the bowl from her outstretched hands and, just for a moment, felt a pang of envy as he wondered what that must feel like.

As they sat in a ring and shared the meal, Jem began to describe the events of the last few hours. He was surprised to find that the words came easily and realised, gratefully, that Ann's stew sharpened his mind and his senses.

"You were incredibly brave. Imagine what they would have done if they'd found you," Tolly whispered after Jem had described hiding in the wooden model of St Paul's Cathedral.

As Jem got to the part about the plot to burn the city, Gabriel slammed his empty bowl to the ground and shook his head in disbelief.

But it was only when Jem took the crumpled contract and the duke's fire map from his soiled jacket and laid them out on the floor of the tent that Ann spoke.

"You say this map came from Cazalon himself?"

Jem nodded.

She stared at the map and traced the outline of the five-pointed star at the place where the quarters of the city met. "What's this?"

"I couldn't see properly, but I think it's the area Cazalon has marked out for himself. The others are to be responsible for starting the fires in a quarter each, but this place in the middle – where the quarters join up around St Paul's – is to be his alone. It's where he plans to build his new cathedral."

Ann pored over the map again and then drew a sharp breath. "This is high magic – beyond my knowledge. Do you see these symbols?"

Jem and the others leaned closer. At the corner of each quarter there was a faint mark – an odd twisted scribble made up from circles, crosses or loops. The symbols were drawn in something brown and crusted – something very like dried blood – and faintly beneath each sigil a name was written in tiny looping script: Avebury, Kilheron, Pinchbeck and Bellingdon.

Ann shivered, her eyes huge. "These are the marks of the Old Watchers. Have you ever heard of them?"

The others sat in baffled silence so she continued. "My grandmother used to say that in the most ancient days, the gates of the world at the north, south, east and west were guarded by four powerful Watchers who allowed nothing from this world to pass to the lands beyond – and vice versa. The Watchers were terrifying beings. They were as old as time itself and they could control the elements. But they had grown weary of their task. Gradually men forgot them – so they slept. I think Cazalon is calling on the guardians of the gates – he is trying to use these four men named here to awaken the Old Watchers and harness their power."

She frowned and added, more to herself than anyone else, "But that's madness, it's like raising a dragon or a demon to do your bidding... I don't understand."

"But surely this is about burning the city and making a profit from building a new one in its place?" Jem said. "The duke and his friends don't know anything about magic."

"Cazalon does," Ann replied. "And I suspect my

dear guardian cares very little about building a new city or making a profit. No, this is about something else…" She paused for a moment, before adding, "Something to do with you, Jem. Why else would he take such pains to bind you?"

She stood up briskly and went over to a pile of furs in the corner. She folded them back to reveal a small oblong casket decorated with bright gems and enamelled panels. Carrying the casket back to the fire she sat down again and smiled at Jericho.

"It's the only thing I have left belonging to my mother and grandmother," she began. "Gabriel has kept it for me ever since they were…" Her voice cracked and she looked down and opened the casket.

Gabriel reached over to put a large hand on her shoulder. "I promised your mother I'd keep it safe until I could give it back to you, and I did," he said gruffly. Ann began to root through the box, and its contents rattled and jingled.

"Ah," she said, producing something small and shimmering. "This was my mother's favourite." She held up the object so that it glittered in the firelight and Jem saw that it was a delicate jewel shaped like a crescent moon. It was studded with small clear gemstones and the curved ends were sharp and tipped with two more clear stones, both cut to a faceted point. The jewel was familiar. Jem realised that he had seen it before – or something very like it – in the portrait of Ann's mother at Malfurneaux Place.

Ann saw his expression and handed him the crescent. "You've seen the painting, haven't you?" she asked.

Jem nodded. "Elizabeth… erm… your mother, was wearing this in her hair. She was very… beautiful."

He blushed as he realised for the first time that Ann too was extremely pretty. Embarrassed, he dropped his gaze and turned the jewel over and over in his hand. When he looked up again Tolly was staring at him.

"She was thirteen when that picture was painted. The same age I'll be next May," said Ann sadly, reaching into the box again. "But that's not what I wanted to show you. Ah, here it is."

She brought out a small, ancient-looking book and leafed through pages covered with beautiful illuminated letters and pictures in rich colours. Arriving at a page marked with a ribbon, she began to read aloud.

The Prophecy of Fire

Oak grove burns and old stones sing
Old stones sing for green blood
Green blood flows in old veins
Old veins fill with new life
New life born as oak grove burns

She looked up expectantly.

They were all silent for a moment.

"What? What does it mean?" asked Jericho.

"I think she's about to tell us…" said Tolly, feeding a scrap of bread to Cleo.

Ann grinned and shifted on her cushion to a more comfortable position.

"The book is called *The Prophecies of Albion*. This version has been in my family for generations. My grandmother loved it because the pictures were so beautiful. There are one hundred and forty-four prophecies in all – they are all supposed to foretell dire events and calamities, but the book is so pretty that it never seemed particularly frightening to me. Did you all notice that the first words and the last words of the verse were the same? It's a very powerful device in old magic."

The others hadn't noticed, but none of them liked to admit it.

"But why read us that verse? What does it mean?" asked Tolly.

Even Cleo was listening in rapt attention.

"Well, that's the question, isn't it?" said Ann. "When I opened the book for the first time since Jericho returned it to me, it just naturally fell open here at this page. But look..." She pointed at a single line of writing beneath the colourful illustration that was opposite the Prophecy of Fire. "When the dark god rises in the Oak Grove only the moon child, the black traveller and the boy of jade can bind him."

Ann laid the book on the ground in front of her. "The boy of jade," she repeated, looking at Jem.

Jem picked up the book and stared at the words. The writing was beautiful and strange. He could tell it wasn't Latin and he was almost certain that it wasn't Greek.

Tolly gasped. "Could it be talking about us? I'm the black traveller, and Jem, you're the boy of jade... and Ann, that would make you the moon child, wouldn't it?" Ann nodded and pointed again at the book. "I think you two should look at the picture, and carefully."

The picture took up the whole page opposite the short verse. At first it looked like an intricate pattern of fire and purple smoke, but as Jem looked closer he noticed towers, rooftops, walls and battlements deftly painted onto the vellum beneath the red and gold painted flames.

But it wasn't the burning city that made him catch his breath – it was the three tiny figures at the bottom left of the page. They were carefully drawn near an archway leading into the walls of the city – two boys, one dressed in green and one completely black, and a girl with streaming hair painted in silver. He couldn't be sure, but as he studied the group, Jem thought that a smudge on the ground next to them looked as though it had a tail.

He swallowed and looked across at Tolly, who was staring intently at the picture.

"Now do you see?" said Ann, adding crisply, "this book is hundreds of years old, but the artist seems to have caught us all perfectly."

The children were quiet and then Jericho spoke. "But what does it mean?"

Ann snapped the book shut. "Well, I can't be sure, but I— "

"We haven't got time for this!" said Jem jumping

to his feet. "We're sitting here talking about old prophecies and dark gods and Watchers, but that doesn't help us get any closer to stopping Cazalon and the plotters! We have this map as evidence – and that roll of paper over there is a contract with their names signed on it. I say we must tell someone immediately, before London gets burned to the ground!"

The tent was silent for a moment, then Tolly spoke quietly.

"Who can we go to, Jem? Who would listen to us? The plotters are some of the most powerful people in the land. Even the king is their friend."

"Then that's exactly who we should go to. I'm taking these to the palace right now," said Jem, gathering the map and the contract from the floor.

Tolly snorted. "Do you really think they'll let you into the palace, let alone allow you to see the king? Forgive me, but you look – and smell – like a beggar, Jem. If you're lucky they'll merely laugh at you, but more likely you'll be whipped... or worse."

Jem was furious. "We can't just sit here eating stew and telling stories! How else can we stop them? I know I might look like a beggar, but—" He stopped suddenly. "Of course!"

Jem looked over at Gabriel. "Your players are to be the entertainment at the king's end-of-summer revels at the palace, aren't they?"

Gabriel slapped his thigh and laughed. It was a deep rich sound. "You're right, lad. A group of us are moving into the palace in two days' time – September the first. We've been practising our play for days now. We can certainly take you with us, inside in one of the wagons. But after that…"

"We're coming too, Gabriel. Jem's not going alone," said Ann. "You'll have to take us all in with you. Isn't that right, Tolly?" She was on her feet now, her little pointed face determined. "This is about all three of us – the prophecy says so – only the moon child, the black traveller and the boy of jade can bind him – we must stay together. I won't—"

Ann broke off as Cleo shrieked and scampered from Tolly's feet to hide behind a pile of cushions. The monkey cowered and shielded her eyes. Ann looked down.

"What is it? What frightened her?" asked Tolly.

"I'm not sure Tolly, there's nothing here… As I was saying, we have to do this together. I don't know what the prophecy means, but I do know it's about us, all three of us. And Jem's right – we have the contract as evidence," Ann continued, picking up the roll of paper.

She screamed.

The contract in her hands began to writhe and lengthen, and as it did so it coiled itself around her arm. Ann yelped in pain as it transformed into a pallid, wormlike creature and wound itself tighter and tighter. She tried to pull it off with her free hand, but as she tugged furiously the thing reared up. It had no eyes.

Jem was rooted to the spot in shock.

As the worm wavered in front of Ann's face, something like a red mouth opened, revealing rows and rows of needle-sharp teeth. Jem realised he'd seen a creature just like it in a jar at Malfurneaux Place.

"No!" yelled Tolly, snapping Jem out of his daze.

"Wait! Stand back!" Jem took careful aim and hurled the silver jewel in his hand through the smoke of the fire. The crescent gleamed and sang as it flew across the tent, scything across the creature's body just below the hideous gaping mouth.

The head fell to the floor and a second later Ann crumpled to the ground – still clutching the contract. Beside her, the huge wax seal now lay severed from the rest of the document, with the red ribbon that attached it cut in two. There was stunned silence.

Then Cleo chirped softly and crept from her hiding place. She nuzzled Ann and batted the rolled contract between her paws. The monkey looked up, chattered again and pulled at the ribbons.

"You all right, lass?" said Gabriel, "What was that… that thing?"

Ann smiled weakly. "I think I'd prefer not to know." She gingerly unrolled the contract and scanned the writing. When she looked up, her face was even paler. "This isn't a business contract at all. At least, it's not the business contract they thought they were signing."

She pointed at the signatures. "All these men have promised to give Cazalon their souls. And they've signed the bond in their own blood."

She shuddered.

Gabriel bent down, picked up the contract and handed it to Jem. "Whatever this infernal thing might or might not be, there's one thing I'm certain of," he said. "It's evidence of treason and somehow, lad, you must get it to the king."

"But just now, what I'm most certain of is that we all need rest," he continued, pointing to the door.

"If it's all right with you, Jem, you'll share with Tolly here. Try to sleep, lad. You're going to need your wits about you in the palace."

Jem nodded gratefully. Suddenly he felt exhausted.

"You'll have to wash first, mind," Gabriel continued, his brown eyes twinkling. "You won't get within a yard of King Charles if you smell like a privy. People turn their noses up at us player folk as it is, we don't need your stink to make it worse!"

As Jem looked at Gabriel's big friendly face, an idea popped into his head. There was an obvious way to deliver the evidence straight to the king – right into his hands in fact – but he would have to involve his friends, Gabriel and all the players.

As the others settled down to sleep, Jem went over and over the plan in his head. It was direct and simple, but it would put all of their lives in danger.

CHAPTER
TWENTY-SEVEN

Jem wiped grime from his forehead. He was perched at the front of one of Gabriel's player wagons as it rumbled along the city street towards the gate leading out to the palace at Whitehall. The hot, dry air was thick with dust. Great piles of muck and slurry, left uncleared, crusted even the most prosperous roads and made the city smell like a giant privy. All around, men and women went about their business holding their noses against the stench, some carrying little bunches of flowers or handkerchiefs drenched in scent to ward off the great stink.

Jem loosened his shirt and pulled at the linen band around his neck. He thought about the plan again. Could it work?

It hadn't been difficult to convince Gabriel, and once Jem had got him on side the other players were easy to persuade – even though they would all be taking a huge risk. Tolly and Ann had also been certain that Jem's idea would succeed. So why did he still feel so uneasy?

He leaned over the side of the wagon and looked back. Several of the players were following the carts on foot. Some were clowning, juggling or performing acrobatic tricks to attract attention to the troupe, others were handing out playbills. In the cart, jolting along behind, Tolly, Ann and Cleo were crammed onto the driving bench next to Gabriel.

Ann waved at him.

Then, just beyond her, out on the busy street beside Gabriel's wagon, Jem caught a flash of blue as a woman pushed through the crowd. The colour reminded him of a dress his mother often wore. There was a bright glint of gold, too – the exact shade of Sarah's hair.

He felt a sharp pang. The last time they'd spoken she had been furious with him and he hadn't had a chance to explain why he'd stolen her keys or, more importantly, to warn her about the duke.

If all went well when they reached the palace that wouldn't matter, but, all the same, Jem still wished he'd spoken to her and made things right. He slumped dejectedly, his eyes locked in an unfocused stare out onto the street.

As the woman in the blue dress turned into a little passageway, he caught a glimpse of her face.

He sat up with a start. It was his mother. What was she doing here?

"You will know him before your thirteenth birthday." Ann's words rang clear in his mind.

Of course! Jem gripped the wooden seat and sat bolt upright.

Sarah had to be meeting his father – that's why she was out alone in the city. It had to be the reason she was here. His heart started to beat very fast. This was his chance to meet his father – and to warn him… but he was supposed to be warning the king… What should he do?

Jem looked at the passageway Sarah had disappeared into and bit his lip. He could always catch up with the wagons later, couldn't he?

Without thinking, he slipped down from the lumbering wagon and pushed through the crowd into the little passage. Sarah was twenty, perhaps thirty feet ahead of him. Every so often Jem caught sight of the distinctive blue of her dress as she swished through the mass of people. He shoved and dodged his way around the crowds to keep up, but he couldn't quite catch her.

She turned into another side street and a few seconds later Jem did the same. It was busy here too, but he could still see his mother ahead, moving purposefully.

Sarah turned into yet another passageway. It was darker here and the air was sour – Jem could tell they were entering a poor part of the city.

Fleetingly, he wondered what his father was doing in a place like this. He was about to call out to her when his mother turned sharply into another passage. Jem quickened his steps. When he reached the narrow entrance he saw that it twisted away into the shadows. At the far end, perhaps fifty feet away, a brief swish of blue showed that his mother had just rounded another corner.

He broke into a run along the deserted alley. He'd catch her easily now. Jem skidded at the corner, caught the wall and swung to the right.

Sarah was nowhere to be seen. But someone else was.

"Good day, Jeremy. It has been some time since we last met, has it not?"

Count Cazalon was there, waiting for him.

The man towered at the end of a blind stone passage. Beside him a fire crackled in a metal brazier and his huge shadow flickered and multiplied over the blank walls.

He was wearing a tall, wide-brimmed black hat with a silver buckle set on a band of blue – he exact blue of Jem's mother's dress. Beneath the hat, the greasy curls of his wig coiled over his shoulder like ink-dipped snakes. His cloak reached to the cobbles and he gripped his knubbled, hawk-headed cane in a red-gloved hand. The bird's crystal eyes sparked in the firelight.

Osiris was perched on the count's right shoulder. This all-too-real bird rocked forward, opened its curved beak and dribbled.

The count's sing-song voice was cracked and hoarse. Jem tried to run, but found that he was rooted to the spot.

Cazalon licked his red lips. "I have returned lately from France and found that several of my… possessions are missing. I wonder, Jeremy, if you know where I might find them?"

He took a halting step forward and Jem saw that the count was sweating. His masklike face was crackled and pitted. The white paint seemed to be melting away in places and patches of skin visible beneath the paint were mottled purple and grey.

Jem could now hear, and see, scores of tiny flies buzzing and hovering beneath the brim of the count's hat. As he stared, a louse crept out from the greasy wig and scuttled onto the man's sheeny cheek. Then it was gone. Jem's mouth went dry with fear and disgust. In that blink of an eye, had he seen Cazalon's long black tongue flick out to catch the insect?

Cazalon smiled. "I think it is a small thing to ask a friend for assistance. So I must try again… Jeremy, where are my things?"

Leaning heavily on the staff, Cazalon began to approach. Jem was almost overcome by the sweet and putrid stench rolling off the man, but he still couldn't unlock his feet. Cazalon's eyes seemed to bore into his very soul.

"Where are they?"

"I don't know what you mean," Jem yelled, hurling the words like daggers.

A look of confusion clouded Cazalon's face. Then he laughed. It sounded like the bark of a dog.

"Oh, I think you do, Master Green. The loss of my idiot servant, Ptolemy, is an annoyance, but the other…" He stopped and limped closer. The tap of his staff and the dragging sound of his lame foot echoed threateningly in the stone passage.

The smell was nauseating.

"Where is she, Jeremy?"

As he repeated the question, the tip of Cazalon's thin black tongue appeared again and seemed to test the air. Jem felt the odd prickling sensation beneath his scalp, as if something was trying to probe its way into his deepest thoughts.

The Eye of Ra burned in Jem's heel – it was shielding him. As the pain in Jem's foot grew stronger, Cazalon's face twisted in frustrated fury. He raised his staff and hammered it into the floor, shrieking, "Tell me where she is!"

The man couldn't read his mind, Jem was sure. With a new defiance, he looked Cazalon directly in the eyes. "If you mean the monkey, I imagine she has gone wherever your servant Ptolemy has taken her." Jem was amazed to hear the words that streamed from his lips as he continued, "And no wonder they ran away. Having seen for myself what happens in Malfurneaux Place I cannot blame them for wishing to leave your service."

He stopped as a high-pitched whimpering noise filled the air. It seemed to come from just behind the count.

Grinning broadly, Cazalon stepped aside so that Jem could see the far end of the alley.

Tapwick's shrunken body was curled against the wall. The little man raised his head to sniff the air and Jem gaped in horror. Instead of blind, milky eyes, the man's empty sockets were now ragged open wounds that wept a thin red trickle of blood.

Cazalon laughed. "Tapwick here has been most careless. And that, dear Jeremy, is what happens to those who… disappoint me."

He continued in a low, menacing tone. "I hope that you will not disappoint me. We are… bonded in friendship after all, are we not?"

The count leaned slowly forward so that his cloaked body loomed over Jem like a shadow. Osiris stretched across, opening his beak to peck at the band covering the birthmark at Jem's neck.

Cazalon continued, "What I want from you, Jeremy—"

"You're not getting anything from him!"

Cazalon was caught off guard as a flash of silver curved through the air over Jem's shoulder. Ann's crescent jewel sang as it flew from her hand and facets of rainbow-flecked light from the gemstones danced into the darkest corners of the alley. It caught Osiris on the head and the bird flapped its huge white wings and soared up from the count's shoulder.

But it was Cazalon who yelped in pain. He dropped his staff, stumbled and brought a crimson-gloved hand to a fresh bleeding gash on his cheek.

At the same moment, a blur of black and white darted across the cobbles past Jem's feet. Cleo retrieved the crescent moon from the dust and scampered back past him again.

Ann's voice came again. "Run, Jem! Run now!"

Tolly and Ann were already pounding back down the alleyway, Cleo racing after them. Jem suddenly found that he could move again. He too broke into a run and within seconds all four of them were stampeding through the maze of dingy passages.

As they emerged into a broad street, they caught sight of the last of Jericho's player wagons rumbling along in the far distance.

"He's back!" panted Ann.

Tolly gasped for breath. "Did h– he f– follow us?"

Jem shook his head "But, now… he knows w– we are together."

He sank to his knees on the dusty road. His dark curls were plastered to his face and neck with sweat. "He tricked me. I don't know how, but he made me think he was my mother. And I was an idiot to think that she might be going to..."

He broke off and thumped the cobbles in bitter frustration, realising that Cazalon had outwitted him again by tempting him with his deepest and most secret desire – just as he had tempted the duke and his cronies.

Ann put her hands on her hips and drew a deep breath. "You shouldn't have gone off like that, Jem! From now on we must stick together. It was Cleo who saw you leave the wagon and she made us follow."

"Then I'm very grateful to you, little one," said Jem, reaching out to stroke Cleo's head. "And to you Ann – that was some shot with the moon brooch!"

Ann took the crescent from Cleo's outstretched paw and turned it thoughtfully in her hand. "I believe this might be a great deal more than a mere ornament," she said after a long moment.

Cleo began to chatter excitedly and Tolly pointed to Gabriel's wagons – now so far ahead that only a cloud of thick dust thrown up into the air showed where they were.

"Come on," he said. "We'll never catch up if we don't get going. And now that Cazalon has come back to London, we have to get to the king before it's too late."

The children took off at a run. They eventually managed to catch the last cart in the line and hauled themselves aboard.

They sat in exhausted fearful silence the rest of the way to the palace. Jem was angry. The count had outwitted him four times now. How could he have allowed himself to be tricked again? He would have to be on his guard.

Jem pushed his damp black curls back from his forehead and frowned. Something else had been nibbling at his mind, and he'd just realised what it was. When they had run from the alley, Cazalon had been laughing.

CHAPTER TWENTY-EIGHT

Jem peered out through the curtains of Jericho's newly built theatre in the gardens of Whitehall Palace. It had taken a day and most of the night to construct the temporary stage – an army of players swinging and swarming over the network of timbers as it rose from the dust of the terrace.

Jem, Tolly and Ann had helped where they could. Jem was strong and Tolly was agile, helping to guide the wooden poles for the roof into place overhead. Ann joined the artists who were painting the backcloths and even Cleo made herself useful, climbing up to the high places that Tolly and the actors couldn't reach.

Then, throughout most of the night and well into the morning, they had rehearsed and practised the crucial new scene that he and Jericho had written into the king's end-of-summer revels.

Now it was time to perform it for real.

The court had just reassembled on the terraces after taking refreshment. Jem could hear laughter and conversation as the audience waited for the entertainment to continue.

The first part of the performance had gone well – dancers, clowns, comic actors, acrobats, songs and a pretty love story had created a jolly mood in the assembled court. Gabriel, dressed as Jupiter, King of the Gods, had taken the role of master of ceremonies and he had ordered his players about the stage as if he truly were the monarch of all he surveyed. The king had laughed good-naturedly as Gabriel referred to him as his 'earthly brother'.

Moving the curtain a little to get a better view, Jem squinted into the bright sunlight. Richly dressed aristocrats paraded on the sandy paths between ornamental flower beds – the women were fanning themselves in the stifling heat, the men talking and laughing noisily. The garden shimmered in a golden haze.

Jem gulped as he caught sight of the king. An elaborate platform with a purple canopy stood directly in front of the stage. Charles and his queen were returning to gilt thrones set upon a raised section in the middle of the platform. The royal couple were surrounded by rows of elegant nobles while other members of the court took up positions on the gravel paths and lawns before the stage. Jem felt his stomach flip. Even though Gabriel, Tolly, Ann and all the players were right behind him, he wasn't sure that he was brave enough. He looked down at the golden sandals that were part of his costume and thought he might be sick.

Tolly patted his back. "Nearly time, Jem. How are you feeling?"

"Terrible."

"Me too… This thing looks ridiculous… and I think it's got greenfly!" Tolly grinned as he adjusted the laurel wreath on his head, but Jem could sense his friend's fear.

Both boys were dressed as Romans, wearing simple tunics that reached to just below their knees. Their faces were painted gold and they carried scrolls.

Cleo was perched on Tolly's shoulder. Tolly offered the little monkey a slice of apple. "Jem, this is a brilliant idea. It will work, I'm sure of it," he said reassuringly, as Cleo spat a pip onto the stage. "Thanks. It's just so… Oh, Tolly, look at them all out there! There must be three hundred people at least. And the king is only twenty yards away."

The other boy opened the curtain just a fraction, peered through, then quickly pulled it back into place.

"Probably better not to look," he muttered, scratching at the laurel wreath.

The stage behind the boys had been skilfully decorated to look like the night sky. A huge moon and hundreds of sparkling stars hung overhead and billowing clouds painted on plasterboard surrounded them.

"Cleo shouldn't be here. We're almost ready, boys."

Gabriel strode out from the wings on the right to take up position between them. Still dressed as Jupiter, with a golden circlet on his head and a trailing purple robe, he looked even broader and taller than usual, but Jem could tell that he too seemed anxious now. He was pale – even beneath the stage paint.

"You two ready then?" asked the showman.

The boys nodded nervously as Gabriel continued, "Every one of us will stand by you today, Jem. Remember that when—"

The big man faltered as Ann stepped from the wings on the left. She was wearing a short tunic, silver-winged sandals and a little shining helmet. Her silver-white hair hung down her back in a thick plait. She gave a small anxious smile.

"Is it... er... is this... all right? Do I look like Mercury, Messenger to the Gods?"

"You look even more beautiful than your mother, lass." Gabriel grinned. "If the king doesn't listen to you today, I'll eat my horse – and the wagon, too!"

Ann straightened her tunic and pushed her hair into place. She looked embarrassed, and smiled nervously at Jem and Tolly as she took up her place on the stage a little way behind them. They watched as she climbed up to stand behind a glittering painted star suspended on ropes. The star hung a foot above the boards of the stage and swayed a little. Ann gripped its points tightly to steady herself.

Gabriel clapped his hands. "To your places!"

Tolly handed Cleo to one of the players and she was carried offstage, protesting noisily. Trumpets blasted and the curtain began to twitch, as a couple of burly players began to turn wheels at the side of the stage to pull the billowing fabric back.

Gabriel squared his shoulders and put his hands on the boys' backs.

"Now or never, lads. May fortune favour us all. And get that monkey off the stage!" he hissed into the wings as Cleo poked her head around a painted cloud.

There was another huge trumpet fanfare, then the thundering of drums and the curtains rolled back.

At first there was silence. Then a round of polite applause rang out as the court took in the beautiful night-time scene.

Jem, Tolly and Gabriel took a single step forward and in unison they made a low, sweeping bow to the stand where the king sat. Jem felt as if his knees were made of custard. He kept his eyes on the boards and didn't dare to look ahead.

A drawling voice rang out from the audience. "Have you got your lines written on your sandals, boy?"

Everyone began to laugh. Jem looked up and saw that the king was smiling. Jericho stepped forward and raised his hands. Gradually the laughter died down.

"As emperor of the heavens, I come to address my brother on earth," he began in a deep, booming voice. "Night has come to England and evil walks the land. I have come to warn my royal kinsman of a plot to burn his city and heap ash upon his name.

"My messengers here," Gabriel gestured to Jem and Tolly, "know of the men who plot this infamy. Their names are scalded into a scroll of vile deeds."

Jericho stared out at the audience as someone

shouted, "I was expecting a comedy, not a tragedy! Bring back the acrobats and the singers!"

There was more laughter as Gabriel continued, "Mercury, do my bidding! Take this proof of treason to my brother."

Ann's little star chariot started to judder on its ropes and pulleys, and slowly she rose into the air, swinging perilously across the stage over the heads of Jem, Tolly and Gabriel. On her back she wore a long silver quiver, but instead of arrows, the quiver was packed with the rolled contract and the maps showing the places where the fires were to be set.

"Now, that's more like it," called out a courtier and there were more appreciative chuckles, whistles and bawdy comments as Ann travelled slowly out over the stage towards the king's stand. As she passed over Jem's head, he saw that she was clinging tightly to the star and her eyes were closed.

"Now, messengers," Gabriel boomed again. "Name the traitors to His Majesty."

Jem's mouth went completely dry. He took a faltering step forward and looked into the crowd. He was struck dumb for a moment as he caught sight of the duke sitting just behind the king on the canopied stand. Next to the duke was a heavily veiled woman, and the Marquis of Kilheron and Lord Avebury were sitting just a little further along the row.

No doubt Aldermen Pinchbeck was here somewhere, too – all of them safe from the flames about to engulf the city.

This was it.

Jem cleared his throat and began. "By the most foul means…" His voice was cracked and hesitant.

"Speak up, lad, we can't hear you," someone called from the audience, while another shouted, "Never mind the whispering boy, look at the pretty player girl there. Up she goes!"

There was more laughter as Ann's star chariot appeared to float out over the edge of the stage towards the canopied stand. Jem gulped as he saw the wires above him pull tight and heard the faintest squeak as the star winched its way towards the king. Moments later it bumped to the ground just in front of the royal stand. Ann curtsied deeply and bowed her head.

Tolly nudged him and whispered "Go on, Jem. Take a deep breath."

Jem cleared his throat and began again, his voice stronger now.

"By the most foul means possible, using sorcery and forbidden powers, the following men have plotted to burn Your Majesty's great capital to the ground today and to murder its citizens."

Jem paused and looked at the crowd.

"George, Duke of Bellingdon. I name you traitor."

Several people gasped. There were shuffles and nervous titters, and even King Charles himself looked surprised.

Jem spoke again. "Matthew, Marquis of Kilheron, I name you traitor."

There was an even louder gasp. Then people began to boo.

"This is no entertainment, it is an insult to His Majesty!" someone shouted.

"Take them away and have them whipped," yelled another.

Then Tolly stepped forward and began to speak in a firm clear voice. "John, Lord Avebury, I name you traitor. Edward Pinchbeck, Alderman of the City of London, I name you traitor."

"Silence the moor!" screamed a woman. "This is an outrage!"

Jem continued, he was shouting now, so his voice still carried. "Sire, these traitors have plotted with Count Cazalon of Malfurneaux Place to raze London to the ground, murdering all inside its walls, and to replace the city with one of their own design."

The crowd was buzzing with a menacing excitement. Some looked furious, staring at Jem with venomous expressions, others were thoroughly enjoying the scandal, gossiping frantically behind their fans.

Jem looked at the royal stand. The king was on his feet beckoning to a man in uniform and Jem saw soldiers rushing down the steps from the palace. They were heading for the stage.

Behind the king, the duke was now talking to Kilheron. The young marquis nodded so violently that his wig slipped and he had to catch it to hold it in place. The duke and Kilheron turned to stare coldly at Jem.

"Sire," Tolly called out. "You must listen. I insist upon it!"

Instantly the crowd fell dangerously silent.

The king strode to the front of the stand. He stared furiously at Tolly.

"*Must* is not a word for kings, boy." His voice was sharp and cold.

"Sire, I apologise for our manners," Jem said as

he dropped to his knees. He yanked hard at Tolly's costume to indicate that he should kneel too. Jem's heart was thumping so heavily that he thought his chest would burst as he continued. "We... we mean no treason. I... that is we..." he gestured at Tolly, Gabriel and Ann, "have discovered a plot against you, but we knew of no other way to warn you."

There was a long silence.

Suddenly Charles began to laugh. "Ah, I see now. Why, this is excellent, Mr Jericho," he said, beaming at the courtiers around him. "The most wonderful and entertaining trick. I congratulate you."

People began to laugh nervously and some applauded. There were shouts of "Bravo!"

Gabriel bowed deeply, but when he spoke his voice was flat and deadly serious. "'Tis no jest, Your Majesty. I only wish it were. These lads speak nothing but the truth. And Ann here can show you."

With her eyes lowered, Ann stepped out from the star. She curtsied and handed the silver quiver up to the king.

"This contains all the proof you need, Sire. The men my friends have named are traitors to you and to your people."

Charles looked confused again.

Jem blurted out, "Our words are true, Sire. We are your loyal subjects and we are here to tell you that these men intend to burn London to the ground and build a city of their own design in its place."

There was a moment of silence. Then a man shouted, "Who are these players to accuse their betters? Vagabond scum! Hang them all! They are the traitors."

Jem felt his cheeks burn. He could feel Tolly trembling beside him, and even Gabriel looked defeated. It had all gone horribly wrong – how could he possibly have thought that the king would listen to them?

Charles raised his hand for quiet. The crowd was expectant. Then a high, clear voice rang out across the terrace.

"Your Majesty. I am proud to say that this boy is no traitor. He speaks the truth."

Jem looked up and squinted into the blazing sun. Two finely dressed women were walking quickly towards the stage down a central pathway between the flower beds. One had chestnut hair that glowed in the golden afternoon light and one was very fair. The fair woman looked like... No! Jem stared in amazement.

This time it really was his mother.

"There – and not before time. I knew my Nelly wouldn't let me down," Gabriel said quietly.

"Remember me telling you about one of my young actresses who had done well for herself at court? Well, that would be Nelly here, and she's our back-up plan."

When the two women were level with the king they each sank into a deep curtsey.

The king stared at Sarah. Jem heard someone say, "Isn't that Lord Verrer's daughter? I thought she died years ago," as another gasp rippled round the assembled court.

By now the king seemed completely bemused. "Sarah? My dear, where the devil have you been?"

He raised her to her feet and stared intently. "Still a beauty, I see. Is this some part of this odd entertainment?" He turned to the other woman.

"And Nell – you too? What is the meaning of this, have you taken to the stage again?"

The red-haired woman rose from her curtsey, her round dimpled face wearing a cheery grin, and said loudly. "I think you should listen to what this lady has to say Char... Your Majesty. Go on, Sarah, tell him."

Jem's mother blushed. "I— I believe the boy on stage to be speaking the truth, Your Majesty. He is my son, Jem – Jeremy – and he is almost thirteen years old."

Sarah spoke the last words slowly and deliberately. A peculiar expression flashed across Charles's face. He turned to look at Jem, and after a long pause he spoke loudly so that everyone could hear his words.

"And a fine boy he is, too. Come here, lad, and bring your friends."

Jem, Tolly and Gabriel climbed down from the stage and came to stand next to Ann. As they made another bow, Jem was aware of a small, black and white shape scampering across the dust to join them. The king's little dogs, who had been loitering beneath the thrones dais, started to bark as Cleo leapt up onto Tolly's shoulder.

Sarah spoke again. "Your Majesty, I do not entirely understand what is happening," she said. "But I would not have come today if I did not know my son to be speaking the truth – and in terrible danger because of it. Mistress Gwynn here was sent by Mr Jericho to fetch me."

Sarah bit her lip and smiled sadly down at Jem, continuing, "Sire, I know my Jem to be a good and honest boy. There is dark sorcery afoot and I can prove it to you."

She looked back, her gaze now directed over the king's shoulder. The Duke of Bellingdon was now trying to push his way through the crowd to the furthest steps, pulling the veiled woman roughly along behind him. The king turned to follow Sarah's gaze and motioned to the guards with his hand.

Immediately, they blocked the duke's path and also that of Avebury and Kilheron, who were trying to sneak down the steps on the opposite side of the platform.

Meanwhile, in the crowd milling around on the lower garden terraces, a space had formed around the puffing forms of Alderman Pinchbeck and his plump, overdressed wife and daughters. Courtiers were now staring at the four of them suspiciously.

Jem's mother called out. "Mary, you must show them. Let them see what you have hidden from everyone except me."

The veiled woman shrugged herself free from the duke's grasp. Jem heard the duchess's muffled cry from beneath the veil. "No! I cannot."

She sounded wheezy, as if she found it difficult to breathe.

Sarah tried again. "Please, Mary, you must, for all our sakes."

The duchess stopped dead, like a dark statue, then she turned slowly towards the king and began to speak.

"I– I too believe the boy speaks the truth, Your Majesty. There is evil abroad in London."

"Silence, you stupid, foolish woman." The Duke of Bellingdon was furious, but Charles raised a hand to stop him.

"Pray continue, my lady," the king said.

The duchess took a step away from the duke and spoke again an odd raspy voice.

"My husband has been thick with Cazalon and the other men these boys have named for many months, although I do not know why."

She paused for moment. "But I do know, sire, that I have been vain and foolish and that Count Cazalon is an evil, vicious man. He promised to make me beautiful again… but look at what he has done to me."

The duchess raised her veil and turned slowly so that everyone present could see her face. There was a horrible silence that lasted just a moment, then a murmur of shock rippled through the crowd.

On one side, the duchess's face and throat were completely black. Instead of skin, the woman was now covered in close-packed, lumpy serpent-like scales that glistened darkly. Her right eye was completely hidden beneath a hood of twitching black scabs that rose across her forehead and crept across half of her hairless scalp.

"Count Cazalon is a sorcerer and a devil," she whispered.

Someone in the crowd began to scream and Mary crumpled to the floor, sobbing.

Bellingdon gasped and backed away from his wife while the king stared at her in pity.

"Call the physician. Take the duchess to him immediately," he said, and two guards gathered her up and helped her from the garden.

The terraces fell silent. Jem felt a stab of sorrow for the duchess as the court watched her being escorted from the garden.

When the doors to the palace closed Ann looked up at the king, her voice quavering a little as she spoke. "Sire, in the quiver in your hand there, is written evidence of the plot – a contract signed in the traitors' blood. It is the scroll with the red ribbon."

Charles pulled the paper from the quiver and

unfurled it. He scrutinised the names signed at the end and swore softly under his breath.

A harsh voice rang out. It was the duke.

"So, I have nurtured a nest of vipers in my own house. Trying to shield your bastard son are you, Sarah – the shameful secret you tried to hide from the world? I gave a place to the pair of you because of your friendship with my wife and this is how you repay me."

Two guards now had Bellingdon in their grasp. The duke glared at Sarah and then at Jem.

"And as for you, boy, you are an ungrateful little thief as well as base born! How dare you steal my papers!"

"I am surprised to hear you speak so coarsely, George." The king's voice was slow and deadly. "But, at least you admit this document is yours?"

The duke blustered for a moment and then all the fight left him. He hung limply between the guards and his magnificent wig fell to the dust. Jem was amazed to see that he was completely bald.

Charles spoke again. "Arrest all of the traitors. Take them to the Tower and interrogate them."

He turned to Jem, Tolly, Ann and Gabriel. "Now, you will all come with me and tell me everything you know. Starting from the beginning. You too, my ladies," he added, looking at Sarah and Nell.

The king and the little party crossed the terraced garden towards the Palace. As they entered Whitehall, the king looked intently at Jem. He nodded, smiled and then turned to Sarah.

"So, madam. You must tell me all that has happened in the dozen or so years since we last met."

CHAPTER
TWENTY-NINE

By nightfall on September the first, the danger was over and London was safe.

Word came to the palace that four of the traitors were now safely imprisoned in the Tower of London, and, using the map Jem had taken from the duke's secret drawer, the king's troops had gone out into the city and arrested all the conspirators' paid henchmen before they had a chance to even start the fires.

The afternoon and most of the evening had passed in a blur.

Charles had taken them all inside the palace, to an echoing council chamber. At first Jem had been tongue-tied and overawed, but the king and his ministers listened carefully as the boy falteringly explained everything he knew about the plot. Occasionally Ann and Tolly were asked about Cazalon and Malfurneaux Place, but Jem noticed his friends were always careful not to mention their powers. Taking their lead, he said nothing that might give them away. Sorcery – of any kind – was punishable by death.

The king's eyes were often on Sarah as Jem spoke. Charles smiled warmly, and, Jem thought, a little sadly, when she nodded or spoke to confirm her son's story.

"The black-hearted blaggards!" the king bellowed when Jem explained that the boxes delivered to Ludlow House contained models of the houses the conspirators planned to build for themselves.

"So, they thought they could burn my city and my people to satisfy their own vanity, eh?" The king brought his fist down hard on the gilded table top in front of him and the little dogs lolling underneath whimpered and darted out into the room.

"I'll have their heads for target practice!" He roared.

⚜ ⚏ ⚜

Stars twinkled overhead as the children and Gabriel sat on the steps to the stage in the palace courtyard. Ann shivered despite the warm night air and pulled a red woollen shawl tight around her shoulders. They were all grateful to have changed out of their costumes.

"I know we should be celebrating, but I can't help thinking that something is still wrong," she said, looking down at Cleo. The monkey was curled in her lap.

Jem nodded. "It was almost too easy, wasn't it? I still can't believe it."

"I know, but we all heard what they said about Malfurneax Place…" Tolly murmured, drawing absent-mindedly in the dust with a stick. "When they went to arrest Cazalon, all they found were the abbey ruins and a great smoking pit where the house should have been."

Jem shuddered.

"Who knows?" Gabriel shrugged his shoulders and took a swig from a large bottle. "When Cazalon's plan was revealed, maybe the Devil rose up and spirited him away?"

"Perhaps," whispered Ann, "But I can't shake off the feeling that something is wrong."

"All that matters now is that Jem's plan worked like a dream – with a little help from good old Nelly."

Gabriel chuckled and took another glug. "Good drop this. From the king's own cellar."

"Er… Mr Jericho, about Nelly and my mother. How did you… I mean, when did you—"Jem stopped short as Cleo suddenly stiffened and stared intently at the doors leading into the palace. Her tail swished.

The double doors swung back and a phalanx of soldiers carrying flaming torches clattered down the steps. There was a fanfare and seconds later the king appeared at the head of a glittering procession of ministers and courtiers, Jem's mother among them.

As the royal party crossed the terrace, the children sprang to their feet. Ann sank into a low curtsey while Jem, Tolly and Jericho bowed.

"Up! Up!" ordered the king. He grinned as he caught sight of Jericho trying to hide the bottle behind his back. Jericho flushed and blustered.

"I– I was just celebrating, Sire."

Charles laughed.

"As well you might, sir! It seems that you and your friends here have saved my city… so I have come to reward you all for your loyalty. And I will begin with the monkey. Cleo, isn't it?"

The children nodded in unison.

"Bring her to me."

Tolly shot Jem a look of surprised delight, took a step forward and looked intently at Cleo. She chattered and leapt up to his shoulder and the two of them approached the king. Tolly bent his head as Charles reached out to stroke Cleo. He grinned appreciatively and chuckled.

"She is a beauty – a fine little animal. Certainly the most loyal monkey in my kingdom. And in recognition of that fact, I present her with this favour."

Charles snapped his fingers and a herald stepped forward with a velvet box. The king opened it and produced a golden medal on a thick red ribbon. He smiled at Tolly.

"Keep her still, lad, while I hang it round her neck. And then I have something for you. Something for all of you, in fact, I—"

A jagged bolt of lightning scythed past the gleaming medal in the king's hand and exploded into the ground just beside him. For just a second the terrace was flooded with a light brighter than midday sunshine.

Jem saw every face, every jewel, every lace cuff, every wig and every wrinkle illuminated with searing clarity.

"God's teeth, but that was close!" The king took a step back. Cleo buried her trembling head in Tolly's neck.

Something hit the top of Jem's head. He winced

as something else hit his shoulder, and yelped and rubbed his head as yet another sharp something caught him above the temple. He looked up in amazement then quickly bent over again, shielding his eyes as hail stones the size of marbles started to rattle and bounce on the terraces around them.

The courtiers gasped and rustled off to find shelter, several of them losing their wigs in the violence of the hailstorm.

And then it began to snow.

As the snowflakes fell thick and fast, they doused most of the torches, and the terrace became grey and shrouded with shadows.

"'Tis extraordinary!" Charles was laughing. "Our end-of-summer revels have brought in the winter!"

A courtier threw a cloak around the king's shoulders and pulled him under the outspread branches of a huge oak that sprouted from the centre of the terrace.

Jem heard Jericho shout behind him, "Over here, lad. This freak weather won't last long!"

He spun round. Through the whirling snow Jem could just make out the shape of the showman's broad bottom as it disappeared beneath the timber platform of the stage. Wrapping his arms tight around his body, Jem battled his way towards the stage, bending low to creep under the boards to join the others.

"W-w-where's Ann?" Tolly's teeth chattered.

"I thought she was with you," Jem answered peering into the gloom beneath the stage. Gabriel, Tolly and Cleo were sheltering there, but Ann wasn't with them.

The wood above began to groan and splinter as the snowstorm became a howling blizzard. There was a jagged tearing sound as the stage hangings were ripped away into the greyness.

"Ann!" Jem called, but his voice was lost in the storm. Tolly and Jericho yelled too and Cleo crouched just beneath the jutting edge of the stage, her shoulders huddled up to her ears as she stared out into the garden. In a short time her nose and whiskers were encrusted with snow.

"Look! Over there," Tolly pointed towards a faint patch of light where the flames of a guttering torch, stuck into the earth beneath a tree, showed a pathway. Jem screwed up his eyes and squinted into the falling snow. He saw a flash of red – Ann's shawl. There she was! But then he saw something else that chilled his blood even more than the freezing snow.

The brief gash of red in the whiteness was instantly masked by something dark and iridescent as a figure stepped out of the whirling snowstorm. bent forward and, in one smooth sweep, folded the girl into its cloak. It was if she had been swallowed by a giant beetle.

Then the torchlight died.

"No!"

Jem slipped and scrambled from under the stage and Tolly followed. Far behind, Gabriel's voice called them back, but the words were lost on the storm.

Jem and Tolly hauled themselves through the blizzard to the spot where Cazalon had snatched Ann, but as they tried to battle ahead, the snow fell thicker and the ice-cold wind burned deeper into their flesh.

Within seconds they were lost in the howling, frozen dark.

"Ann! Where are you?" Tolly's stricken voice was deadened by the storm. Even if Ann had answered they wouldn't have heard her.

"It's no good, Jem. She's not here." Tolly sounded desperate.

"We can't let him take her," Jem shouted back. "We have to keep going. If we can't move in this, then neither can Cazalon. Come on. Stay with me."

The boys pressed forward again, but now the snow was up to their knees. Their light summer clothes were frozen against their skin.

After several yards more, Jem stopped. "I– I c-c-can't see anything, Tolly. C-c-can you?" He was so numb he could hardly speak, but he forced himself to call out, "Ann! Are you there?"

The answer was a single massive clap of thunder that rocked the terrace. Then everything was silent.

Instantly, the blizzard ceased and within seconds stars began to twinkle again overhead.

Snow-crusted people began to move. They crawled out from their hiding spaces, wrapped their arms around their frozen bodies and crunched through the snow.

"Ann! Ann!" Tolly's eyes were huge as he scanned the dazed people now surging forth around them. Cleo scurried from beneath the stage and raced through the snow to leap up to his shoulder. She too scoured the faces of the courtiers, her nose twitching and her tail flicking.

"Jemmy. Thank the Lord you are safe." Sarah staggered out from beneath the tattered royal stand and reached out to touch her son's ice-dusted face.

Then she enveloped him in a fierce hug.

"The lad is safe then?" The king crunched over to them carrying a flaring torch. As he scanned the devastated gardens, his face was grim. He was no longer amused. "Sorcery!" he muttered.

Jem broke from his mother's embrace and climbed onto an ornamental plinth that jutted up through the whiteness. He slipped as he tried to balance on the icy stone, gripping the handles of the huge urn that stood on the top of the plinth to keep himself upright.

"Ann, where are you? Are you hurt? Please try to answer me!" he shouted.

"Ann!" yelled Tolly, searching the frozen terrace with desperate eyes.

They both knew she wasn't there.

"He took her," muttered Jem. "Cazalon took her!"

Suddenly, a man appeared at the doorway that led out of the palace. He stopped and stared in amazement at the snowy scene. Then he pulled himself together and ran down the frosty steps, skidding to a halt at the centre of the terrace.

"Where is His Majesty? I must see the king," he shouted urgently.

The man's eyes were bulging in his red face and

sweat ran down his forehead. When he spoke again it was as if the words were wrapped around his tongue.

"F– fire! It started in P– Pudding Lane and is spreading like the plague. London is burning!"

CHAPTER THIRTY

"We've failed completely," Jem groaned, then sank into the melting snow, cradling his forehead in his hands. "We thought we'd defeated him – him and the rest of them, but he outwitted us. If Ann were here, she'd…"

He felt tears of anger, frustration and something much more painful prickle behind his eyes.

"At least we know where he's taken her."

Jem looked up. Tolly's face was a mask of fury as he continued, "I'm sure he's taken her to St Paul's. Remember the model cathedral where you hid, Jem? That was Cazalon's only demand, wasn't it? He didn't care what the others wanted as long as he got that. It has to be the key to all this. The old cathedral has to be where he's taken her."

Jem nodded, then clenched his fist as a terrible thought occurred to him. "Tolly, do you think he means to sacrifice Ann? Is that what he wanted all along – is she the sacrifice he needs to transform himself into a god, like the old druids in *The Prophecies of Albion*?"

Tolly spat into the snow. When he looked at Jem again his face was set like stone. "I don't know about that. But one thing I do know: we can still stop him. The prophecy says so, remember? When the dark god rises in the Oak Grove only the moon child, the black traveller and the boy of jade can bind him."

Jem scowled. "Well, now it looks as if only the black traveller and the boy of jade are left. We have to get into the city, Tolly."

Gabriel crunched across the courtyard. When he saw the boys' expressions, his face crumpled.

"We'll find her, lads. I'll not lose that girl again…" The showman's voice cracked and he stopped and bit his lip.

Jem spoke in a rush. "It's St Paul's. We think… that is, Tolly thinks, it's where Cazalon has taken her. And I know he's right."

Gabriel nodded slowly. "If that's so, I bet he's burning the city to cover his tracks. We have to find her before—" He broke off as a shout echoed across the courtyard.

"Gabriel! Here man!"

It was the king.

Gabriel squeezed Tolly's shoulder, then turned, bowed and splashed quickly through puddles of melted snow to King Charles, who was surrounded by a knot of ministers. Even at a distance, the boys could hear the king swearing.

"Damn and blast you all! I'll not sit by while my city burns! Ah, Mr Jericho, walk with me."

The king clapped the showman on the shoulder, took a flaming torch from the hand of one his ministers and guided Gabriel away from the rest of the courtiers.

Several minutes of urgent conversation followed and as the boys watched, Gabriel nodded twice and turned to point at his snow-battered player wagons drawn up in a line along the wall beyond the stage. Then the king clapped Gabriel's shoulder again, strode back to the courtiers and issued some swift instructions. Jem caught the last words, "… and all to be ready before daybreak."

Gabriel hurried back to the boys. His face was serious, but now his eyes gleamed with hope. "Get yourselves ready, lads," he said. "We're going into the city – and the king is coming with us."

※ ⚏ ※

It was early morning on Sunday, September 2nd, when a procession of painted player wagons rumbled along a dusty road towards the city. Jem was not surprised to find that the snowstorm had only battered the garden terrace inside Whitehall Palace.

From his perch high up on the seat between Gabriel and Tolly, Jem saw that an inferno was already raging in London's oldest and most crowded streets.

The sky above had turned a shade of grimy orange and the air was thick with the smell of burning wood as, one by one, the City's jostling wooden houses were consumed by flames.

A small voice in his head whispered again and again.

"Trying to shield your bastard son are you, Sarah – the shameful secret you tried to hide from the world?" That was what the duke had said, wasn't it?

In the confusion of the snow and Ann's disappearance, Jem hadn't had the chance to speak to his mother properly, but now, at least, a lot of things were clear to him.

His mother had never married his father – a man who was probably a soldier right here in the city, a soldier who might perish in the fire without Jem ever knowing him.

As they neared the western gate in the old city

wall, their carriage was surrounded by hundreds of people. All of them – from the smallest children to the most ancient, crooked women – were staggering beneath bundles of possessions. Some pushed loaded hand-barrows, or, if they were lucky, they dragged the reins of an unwilling horse or donkey with the contents of half a house packed precariously upon its back.

Frustrated by the slow progress of the wagons, Tolly pulled at his friend's arm and tried to scramble down. "We'll never get through this crowd, Jem. We should go on foot," he yelled above the sound of the street.

"No you don't, lad." Gabriel grabbed his shirt and yanked him back. "You'll be crushed by the mob down there. Look around you, Tolly. We're about the only ones going into the city. You'd never make it through on foot."

Tolly sank back onto the seat and glowered.

Around them the streets were almost impassable. It seemed that all of London was pushing in the opposite direction. A strong wind – the first for days – seemed to have risen from nowhere to blow them on their way.

"It is a judgement come upon us," called a preacher

standing on a corner, clutching his hat to his head. "We are being punished for our wickedness."

The rich had packed their possessions into coaches that blocked the streets. Fat city merchants and their wives leaned from carriage windows and swore at their drivers and the people around them. Jem saw one distraught couple left marooned in their coach at the entrance to their yard. Someone, perhaps their coachman, had cut the horses from the traces and made off with them.

London was melting.

"I never thought it would come to this," said Gabriel, pulling hard on the reins to keep the bucking wagon horses steady. It was as if they could smell the fear from the crowd pushing around them.

"I thought we'd stopped the fire, but... Whoa there! Easy, girls." Gabriel pulled hard again on the reins.

"Look!" Jem said, pointing.

Two masked horsemen, both wearing red and gold player costumes, were pushing back through the crowd ahead of them. One of the men drew his prancing white stallion parallel to Gabriel's wagon and leaned closer.

"Well, Mr Jericho." The voice from beneath the half

mask was a familiar one. "First you helped to unmask the traitors and now you are helping to mask me!" It was the king.

The king turned to the other disguised rider. "I know you don't approve, Captain, but God's teeth, man, I'm damned if I'm going to stand idle while my capital burns."

The captain, who was wearing a long-snouted mask and a pair of chequered breeches, borrowed from Gabriel's stores, snorted. "You put yourself at great risk, Sire. Not just from the flames but from the citizens. If you are recognised, who is to say that the Londoners will not blame you for the fire? Some may even think that you've come to see the city burn."

Charles laughed grimly. "Let them say what they wish. But if any of them recognise me today, they will see a king willing to stand side by side with his subjects to fight for his capital." He slapped Jericho's wagon. "Is everything ready?"

The showman nodded. "Every one of my wagons is packed, Sire."

He jerked his thumb to the contents stacked behind Jem and Tolly. Instead of the troupe's usual jumbled possessions, the cart was now full of giant leather buckets, ladders, pike staffs, axes and long metal poles with hooks on the end.

"Twelve wagons in all, Your Majesty, carrying your men, my players and the tools to fight the flames. We're ready to help, Sire"

Charles grinned beneath his half mask. "I won't forget your loyalty, Jericho. Come!"

The king wheeled his horses about and pushed through the surging crowd back to the head of the wagon train. Jem caught sight of a boyish grin on the king's face as he called over his shoulder to the captain, "Almost like the old days, eh?"

Gabriel grunted and urged the horses forward. Their wagon clattered over the cobbles under the gate arch and immediately the streets narrowed as they entered the old City. Tolly gasped as they looked ahead, and Cleo wrapped her paws around her eyes as she huddled between the boys on the wooden seat.

"Keep Cleo with you at all times, lads. You won't want to lose her in all this. If I'd known you were bringing her with you, I'd—"

But Gabriel's complaint was cut short as they turned into a wider street and saw the glowing heart of the city ahead.

The sky was black. But this wasn't the darkness

of night. Above the rooftops the air was filled with a billowing plume of inky smoke. It swayed and throbbed like a living thing and the leaping flames beneath its canopy made the underside of the cloud blush with pulses of violent orange and red.

Even from this distance the boys could feel the heat on their faces and the skin beneath their shirts began to prickle with sweat.

They could hear the fire, too. Above the cries of the people around them the air thrummed and crackled. The sound was like a constant muffled roar. Jem found that he had to keep swallowing hard to make his ears pop and his head clear.

The wagon horses were terrified now. They rolled their eyes and their ears lay flat against their heads.

Tolly gripped Jem's arm. "I just heard her! Ann's alive!"

"Where is she? Can you tell?"

Tolly shook his head. He covered his ears and bent forward for a moment. "She's very faint... There's darkness and fear... and... pain. Terrible pain." He sat bolt upright. "Jem, we have to find her, now!"

Jem saw that his friend's knuckles were clenched so tightly that the bones showed white through the taut dark skin.

"Mr Jericho, we must go faster!" Jem yelled angrily above the tumult.

He didn't know what else to do. He felt utterly powerless. The showman hunched his shoulders and flicked the reins.

"Come on, ladies, be brave ponies for Jericho now."

꙳꙳ ⚎ ꙳꙳

When they finally reached St Paul's Cathedral they found that the narrow lanes and roads ahead were completely blocked by fleeing people. The fire was so close here that when ash fell upon their heads it stung their scalps and singed their hair.

The eastern side of the cathedral's square tower glowed in the light of the flames that danced over the city streets. The flickering shadows cast by the spider-leg scaffolding that propped up the rickety old building made the ancient stones seem oddly alive.

It was as if the cathedral was breathing – and waiting.

The great west doors stood open and scores of people scurried up the steps carrying bundles of papers, books and goods into the gloomy depths.

Gabriel pulled up the wagon on the northern edge of the churchyard. He looked at the men swarming over the steps and shook his head. "I suppose it's as safe a place as any in the city to store your valuables. Those walls are thick enough to withstand any fire. But tonight I think it's the last place in London I'd want to place my trust or my belongings."

Jem was reminded of the time, years ago now, when he'd poked an ants' nest in the gardens at Pridhow House. He'd goaded the tiny creatures into a frenzy of activity until a steady stream of them marched from the nest, each of them carrying a precious egg to safety.

He stared at the jostling queue and shuddered. St Paul's was the place he most feared. If Ann was here somewhere, Cazalon was too.

The roaring sound of the fire had turned to a death bellow of terrifying groans and juddering rumbles as six-storey buildings in the streets beyond collapsed into white-hot mounds, consumed by the flames.

As the old buildings fell, the strong east wind scooped glowing ash into a cloud of smouldering destruction, whirling it up into the air until it fell upon roofs and wooden gutters like raindrops from hell.

"Stay close, lads. I want to find Ann as much as you two, but I don't hold with heroics." Gabriel jumped heavily from the wagon and started to direct his players as they unloaded.

Moments later, Charles called him over to a patch of scrubby grass where street maps of the city were laid out on the ground. The men knelt to examine them.

Gabriel had told Jem and Tolly that the king planned to create firebreaks in the heart of London to prevent the flames from spreading. This would mean tearing down houses and perhaps whole streets so that the fire could not jump from house to house. Old wooden buildings burned easily but they were also easy to pull down, so it was work that anyone could help with – man or boy.

Jem and Tolly leapt from the wagon. Cleo chattered angrily and scrabbled onto Tolly's shoulder, but he lifted her off and placed her firmly back on the seat. She stared at the boys furiously for a moment and then turned her back.

"I shouldn't have brought her. Mr Jericho was right," Tolly sighed. "Everything happened so fast I didn't think clearly."

"Well, she's here now," said Jem. "And if she

stays under cover she'll be fine."

He looked up at the looming cathedral and shuddered. "Do you really think Ann's in there, Tolly?"

The dark boy was silent as he stared at the building. He nodded slowly.

"She's definitely in there. I know it. The connection is stronger than ever. She's…she's very frightened… and she's not alone."

Tolly's face hardened. "I'm going in. I'll pretend to be carrying valuables inside like the people over there – and I'll just walk straight in through the main door."

"I'm coming with you."

"No, don't! At least not yet. I need to be completely focused to follow her trail. Look, I'm sorry, Jem, but if you come too I'll pick up your thoughts and everything will be muddled. When I can track Ann I'll come straight back and lead us both to her."

He smiled and added more gently, "I can't beat Cazalon alone, can I?"

Jem shook his head. "But you can't go on your own, Tolly. What if something happens to you? How will I know? Listen, this makes no sense. We have to go together. Remember the prophecy?"

"Jem, trust me, please. This is our best chance to

find her, but I have to be alone in there. My mind must be as clear as possible. Remember, I can pick up the feelings of anyone I care about. If you were there too I'd only be confused…" Tolly's expression clouded for a moment. "Jem… you've been thinking about something else too, haven't you? For days now… I'm right, aren't I? Your feelings are so jumbled and strong that sometimes I…"

Jem knew immediately what Tolly was hinting at – his father. He scowled as Tolly continued, "I'm sorry, but what I need right now to help me pinpoint Ann's location is clarity. Your mind is like a soup and it… it gets in the way."

Jem bit his lip. He knew that Tolly was only speaking the truth, but he still wanted to go with him.

"Please. I need some time alone, just a short time," Tolly said.

After a moment Jem nodded curtly. "All right then. But as soon as you find a trace of her, let me know. Promise?"

Tolly gripped Jem's arm and squeezed it tightly. "I promise."

He grabbed a scrap of material from the cart and gathered up some stones. He wrapped them into a small bundle and then winked at Jem. "My valuables."

Jem watched his friend lope across the parched grass and tumbled gravestones to join the queue snaking up the steps of the cathedral. Within a minute Tolly disappeared through the door.

Jem kicked a pebble in frustration. He felt useless.

"Here, lads!" Gabriel's voice carried, even above the rumbling sound of the fire.

Over on the far side of the churchyard the players and the king's men were forming a bucket chain to carry water up from the Thames. Jem knew that part of the plan was to soak the wooden scaffolding around the cathedral so that it wouldn't burn so easily.

Jericho's voice came again. "We need more hands."

Jem took a deep breath and pushed the mass of sweaty black curls back from his forehead. If he couldn't fight Cazalon – yet – at least he could fight the fire.

As he sprinted across the churchyard, Jem didn't notice the tiny black and white form of Cleopatra leaping from the wagon to follow her beloved master into St Paul's.

※ ⚊ ※

Slopping, stinking buckets were passed from person to person, but not even the cool water soaking into their shirts could guard them from the heat of the flames that burned ever closer and with increasing ferocity as the hours passed.

"Zounds, man, but this is hot work!" said Charles. He was standing just down the chain from Jem.

The king stopped for a moment, stretched his back and bent down to dampen his face and neck with water from a passing bucket.

"Not the finest perfume, eh, lad?" he laughed as he pulled off his linen shirt and ripped the mask from his face.

Jem felt as if his heart had stopped beating for a moment.

The king was not wearing his usual long wig, so when he removed his shirt and pulled away the hanging ribbons of the mask, the back of his neck was exposed for all to see.

It was stained by a livid red birthmark… exactly the same as the one Jem had always taken such pains to conceal.

For a moment Jem was frozen to the spot. He simply stared at the king, who was now deep in conversation with Jericho.

It was as if the entire world had shifted on its axis. Jem didn't know what to think or do. His mind felt so crowded that it might explode, but at the same time, it was completely empty, as if everything he had ever known had suddenly drained away.

Then slowly, from somewhere deep inside, it began to feel as if a small golden ball of light was beginning to expand and shine through every fibre of his being.

The strange conversation he'd witnessed between his mother and the king a day earlier now made perfect sense.

He remembered the king's words, "*A fine boy he is, too.*" Despite the danger and the horror of the night around him, Jem smiled.

Charles II, King of England was *his father* – and they had met just before his thirteenth birthday, exactly as Ann had predicted.

Charles threw down his shirt, looked around and caught sight of Jem's shining face. He winked.

Jem grinned and bowed his head, and then, fizzing with a feeling of confidence and completeness that he had never known before, he stripped off his own shirt and removed the band from around his neck.

"Here, lad, I'll take those for you. It's sweaty work, ain't it?"

"Thanks," said Jem, gratefully handing the shirt and the neck band to the man standing just behind him.

Immediately he felt cooler and less constricted. Every sinew of his body tingled with purpose and energy. He'd play his part here to fight the flames and as soon as Tolly came back for him the pair of them would rescue Ann.

Jem leaned over to grasp the straps of another huge overflowing bucket coming up the line, completely unaware that he had just fulfilled the last of Cazalon's rites of binding.

CHAPTER
THIRTY-ONE

As the great bell of St Paul's tolled midnight, Jem began to feel odd.

It wasn't just the heat and the relentless work that were affecting him, it was as if everything around him – the sounds, the sights, the smells – were distorted.

The cathedral seemed to be moving. Its outline quivered in the smoke and appeared to throb like a beating heart. As Jem looked up at the tower he thought he could see the stone carvings along the parapet stretching down to touch him.

Despite the heat, he shivered and stepped back from the chain, bending double for a moment to clear his head. When he looked up again, St Paul's seemed to have crept a little closer, like an old woman who had lifted her skirts and tiptoed silently across the floor while he wasn't looking.

The sounds around him were changing, too. The constant roaring and splitting that had filled his ears for the last few hours now came in waves like the sea on a beach – sometimes the noise was deafening, then it would fade to nothing, gathering its strength to come rushing in again with such incredible force that it actually hurt. He took another step back.

The churchyard began to spin, the scene before him becoming a confusing whirl of black, orange and red, punctuated by giant shadows and wavering human forms.

Jem staggered over to a little patch of grass at the entrance to the churchyard intending to rest for a moment. As he tumbled to the ground his mind lurched into a tangle of strange images and words.

Tolly rode on a lion.

The duchess was a serpent.

The king was a tree.

Ann shone like the moon.

The cathedral was a forest.

His mother was a monkey.

Cazalon was standing over him.

Jem jerked upright and was immediately violently sick. Cazalon *was* standing over him. He was leaning on his staff and watching Jem. His thin lips twitched as a sneer spread across his face.

The count's eyes glittered in the light thrown by the torches around the cathedral. He was swathed in a long, black cloak that covered his entire body from his neck to the ground. Only his head was bare and his snakelike blue plait almost reached the dust of the graveyard. His face was caked with white chalk and his eyes were lined in thick black paint. When he blinked, Jem saw that the count had drawn another eye on the skin of his heavy lids.

Cazalon smiled. "I believe that congratulations are in order, Jeremy. It is now the eve of your thirteenth birthday and I have prepared a very special... *celebration* for you."

Cazalon began to laugh. The horrible dry noise that came from the man's mouth gradually built to a howl that burrowed into Jem's head and coiled itself so tightly and painfully around his mind that he couldn't think or move.

Cazalon stopped and stared intently at the boy.

"And now I would like you to get up and follow me like a dog. Do you think you can do that? I think you'll find that you have little choice in the matter."

From the depths of his cloak the count produced a bundle of grey linen. He flicked a red-gloved hand and as the material unfurled Jem saw that it was a shirt. His shirt.

Cazalon stared at the boy for moment before

speaking slowly and distinctly. "It's sweaty work, ain't it?"

Jem's blood froze.

Cazalon continued, "Although it is customary to offer a gift on the occasion of a birthday, I have taken the liberty of reversing that charming ritual. I must thank you, Jeremy, for freely giving me the most splendid present of all – your soul. Come."

The man turned in the dust, and resting on his staff, stalked towards a narrow alleyway leading away from the churchyard. As he moved, his cloak was caught by the wind and flapped around him like the wings of a huge black bird.

Unable to stop himself, Jem jerked to his feet and stumbled after him.

࿓ ⚏ ࿓

Cazalon wove through a maze of dark, smoke-filled passages and stopped outside a tall, ancient house. He stepped through the open door and Jem followed. No matter how hard he tried, Jem couldn't free himself from the count's control. He tried to swallow his terror. His body was bending to Cazalon's will, but his thoughts and feelings were still under his own control.

Cazalon limped through the deserted hallway to a small chamber at the back of the house. He stooped and threw aside a tattered rug. In the thin orange firelight from a small window high on the wall, Jem saw a trapdoor set in the floor.

The count bent to pull open the trapdoor, revealing a flight of stone steps that spiralled down into darkness.

He clicked his fingers and an orb of sickly green light appeared in the air above him. The orb revolved slowly, hovered and then swooped down the steps, casting just enough light to show the way. At the same time, the crystal bird's head at the end of Cazalon's twisted staff began to glow.

Cazalon stepped down onto the stairs and moments later Jem followed.

He couldn't stop. It felt as if someone was riding in his head, controlling every movement of his body.

At first the air was thick with the smell of burning, but as they went deeper, it was overpowered by the stench of damp and rot.

The stone staircase seemed to spiral down an impossibly long way. Jem felt dizzy again as he followed the black hem of Cazalon's cloak, which slipped around and around the stony turns just ahead of him as they descended. Jem had to clasp the cold, moist walls to steady himself… but still he couldn't stop.

At last they reached the bottom of the spiral staircase and entered a domed chamber that branched off into several arched passageways. In the dull, green light, Jem noticed that there were symbols scratched into the stone above the arches and the walls were carved with strange figures. A grinning demon spewed leaves and flowers from its mouth, a woman held a flaming wheel above her head, a mermaid rode upon a dragon and, most unsettling of all, a man with the head of a huge bird soared across the ceiling carrying a figure between his taloned feet.

Cazalon turned to look at Jem. He smiled and moistened his lips, and Jem shivered at the sight of his pointed black tongue. The count gestured at the walls with the glowing staff.

"London is ancient, Jeremy. This cavern is over four thousand years old. It was here long before the Romans built their city on the banks of the Thames. Come. I will show you the Roman catacombs."

The passageway they followed was low and narrow to start with, but then it broadened and Jem saw that the walls were lined with shelves carved into the stone. He stared into the black depths of one of them and gasped as, just for a second, Cazalon's orb of light illuminated the crumbling eye sockets of a skull mounted on top of a heap of bones.

Cazalon laughed.

"Use your eyes, Jeremy. There are thousands of skulls around you. This is a necropolis. Do you know what that is?"

Jem swallowed hard and did not answer. He could not stop himself following the man, but he would not speak to him.

Cazalon feigned sadness. "Ah – such ignorance in the young these days. Permit me to enlighten you – this, Jeremy, is a city of the dead."

The light from the green orb intensified, revealing hundreds, perhaps thousands, of shelves in the tunnel stretching before them, each one filled with jumbled, dusty bones.

Jem's eyes widened and Cazalon laughed again, moving deeper into the catacombs The tunnels were like a maze. Every so often Cazalon stopped when the passages came to a double, triple or even quadruple fork, scanning the incised symbols that covered the walls.

At last they turned into a particularly broad passage. At the far end, Jem saw a massive black doorway surrounded by an arch. As they neared the door, Jem had a strange feeling that this place was incredibly powerful.

A dark sense of foreboding, invisible but thick as treacle, rolled down the corridor to engulf them. He tried to stop his feet but they wouldn't obey.

The arch was the height of five men and carved from black marble. Enormous twisted tree trunks were carved into the stone, making it seem as if the door led into a dark forest, but as Jem looked closer he saw that some of the trunks had mouths, eyes and rows of jagged fangs. There were serpents hidden among the branches.

Jem began to tremble. He was unable to ignore his terror any longer.

Cazalon must have felt something too. The count turned and stared intently. For a second, Jem felt a flare of pain from the scar on his heel. Cazalon smiled bleakly.

"I don't think that such simple magic will be able to save you now, Jeremy."

Jem's jaw dropped as the count continued with a sneer, "Oh, yes. I know all about that pathetic charm.

My little ward has told me everything. Perhaps you would like to see her?"

Cazalon turned, and, using his staff, knocked three times on the soaring carved doors that hung between the marble trees.

"Behold – the Oak Grove!"

The doors swung back silently to reveal a huge circular cavern lit by hundreds of candles set into niches around the walls. Three other passages set at equal distances along the curved interior appeared to lead out of the chamber. Seven more of Cazalon's glowing green orbs hovered overhead at the centre of the space, giving off a steady, sickly light.

The cavern was domed, like the place Jem had seen earlier. It was dominated by a monstrous carved centaur that galloped across the ceiling, and the walls here were inscribed with a thousand more carvings – some were copies of the ones he'd already seen, others even stranger and more intricate.

Jem stumbled forward and stared, unable to comprehend where he was or what he was seeing.

"Beautiful, isn't it?" Even Cazalon's voice had taken on a note of awe.

The man limped forward to a pile of fallen columns near the centre of the great chamber. He stepped up onto a broken stump and raised his arms.

"We are far beneath St Paul's, Jeremy. Beneath the ugly cathedral that will soon burn to the ground; beneath its undercroft; beneath its crypt; and beneath its bone-packed tombs."

Cazalon stopped to note the effect of his words on the boy. Jem looked up in amazement. Was it true? Were they really under the cathedral? Was Tolly up there somewhere?

Cazalon continued, "The stones you are standing on now, boy, were sacred to the Romans, who built their great temple here. And they were sacred to the druids of this land, who came before them. They called it the Oak Grove. I believe that name might be familiar to you?"

The words of the old prophecy rang out in Jem's mind. *When the dark god rises in the oak grove…* His mouth went very dry and he was suddenly aware of his heart thumping under his ribs.

The count watched him for a moment then smiled. "In the time before time, this place was an ancient forest open to the sky. Indeed, I imagine that it was sacred even to those who came before the druids, but that…" he began to laugh hoarsely, "was before I was born."

He breathed deeply for a moment and closed his eyes. "Can you feel it, Jeremy? This is the place of power where I shall become immortal. It is the great portal I have sought for more than a thousand years."

The count limped over to the far side of the cavern. As Jem's eyes grew accustomed to the odd light, he saw that Cazalon was standing beneath a curved, shimmering object set on one of the pillars. It was a gigantic hourglass. Cazalon looked up at the glass and pressed one of his gloved hands against the surface of the lower bulb. He watched for a moment as the thin thread of sand trickled down from the bulb above.

"And it is not a moment too soon," the count whispered. His words hissed and reverberated from the stone walls – the last word, 'soon', coming again and again in a sibilant echo.

"Now," Cazalon turned and limped to the centre of the cavern. "I suppose you will want to be reunited with your friend?"

The count brought his staff down heavily to the stone floor. The noise rang out around the chamber and suddenly the huge space was light as day.

In the brightness, Jem saw Ann for the first time. She was curled up on the floor on the other side of the cavern, Tapwick crouched on a broken pillar next to her. The twisted little man leapt from his perch and aimed a swift, vicious kick at Ann's legs. She moaned and curled into a tighter ball.

"Up! Up! Master's here."

Ann moaned again and slowly pulled herself into a seated position. Jem wanted to run to her, but he couldn't move his feet. He felt as if his head would burst and his eyes stung with unshed tears of anger and frustration.

Ann's face was horribly bruised and fresh red blood stained the linen at her sleeves. Cazalon had clearly made the blood bridge again, and recently. She opened her eyes.

"Jem!" Her voice was cracked and dry, but then she spoke in a rush, "You must run. Listen to me. Get away from here, it's you. He means to—"

"That's enough, you stupid girl."

Tapwick's blow sent Ann sprawling to the dust again.

Cazalon sneered at her. "You ignorant little fool. Did you really believe that I knew nothing of your schemes – all those feeble conjuring tricks? You have played your part to perfection, Lady Ann. But now I no longer have a use for you. Of course, I am grateful

that you enabled me to speak to your mother –
who is, I must say, a vastly superior species of sorceress
– but I am even more grateful that you proved to be
such excellent bait."

He paused for moment.

"I doubt the boy of jade here would have come to
his death, so quickly and so willingly, if it hadn't been
for you. And now that he has completed the rites
of binding, just as your clever mother so carefully
explained, he is my creature. I think the game is over."

Cazalon allowed his words to sink in. Then he
began to laugh. The harsh noise coiled around the
chamber so that the stones themselves seemed to ring.

Ann's eyes blazed. Painfully she pushed herself
up and stared defiantly across the chamber. "But my
mother has a last message for you."

Cazalon's eyes sparked with interest and he
limped over to grab a hank of Ann's matted white
hair, pulling her face back so that she looked directly
into his eyes.

"And what is that, little one?"

Ann glowed with hatred.

"My mother says that you are a fool, Cazalon.
And you will fail because your servant will betray
you."

She spat the last words into Cazalon's face.

Without warning, Cazalon raised his hand and slapped Ann's cheek so ferociously that her head snapped back, hitting the floor behind her.

Every muscle and nerve in Jem's body strained to move, but he was trapped – rooted to the spot. As he watched in horror, he felt a single tear trickle down his face.

Cazalon contemplated Ann's motionless body for a moment, then he turned and regarded Tapwick through narrowed eyes. He repeated Ann's words softly.

"Your servant will betray you."

As before, his voice echoed strangely around the chamber so that the stones seemed to whisper '*betray betray betray*'.

Tapwick twitched and cowered against a broken pillar.

"No master! I wouldn't… never. Not me… Please, I—"

But as the little man whimpered, Cazalon slowly raised his staff and pointed it at his steward. Instantly Tapwick fell silent – all the colour drained from his terrified face, even from the red-raw sockets of his eyes. A peculiar greyness flowed over his body like a shadow, from the curls of his ragged wig, down over his hunched shoulders, around his arms, chest and legs all the way to the tips of his pointed shoes.

The steward simply froze like a small stone statue.

Cazalon struck the ground just once and Tapwick shattered into a million tiny pieces. The count stirred some of the fragments with the end of his twisted staff, smirking as he did so. He turned to Jem and laughed aloud at the expression of horror on the boy's face

"It is such a pity that I am going to have to kill you too, Jeremy. For you would have made such an amusing pet. So much better than the mute halfwit and the monkey!"

The man seemed suddenly weary and sat heavily on a fallen column. He clicked his fingers and the light from the orbs dimmed.

Cazalon thought for a moment and then leaned forward to draw something that looked like a man with the head of a hook-beaked bird in the dust. After a moment he looked up.

"Do you like stories, boy?"

Jem was silent. He refused to look the man directly in the eye.

"Ah. The young prince is angry with me."

Jem flinched.

"Oh yes! I know who you are, Jeremy Green. I have known for a very long time. It is the only reason I befriended that fool Bellingdon and gave the elixir of youth to his vain wife. I needed to gain access to you."

The count grinned. "I always knew a greedy woman like the duchess would use the mummia in dangerous, not to say fatal, quantities."

Cazalon seemed to relish the word 'fatal', rolling it around his tongue like a delicious sweetmeat. "To be frank, it has all been such an entertaining game. It passed the time most enjoyably… while I waited for your thirteenth birthday.

"Do you not see?" he continued. "It was you I wanted all along. Not her money. And certainly not her husband's ridiculous scheme to profit from building a new city. Although, I concede…" he paused for a moment and rubbed out the image in the dust with his foot, "that Bellingdon's ambitions did prove rather useful. He and his stupid, greedy friends are exactly the sort of souls I need."

He stared speculatively at Jem, before adding, "But you shall be my most important soul of all."

CHAPTER THIRTY-TWO

Cazalon stood up wearily and limped over to where Ann lay. He prodded her with his foot, but she didn't move. Was she alive? Jem wanted to run to her but his legs wouldn't obey him.

Cazalon's voice rang across the chamber.

"Let me tell you something about myself, Jeremy. It would amuse me to see your reaction. And anyway, as you will not leave this place alive, I feel that I can trust you with my greatest secret."

Jem stared at the floor. He didn't want to listen to the man, but he didn't really have much choice.

"I am more than three thousand years old, boy. What do you think of that?"

Jem glanced up in shock and disbelief. Cazalon smiled bleakly.

"Yes, I thought that might capture your attention. What is more – Cazalon is not my real name. I purchased the title many hundreds of years ago. The library of the Court of Cazalon in the Pyrenees possessed the greatest and oldest collection of books in Europe at that time and so, of course, I had to have them. Knowledge is power, Jeremy, and I needed power to help me avoid a terrible debt."

Jem was listening now, despite himself. He watched as Cazalon walked haltingly back to the broken column and sat down again. The count swiped some dust from his cloak and continued.

"My true name is Kaphret. Three thousand years ago, I was a priest at the temple of Horus in Thebes. We called our land the Nile Kingdom. You would know it as Egypt.

"I was young, clever and ambitious. The pharaoh was a fat and stupid youth and yet people revered him as a god. I was jealous. I knew that I had more worth in a single lock of my hair than that dullard. But the people still worshipped him... Or so I thought."

Cazalon bent his head and stared at the floor, before continuing, "You must always be careful what you pray for, Jeremy. I prayed to the dark god Set to give me power... and he answered.

"In return for three thousand years of life he demanded my eternal soul. I accepted his bargain. Who wouldn't? But what I didn't care about all those years ago was that I sold the afterlife of my soul for the merest speck in time. I exchanged eternity for a just thirty centuries, Jeremy. Do you

406

know what that means?"

Jem shook his head slowly and Cazalon's mouth twisted into a bitter smile.

"It means that when Set comes to claim his dues I will utterly cease to exist. There will be no world beyond this one waiting for me, no Land of the Dead, no Heaven, no Valhalla, no Elysian Fields, no Isles of the Blest. There will be only the void. An eternal nothingness. And Set is coming soon. Very soon."

Cazalon shuddered and Jem realised, with a jolt, that the man was frightened.

"Three thousand years go very quickly, boy. I first started to worry about my... future many centuries ago. I travelled the world to find a way to escape my debt.

"From shamans in the frozen wastes of the north to mystics in the mountains and temples of the east, and from the seer tribes of the southern deserts to the shapeshifters of the plains of the New World, I have learned the deepest secrets of earthly magic from the wise ones.

"And recently I have dabbled with the new magic, the science that so fascinates your royal father, he has established a special society to investigate it. I must admit, Jeremy, I had great hopes for the experiments I carried out to capture a soul on the point of death. You saw the experiments on those wretched animals. Obviously, the next step would have been to transfer my soul to another living vessel. I did think that Ptolemy might be suitable, but as he is so very stupid and damaged, the risk to myself—"

Cazalon stopped himself. "But I must return to our story. Many years ago now, in the time of Queen Cleopatra, I found a scroll in the great library at Alexandria. It was written in Greek, but the knowledge was much older. It spoke of the Androtheos – the man-god of the Western Isles.

"The Druids of Albion, from whom your little friend Ann over there is directly descended, had perfected a rite to endow an earthly man with all the powers of a god. And I knew then, Jeremy, that if I could meet Set as his equal, then he could not claim his payment. I too would be an immortal."

Ann... descended of the Druids of Albion! Jem was astounded. Had she known this already?

"I'm sure you can imagine my disappointment when I discovered that Elizabeth Metcalf, Ann's mother, the most powerful druid priestess in these lands was... indisposed," Cazalon continued.

"But when I heard that her only child, a little girl of just six years, was alive, I made it my business to find the girl and to use her blood to communicate with her departed mother."

Cazalon shifted and arched his back as if he was in pain.

"It has cost me a great deal to make the blood bridge, Jeremy, more than it has cost my white-haired ward. It is the most dangerous, terrible magic imaginable. Every time I crossed back over the bridge I left a little piece of my life force behind in the dead lands, but I had to do it. From Ann's living lips I have heard the voice of her dead mother – and she told me how I could become the equal of a god."

Cazalon paused for a moment and stared at Ann's huddled body.

"And so, Elizabeth directed me to this ancient place – known to her druid ancestors as the Oak Grove. It is a portal where the ancient power of the earth can be harnessed. But first that power needs to be awakened… and fed."

Cazalon smiled, "And that, Jeremy, is why I needed Bellingdon and his greedy friends. To awaken the spirit of the grove I must sacrifice a bonded soul to every point of the compass – so that the power of the four Guardians of the Gates to the World will flow to this very spot."

Still rooted to the ground, Jem's horrified expression must have given his thoughts away: He is mad.

Cazalon merely laughed. "Oh foolish Jeremy – I was never interested in burning London and profiting from a new city. It was only this place, this very spot, that I wanted. I will use it to magnify my power. When I am a god I will build a new temple for myself above the Oak Grove on the site of St Paul's. The land for my wonderful temple will be purified by the fire that is raging above us at this very moment.

"I believe you have already seen my design for the building where people will come to worship me for ever?"

Without pausing for an answer, the count continued. "The contract that Bellingdon, Avebury, Kilheron and Pinchbeck signed in their own blood has delivered their souls into my care and soon I will use them... Then I will use you."

Cazalon stopped and caught his breath. He bent double for a moment and rubbed his leg through his black breeches. He looked across at Jem and his mouth curved into a cruel smile. "Would you like to see what three thousand years do to a body?"

Jem gulped and tried to turn away, but he couldn't move his eyes from the man sitting in front of him.

Cazalon drew back the lower folds of his cloak and removed one of the elegant leather boots that covered his legs to the knee. Jem flinched when he saw the man's foot. It was black and twisted. Peeling skin clung tightly to grey bones clearly visible beneath the desiccated flesh. Narrow yellow toenails appeared to sprout from the wrong places on the count's withered foot. After a moment Jem realised they seemed unnaturally long because the flesh around them had shrivelled and died. A fat grey maggot crept from beneath one of the toenails, reared up, wriggled and then burrowed beneath a tattered flap of blackened skin. A foul smell filled Jem's nostrils.

It was the stench he had come to recognise. Cazalon was rotting alive.

The count's painted eyelid twitched as he regarded his foot. He was silent for a moment, before he spoke again.

"The powdered mummia helps, but death is slowly creeping through my body – and I fear that making the blood bridge has hastened the decay. I have ten years at most before Set claims my soul."

Cazalon stood up and grinned broadly. "And that, my dear Jeremy, is why I need you so very badly to achieve my transformation. For a long time Elizabeth babbled about spilling green blood in the Oak Grove and, I'll admit to you, I was confused. Then she started to talk about sacrificing 'the jade boy' and things became much clearer.

"Her words led me to you, Jeremy Green," Cazalon placed a heavy emphasis on Jem's last name. "You see, to become the Androtheos, a man must sacrifice the first-born son of an anointed king. The deed must be done on the cusp of the boy's thirteenth birthday and the victim must have come willingly to his fate. Guided by a dead witch and a greedy duke, I found exactly the child I needed.

"When you gave me your shirt and your neck band back there, you completed the last of the rites of binding and allowed me to control you completely. And so, we might say, that you have come willingly to this place to complete the ceremony. The fact that you came to the city to find your little friend has only strengthened the magic. It is almost too perfect!"

Jem tried to shout but no words came. He couldn't even twitch a finger. He scanned the cavern, desperately seeking some means of escape.

Cazalon smiled at Jem's stricken expression. "Tonight you should be journeying into manhood, Jeremy, but instead you will be taking a very different path."

It was no use – they had failed. Tolly was searching in the wrong place, Ann was surely dead, he was about to be sacrificed and Cazalon was about to become more terrible and powerful than ever. Something inside Jem seemed to break.

His feet started to move involuntarily and he walked stiffly, like a stringed puppet, to stand in the very centre of the cavern, beneath the domed ceiling. He didn't even try to resist.

Cazalon leaned on his staff and watched.

"Well, my young princeling, enough stories for today. I think it is time to begin."

He snapped his fingers and Jem's world went black.

CHAPTER THIRTY-THREE

Somewhere far away someone called Jem's name. As his senses returned, he saw that he was surrounded by a ring of blue flames. Tongues of cold fire licked hungrily at his boots as the dancing circle closed in on him. A deadly numbness began to creep up his legs. This was no dream. It was terrifyingly real. The odd blue flames glinted on the massive hourglass and Jem saw that several hours had passed.

Cazalon stood on the other side of the flickering circle. He had removed his cloak to reveal his bare torso and now a pleated white cloth fell from his waist to his knees. Jem saw that Cazalon's skin was covered in a coiling, snake-like pattern etched in blue. The count had released his hair from the plait and it now hung to the floor like a thin blue mane sprouting from the crown of his head.

But it was the man's hands that horrified Jem most of all. For the first time, Cazalon had removed his gloves – and now the boy could see why he had never done so before.

On the right side, from the fingers to just below the knobbled elbow, the count had a skeletal claw. Hardly any flesh remained and the little strips that clung to the long yellow bones were ragged and black. On the left side, the count's hand was intact, but the skin was puckered and weeping. The flesh was mottled yellow, green and black and studded with gaping sores that oozed a foul yellow liquid. Jem felt his stomach lurch in revulsion.

Cazalon was intoning some words in a language Jem couldn't understand, and drawing patterns in the dust with his staff.

Just beyond him Ann's body lay motionless in the dust, her bloody head turned to the wall.

Ann! Tears began to stream down the boy's cheeks as he realised he had failed her too. He wanted to sob aloud, but his body wouldn't obey him. He couldn't move, he couldn't speak. All he could do now was weep silent tears of despair.

Cazalon looked up from the pattern on the ground and stared at Jem. His black eyes glittered.

"Ah, Jeremy, you are awake at last," he whispered across the flames.

Suddenly Jem's voice returned. But the words that came were not his.

"I am, master," he said. The words tasted like vomit in his mouth.

Cazalon smiled. "And so we begin."

The count began to chant. His voice echoed around the chamber, reverberating from the walls, which picked up the rhythm and amplified the sound so that the air itself seemed to hum.

Gradually Jem became aware that the slabs of the stone floor within the circle beneath him were beginning to give off a blue glow.

Cazalon stopped chanting, but the humming sound continued, growing louder and deeper. He threw back his head so that his hair swept the ground, then he called out, "Richard Pinchbeck, Alderman of London, come forth. I cast you to the east.

Matthew, Marquis of Kilheron, come forth. I cast you to the west.

Edward, Lord Avebury, come forth. I cast you to the south.

George, Duke of Bellingdon, come forth. I cast you to the north."

The floor of the burning circle glowed more strongly. Four wispy, ghostly figures began to take shape around the edge of the circle and, as Jem watched, he realised that he was seeing the men Cazalon had just named – the duke and the other plotters.

As the figures became more substantial, Jem could see the men's faces clearly. They were terrified and seemed to be calling out, although what they were saying couldn't be heard. Bellingdon held out his hands as if imploring Jem to help him, but the boy couldn't move.

Cazalon struck the dusty floor four times with his staff.

"Watchers at the Gates, take these mortal souls in payment for your power!"

The cavern was utterly silent for a second and then it was flooded with a blinding explosion of white light that flared from the eyes of the crystal hawk at the tip of the staff.

The figures now found their voices. With terrible screams, each one of them burned brilliantly and then collapsed in on themselves, shrinking to tiny black pinpoints on the stone floor before disappearing. It was if they had been sucked down into the earth.

Cazalon smiled in satisfaction as the air began to fill with sound. The noise was like a thousand church organs – all playing different, discordant notes. It was beautiful and terrible at the same time and it made the chamber pulse with an unnatural life of its own. Colour glowed in every stone and the carved walls seemed to ripple and move.

Cazalon watched him through the flames for a moment and then spoke.

"Have you come here of your own free will, boy?"

"I have, master." Jem struggled, but the foul-tasting words came of their own accord.

"Did you give me clothing and food?"

"Yes, master."

"You are the first-born son of an anointed king?"

"I am, master,"

"Will you allow me to cross the barrier of fire to join you?"

"Surely, master."

Jem felt prickles of terror run down his spine. Inviting Cazalon to join him was the last thing he wanted to do, but he couldn't stop his tongue.

The count smiled in triumph, and, leaning on his staff, he stepped through the ring of flames.

He grinned down at the boy and the pointed tip of his black tongue licked the corner of his mouth. From the folds of his waistcloth, he revealed a curved dagger.

"And will you allow me to cut out your beating heart?"

"No!"

A great shout rang around the chamber, but the words were not Jem's.

Tolly barrelled through the ring of the flames, knocking Cazalon to the floor. The count's staff was jolted from his hand and skittered through the flames, coming to rest next to Ann's body.

At the same moment a tiny black and white blur dropped from above and wrapped herself around the man's head, knotting her tail and limbs into the mane of blue hair. Cleo shrieked and growled as she bit and scratched at the count's ears and nose with her sharp little teeth and claws.

Cazalon staggered to his feet and grasped the monkey by the neck. He ripped her from his head and flung her to the floor. Cleo yelped, but Jem noticed that as she fell, she took with her a hank of the man's hair and a bleeding scrap of his scalp.

Cazalon spun to face Tolly, drew his dagger and made a swift, vicious lunge in the boy's direction.

But Tolly was too quick for him, stepping deftly to one side so that instead of sinking into his throat, the blade merely pierced the linen of his shirt at the shoulder.

Tolly yelled in pain and gripped the top of his arm.

He was wounded. Jem saw bright drops of blood seeping through his friend's fingers.

Cazalon's eyes narrowed. He stood a few feet away from Tolly on the inner edge of the flaming ring and began to laugh.

"Who would have thought that my animal could talk?" he sneered. "After all this time it seems that my most tedious pet has found a voice."

Tolly's eyes flashed. "I have always spoken, Cazalon, but only to those worthy of hearing me."

The boy's voice was clear and defiant and the words rang around the chamber.

Cazalon kept his eyes fixed on Tolly and he began to trace a pattern in the air with his withered hand.

After a moment he spoke. "It seems I may have underestimated you, Ptolemy. Still, the only thing I hear in your voice now is despair. You cannot save your friends. It is too late, even now your feet are turning to dust. Look boy, look at the ground beneath you. Do you see how you and stone are fused?"

Tolly looked down and Jem saw that his friend's bare feet appeared to be part of the cavern floor. As he watched in horror, the dark skin of Tolly's ankles began to change colour and gradually a dull greyness crept up his legs.

Cazalon started to laugh again and the rasping sound scraped the walls of the chamber. "What a pity it is that the moment you find a voice I have to silence it for ever."

Tolly yanked desperately at his feet and as he did so, a few drops of bright red blood fell from his shoulder to the stone floor. Immediately there was a hissing, spitting noise, like the sound of fat sizzling in a pan.

The globules of Tolly's blood formed a little pattern on the ground near his feet, but after a few seconds, instead of sinking into the dust, the blood began to move.

At first the droplets rolled towards each other to form a single stain no larger than a robin's breast.

Then the patch began to spread. Very soon it was the size of a plate and then a coach wheel, all the time spreading faster and wider.

From the centre of the flaming ring, Jem watched as little red tendrils began to shoot off from the edge of the bloodstain, winding and weaving their way across the stone.

"What have you done?" Cazalon hissed at Tolly as the veinlike channels rippled swiftly across the circle. The count had to step back to avoid the pulsing red network that now covered most of the ring. It was as if the blood was searching for something.

Rooted to the spot, Tolly watched in silence as the tendrils finally reached Cazalon's feet.

Still holding the blade outstretched, the count was now surrounded by a network of threadlike whorls and patterns on the stone.

As the first of the tendrils touched his skin, Cazalon let out a horrible scream, as if he had been burned. He stepped back, but the weaving red filaments burrowed through the dust and quickly sought him out.

Jem watched as the man's rotten feet quickly disappeared beneath a growing network of wriggling scarlet veins.

"This is not possible!" Cazalon gasped in pain, flailing desperately with the blade to cut at the heaving mass around his feet.

He stared wildly at Tolly. "Who are you, boy? A witchdoctor?"

"I too am the first-born son of a king. My father did not wear a crown or sit on a throne, but to my people, he was a mighty ruler," replied Tolly coolly. "You bought a prince to be your servant."

Cazalon's eyes widened. He looked at the seething

red mass around him and then stared back at Tolly. A strange look crossed his face; his mouth opened but no words came. It was if he had suddenly discovered some terrible secret.

"It's the blood!" Cazalon eventually whispered. "I have spilled the blood of a prince in the Oak Grove, but not the prince made ready for the ritual. Why did you not tell me who you are?" He spat the words at Tolly.

"You were not worth speaking to. You thought I was nothing more than an animal," Tolly replied flatly.

Cazalon twisted violently but he couldn't move. Like Jem and Tolly, he was now rooted to the spot.

The twisting, glistening veins gathered momentum as they climbed up Cazalon's thrashing body, winding themselves tightly around his legs.

The boys watched calmly as Cazalon continued to flail and writhe, hacking at the creeping veins.

His voice grew wild and shrill. "Where is my staff?"

"Here."

Ann's voice was hoarse, but it was firm.

The count's head whipped round and he yelped as his hair was tugged by the veinlike tendrils that now curled around his waist. Ann was standing on the far side of the flames, supporting herself with Cazalon's gnarled staff.

"I think you will find, dear guardian, that the offering of royal blood was given, but it was not given willingly. Therefore everything will be inverted. A sacrifice must still be made today… but now, you will become that sacrifice!"

"Never!" he snarled. "Give me my staff, now." Ann shook her head.

"I command you… you must…"

His voice became a high-pitched shriek of agony as the wriggling scarlet filaments wound and curled into his blue hair, binding the arm and hand that still held the dagger. "I am not ready. It is not time. I cannot…"

The count fought to stop the probing tendrils from creeping into his mouth and nostrils, spitting and jerking his head about.

Then a thunderclap ripped through the air and the ring of blue flames disappeared. Instantly, the walls of the cavern dimmed, the humming ceased and the floor seemed to tilt.

Jem suddenly felt a great jolt run through his body and he collapsed to the stone like a puppet whose strings had been cut. He could move again!

"Cleo!"

Tolly raced to the spot at Ann's side where a tiny body lay crumpled in the dust. Gently he scooped the monkey into his arms.

Jem was with them both just a second later.

"Is she…?" he gasped.

"Oh no. Please, no," whispered Ann, her eyes glittering with tears as she looked down at the battered little body.

Cleo still had a clump of Cazalon's blue hair gripped in her paw. As the children looked, the tiny hand opened and the hair fell to the floor.

Then Cleo took a deep shuddering breath… She was alive.

Huddling the monkey close to his chest, Tolly scanned the tunnels leading from the chamber. "We have to get away from here! I think it's this way." He jerked his head.

They began to run.

"Stop. I– I command you to free me." The pain-wracked voice was Cazalon's. He was now almost completely encased in a bulging, twitching mass of wriggling veins. His head was pulled oddly to one side by the hair trapped in the throbbing scarlet network.

"If you leave me here I will… I will…"

Tolly stopped suddenly and turned to stare at the hideous figure.

"What will you do?"

He took a step towards Cazalon.

"Tolly come on. What are you doing?" Jem was almost at the gaping entrance to a tunnel. He grabbed a candle from a niche and reached for Ann's hand. Even in the odd grey light that now filled the cavern, he could see that she was weak with pain and exhaustion. Blood glistened on her temple.

But Tolly took another step towards Cazalon. "What will you do?" he asked again, his voice dripping with defiant sarcasm.

Cazalon was suddenly still. He stared at Tolly and his bloodshot eyes narrowed. When he spoke, his slow deliberate words were dipped in venom. "I will hunt you down to the ends of the earth and beyond. And when I find you, every one of you, I will ensure that the pain you have inflicted upon me today is visited upon you sevenfold."

Tolly took one more step so that he was almost standing next to the glistening red mummy that was Cazalon.

"No! Tolly, don't." Ann tried to run to him, but Jem held her tight.

Tolly shielded Cleo's body, leaned closer and whispered something.

Cazalon's eyes grew wide with astonishment and confusion. And then he let out a huge roar as the creeping veins began to cover his eyes.

Jem felt a sudden searing pain on his bare right shoulder. He yelped and felt for the spot. A patch of skin the size of a penny stung beneath his fingers.

He looked up. Rain seemed to be falling from the ceiling above, but the droplets were made of flame – hot, red flame. Ann cried out as a fiery ball no bigger than a marble spattered and sizzled on her hand. Jem leaned over to shield her.

"We have to get out of here. Now!" he yelled. "Come on, Tolly."

Tolly hugged Cleo closer to his chest as he hurried back to them. He scanned the four exits to the cavern and frowned.

"Not this one. It's that way," he said, pointing to the dark mouth of one of the other passages.

Jem squeezed Ann's hand. "Do you think you can run?"

She nodded.

The children and the monkey pelted across the

chamber, dodging the fire-rain that was falling more heavily around them now.

They were just a few feet from the passage when a great booming noise rumbled overhead and the cavern juddered. A cloud of dust fell from the ceiling, coating their hair and skin in a layer of fine white powder.

Tolly began to cough. "What was that?" he spluttered, trying to shield Cleo with his body.

The noise grew louder and deeper and a crack began to fracture across the dome, dividing the head of the carved centaur from its galloping body. Ann looked up. "The cavern is splitting in two," she shouted.

Huge balls of fire now fell through the gaping fissure overhead and spurts of molten white-hot liquid began to cascade through the crack, splashing and fizzing on the stones around them.

Jem shouted. "St Paul's is on fire above us – and it's collapsing! We have to get out of here, now!"

The little group ran into the entrance of the passage. Jem grabbed a candle from a niche in the wall to light their way. As they disappeared into the darkness there was an odd wheezing crackling sound. Then a rasping voice rang out around the cavern.

"Remember, I have already been to the land of the dead. I have crossed the blood bridge many times and returned. I know how to cheat death! You cannot defeat me."

A deafening groan grated and echoed around the vast chamber and then the children were enveloped in dust and stones as a thunder of falling rocks sealed them into the tunnel.

CHAPTER
THIRTY-FOUR

Jem coughed in the dust-thickened darkness. His candle had been extinguished by the rock fall. He felt for the stone wall, carefully pulling himself to his feet.

"Tolly? Ann? Can you hear me?" he choked.

"Jem!" Tolly's voice came from a little way off.

There was a rustling noise, a sharp cry of "Ouch!" and then Jem felt a small hand on his arm.

"Jem, is that you? Are you all right?"

He grabbed Ann's hand in reply. Her voice came again. "Have you still got the candle?"

Jem handed her the stub and seconds later he jumped as her pointed little face glowed eerily into life beside him.

"Even an inferior sorceress like me has her uses... sometimes."

She grinned wearily, shielding the tiny flame with her hand.

Moments later, Tolly, still cradling Cleo, scrabbled across the rock-strewn floor to join them.

"We have to keep moving. This place isn't safe," said Tolly. He shuddered as Ann raised the candle and revealed the ink-black passage ahead of them.

"But how will we find the way out?" said Jem. "This place is a maze. We could get lost down here for ever."

"I think I can find the way," said Tolly. His eyes were huge and fearful in the gloom and he had to take a deep breath before continuing.

"In the cathedral, I picked up Ann's fear and it led me down to the crypts. But I– I froze down there, in the dark. I couldn't move. I don't know how long I stayed there, but then Cleo found me. She'd followed me into St Paul's and then, down in the crypts, she found an ancient vault with a cracked wall. The gap led through into the old catacombs beneath the cathedral, where I knew you were."

Ann gasped. "Tolly, you must have been terrified. The darkness, the cramped space. I can't believe you found us." She cupped his cheek in her hand. "You were very brave."

Tolly smiled tightly. "Thank Cleo. She wouldn't let me give up."

He snuggled the monkey closer.

"So that's how you found us?" asked Jem.

Tolly shook his head. "Do you remember that

time on the ice, Jem, when we saw the poor drowned pedlar girl? I'll never forget that day. It was when I discovered that, along with animals, the dead can talk to me."

He laughed grimly. "So when I came into the catacombs to find you, I– I simply asked the way."

Jem shivered. "You mean you... you talked to the skulls?"

Tolly nodded. "The worst thing is that most of them don't understand. They don't know they are dead. They all want to talk. Like that girl in the ice – she asked me when she could go home."

The children were silent for a moment then Jem spoke decisively.

"We have to get out of here before this becomes our tomb too. Tolly, can you lead us back?"

Tolly nodded and squared his shoulders. "Give me the candle Ann. I will get us out."

※ ⚓ ※

When the children and the monkey finally emerged from the tunnels beneath St Paul's on to the banks of the Thames, the London they had known was gone.

Jem cleared his throat – the air was hot and dusty. "How long were we down there?"

"I don't know, but at least the fire has passed," said Ann softly, trying to make some sense of the landscape around them.

They had been underground for so long that the fire was indeed over, but it had scorched the city they knew from the face of the earth. Ash fell like rain from the sky as they clambered up the riverbank. They were met by the sight of hundreds of grey-faced people, picking through the cinders and climbing over the smouldering ruins.

"Do you feel that?" whispered Tolly as they stared in horror at the devastation. He prodded the ground with his bare foot. "The earth itself is still hot."

The children turned about slowly trying to get their bearings. It was as if they could see from one end of the city to the other across jumbled piles of smoking rubble. St Paul's Cathedral towered above the wreckage, but it was blackened, roofless and utterly ravaged.

Jem looked down to the water. He was surprised to see hundreds of small boats moving purposefully up and down. He could even hear water traders calling out their wares.

A scruffy man carrying a large leather pouch popped up from behind a ragged wall beside them.

"Read it here, young sirs and little lady. The true story of the Great Fire of London. A pamphlet for a penny – and that's money well spent."

"The true story of the fire, you say?" asked Ann.

The man nodded eagerly.

"Well, if I had a penny I would most certainly buy it," she grinned.

Tolly and Jem laughed as the man scowled and stumbled away.

Jem looked west to the palace at Whitehall. It was intact. He whispered a brief prayer for his mother – and his father – and then he kicked angrily at the hot earth.

"So much for your ancient prophecy, Ann! We failed miserably. London is a smoking ruin."

"Perhaps that isn't true," said Tolly, scrambling onto a pile of blackened bricks. "Look at the river down there. It's business as usual. Even the pamphlet writers are hard at work. Life will go on, Jem."

He smiled down at his friends.

Ann placed Cazalon's staff on the ground and took Jem's hand. She led him up to Tolly's vantage point where she caught hold of Tolly's hand too.

The three of them stood side by side, looking out over the busy river.

"In one very important respect the prophecy did come true," she said solemnly.

"The boy of jade, the black traveller and the moon child did bind the dark god. And that was probably the most important thing of all."

She shuddered. "Just imagine what Cazalon would have done if he had become a man-god."

They were silent for a moment as they looked down on the busy river.

"Is he really dead?" asked Jem.

Tolly nodded uncertainly. "He must be. No one could survive that. For all his three thousand years, Cazalon was just a man."

"What did you say to him, at the end there, Tolly?" Ann's green eyes were alight with curiosity.

Tolly shrugged. "Nothing important."

Cleo wriggled and chirruped softly in the crook of Tolly's arm. He grinned and lowered her gently to the ground. The little monkey looked up, twitched her tail, wrinkled her nose and chattered indignantly.

"And it wasn't just us who defeated him, was it?" laughed Jem. "Cleo appeared in the prophecy too, remember. She was the ink blot with a tail."

Epilogue

On a dusty road just beyond the gates to the smoking city ruins an elegant carriage drawn by four grey horses juddered to a halt.

A graceful hand, encased in an elaborately embroidered lavender glove extended from the window. Seconds later a huge white bird circled from the sky and landed on the outstretched arm. It pecked at the expensive leather of the glove.

The woman wearing the glove leaned from the interior of the coach. One eye was covered by a jewelled eyepatch. Her other eye was golden and glinted in the light as she caught something that dropped from the bird's dribbling beak.

A silver crescent moon studded with sparkling gem stones.

✄ ⚒ ✄

ACKNOWLEDGMENTS

There are so many people I'd like to thank for their encouragement and support throughout the writing of *The Jade Boy* that I could easily fill another three chapters... I won't – I'll try to keep this brief, although that will be hard for me!

Firstly, I'd like to thank my family – my long-suffering husband Stephen and my dad, John Cain. I'd especially like to mention my late mum, Sheila, whose passion for history – and particularly the gory details – ignited my own fascination from a very early age. There's a Cain family story about the time I had my tonsils removed at the age of four and 'entertained' the inmates on my hospital ward with a spirited reenactment of the beheading of Mary Queen of Scots, complete with her little dog (a stand-in teddy bear) hidden under her skirts. When my parents came in to see me the next day, the matron took them to one side and told them crossly that I'd given several small patients nightmares. Thanks, Mum!

Secondly, I'd like to thank my friends, who have been almost as amazed and excited as me at the prospect of *The Jade Boy*'s publication. I'd particularly like to thank the Wells family and my 'nodson' Henry Wells, who was the first person to be frightened by Count Cazalon. Henry read the initial version of *The Jade Boy* and made some very clever comments.

Thirdly, I am enormously grateful (and slightly in awe of) the team at Templar Towers, who have been so fantastic to work with. I must mention lovely commissioning editor Helen Boyle, who fished me out of the slush pile, my brilliant editor Emma Goldhawk, whose forensic eye for detail made Jem really shine, and designer Will Steele for knowing exactly what I saw.

Will also commissioned the amazing cover by award-winning artist Levi Pinfold. When I first saw his stunning artwork, I couldn't believe how beautifully sinister and right it was!

My mum's favourite period in history was the Tudor age. I love that era too, but as a teenager, I decided that I would make the seventeenth century – and especially the colourful, roisterous, fancily dressed reign of King Charles II – my particular enthusiasm.

I hope this book might inspire you to 'adopt' an era yourself.

ABOUT THE AUTHOR

Cate Cain is a true cockney, having been born within hearing distance of the church bells of St Mary-le-Bow in the City of London.

She studied English Literature at the University of London and trained to be a teacher. After leaving teaching, Cate became a journalist and worked in newspapers for more than ten years.

Cate has always loved history and now, appropriately, works for the Society for the Protection of Ancient Buildings in Spitalfields, London. Her office is in the attic of an old Georgian building and, like Jem, Cate often daydreams, looking out of the attic window over the London rooftops around her office.

Cate lives in St Albans with her husband, Stephen.

COMING SOON...

The MOON CHILD

Jem and his friends are now free from Count Cazalon's clutches, and enjoying the sort of life they'd always longed for. But when a party at Jem's elegant new house goes terribly wrong, they find themselves flung headlong into danger once more.

Look out for Jem, Tolly, Ann and Cleo's next thrilling adventure, coming in September 2014!

templar publishing

www.templarco.co.uk